Tempt Me

NEW YORK TIMES BEST SELLING AUTHOR

SAMANTHA
CHASE

Cover Design: Kari March Designs

Edits: Jillian Rivera

Praise for Samantha Chase

"If you can't get enough of stories that get inside your heart and soul and stay there long after you've read the last page, then Samantha Chase is for you!"

   -*NY Times & USA Today Bestselling Author* **Melanie Shawn**

"A fun, flirty, sweet romance filled with romance and character growth and a perfect happily ever after."

   -*NY Times & USA Today Bestselling Author* **Carly Phillips**

"Samantha Chase writes my kind of happily ever after!"

   -*NY Times & USA Today Bestselling Author* **Erin Nicholas**

"The openness between the lovers is refreshing, and their interactions are a balanced blend of sweet and spice. The planets may not have aligned, but the elements of this winning romance are definitely in sync."

   - ***Publishers Weekly, STARRED review***

"A true romantic delight, *A Sky Full of Stars* is one of the top gems of romance this year."

   - ***Night Owl Reviews, TOP PICK***

"Great writing, a winsome ensemble, and the perfect blend of heart and sass."

Chapter One

Ultimately, the eight-foot-tall smiling ghost was the last straw.

Liam Donovan certainly didn't consider himself to be the kind of guy who didn't enjoy some festive Halloween decorations, but for some reason, this year it annoyed the hell out of him.

"Hey," his brother Jamie said with a smart-ass grin. "Nice ghost. Didn't realize you were decorating this year."

If it weren't for the fact that his brother was carrying a box of glasses, Liam would have punched him.

Or tripped him, at the very least.

This so wasn't the way he wanted to go about meeting his neighbors as he moved into his new home. But unfortunately, over the last week as he'd been going about doing some work on the house before he moved in, the yard decorations at the house next door just got progressively more obnoxious. Even now as he stood in the middle of his front yard and glanced over at theirs, he couldn't believe anyone would go to that much trouble to decorate for Halloween.

And then there was the ghost that wandered onto his property.

Yeah, that was the last straw.

Liam had picked this particular house because of the neighborhood and the fact that each home had a decent amount of space between them. He was looking forward to the privacy and not having anyone living right on top of him.

And that included inflatable ghosts.

"Dude, you know I don't mind helping you move," Jamie said as he walked back to the moving truck, "but you have to at least give a hand." Chuckling, he went and grabbed another large box before heading back into the house.

He hated that his brother had a point and, with more force than necessary, he kicked the ghost back over to his neighbor's yard. He'd talk to them later about boundaries and property lines.

"Should have gone with a newer subdivision with an HOA," he mumbled as he grabbed one of the boxes from the truck. "I could complain to them anonymously and go about my day."

When he got out of the Marines a few months ago, one of his first goals was to buy a house. He'd been renting an apartment in town that he'd kept for years, even though he rarely used it. The logic had been that he wanted a place to come to and have some privacy when he was home on leave. With four siblings, it was important for him to be able to come back and visit and see everyone without having to stay in his childhood home and sleep in the same bed he'd grown up in. Everything had fallen into place and gone so smoothly that he'd felt like he'd hit the jackpot.

And now this.

"What are you frowning about?" his sister Ryleigh asked as he put the box of dishes down on the kitchen counter. "We're all working and things are getting done. I thought you'd be thrilled."

"Just...thinking," he murmured before turning and walking out of the house again.

"It looks like the Halloween version of Candyland over there," his other brother Patrick said as they worked together to heft a sofa out of the truck.

"Don't remind me."

With a small laugh, Patrick picked up his end of the sofa before they carefully made their way down the ramp.

"You should have warned me about this," Liam grumbled.

"About what? That your neighbors celebrate holidays?"

He had a point, but...

"As my realtor, you should have pointed out this sort of thing to me. It's an eyesore and if I'd known about it, I wouldn't have bought the house."

"Bullshit," Patrick retorted.

"Excuse me?" He wanted to drop the sofa and argue this out, but he was the guy walking backwards while his brother was pushing forward.

"Liam, be serious. Are you saying you would have passed on this house because a neighbor puts up holiday decorations? I mean, I know you're uptight, but that's ridiculous. Even for you."

That made him laugh. "I'm uptight? Dude, you are the king of uptight."

Grinning, his brother shook his head. "I learned from the master. You."

They put the sofa down in the living room before pausing and staring at each other. Maybe he was just itching for a fight because it seemed like everyone was grating on his last nerve. He was about to say something—definitely not an apology—when their mother walked in with a big smile and announced that she had lunch for everyone.

"Finally!" Jamie called out before running over and taking the box of food from her. "Your eldest child is working us all to death! He hasn't allowed us to even take a break! I'm telling you, it's almost criminal."

"Seriously?" Liam huffed with annoyance. "What about on the ride over here?"

"That was a twelve-minute drive," Jamie countered. "I'd hardly call that a break."

"My poor baby," Kate Donovan cooed as she patted her youngest son's cheek. "You'd think a strapping young man like yourself could handle this sort of thing. After all, wasn't that what you told that pretty girl the other night at the pub?"

Everyone stopped and watched as Jamie's cheeks turned a little red.

"Wh...what are you talking about?"

"Jamie, please," she said as she poked around the kitchen, looking in all the boxes. "There isn't a night that goes by that you're not flirting with one girl or another. You're the town Casanova and everyone knows it." She shrugged. "Of course, there are some things a mother doesn't need to hear."

"Mom...what the heck?" Jamie hissed.

"What?" she asked with amusement. "The cute blonde who was hanging on your every word Thursday night. She wore that very low-cut pink blouse and practically put her breasts in your face." Pulling out a stack of napkins, she went on. "You mentioned something about your stamina and..."

"Mom!" he cried. "Oh my God! You were listening to that?"

And just like that, Liam's foul mood dissipated a bit.

Stepping into the kitchen, he kissed his mother's cheek and figured he'd help his baby brother out a bit. "Thanks for bringing lunch over. I'm sure things are busy at the pub, so..."

"Nonsense. We have a wonderfully competent staff and I always have time for my family," she told him as she began pulling food out and placing it on the counter. "I brought you a bacon cheeseburger. Patrick, I made you a turkey club. Jamie, I got you the Swiss and mushroom burger. And there are fries and drinks for everyone."

Behind them, Ryleigh cleared her throat. "Um...hi," she said with a hint of annoyance. "Did you happen to bring anything for me?"

"Of course I did!" Picking up a container, Kate handed it to Ryleigh. "I made you a nice salad with grilled chicken and the light dressing on the side. Use it sparingly."

"What? Why? Why do the guys all get burgers and I get a measly salad?"

"Your jeans look a little snug."

Now it was Ryleigh's turn to cry out in frustration. "Mom! Jeez! These are not snug!" Tugging on the waistband of her jeans to prove the point, she let out a low growl before walking out of the room.

"Are Arianna and Will here?" Kate asked as she looked around. "I didn't think I saw their cars, but I brought lunch for them."

"They stayed behind and are cleaning up at the apartment," Liam explained. "And to pack up anything we left behind."

"If you ask me, it's an excuse for them to get out of doing any of the heavy lifting," Jamie murmured around a mouthful of burger. "We all know there's nothing left there."

All Liam did was shrug. "Doesn't matter. Arianna volunteered to clean the place and I sure as hell didn't want to, so…"

"That was very sweet of her," his mother said as she unwrapped a sandwich for herself. "Now you'll certainly get your deposit back. Be sure to thank your sister."

"We could've used Will over here," Patrick chimed in. "One more set of strong arms to move the furniture. You and I can't do it all."

"Hey!" Jamie snapped. "I'm right here and I've been helping too!"

"Yeah, you've been a real champ with the boxes," Patrick countered. "I think Ryleigh carried in heavier stuff than you."

"Okay, that's enough," Kate said as she tried hard not to laugh.

Liam always got a kick out of how she tried to keep the peace between her children without showing favorites, but it was definitely fun when she had to hide her amusement.

"Your brother works very hard at the pub and does heavy lifting all the time. It's exhausting," she explained to no one in particular. "And no matter how much stamina he claims to have…"

"Oh my God, Mom!" Jamie snapped again. "*Stop!* Please!"

"What? What did I say that was so wrong? You do this

sort of thing all the time when a pretty girl comes into the pub. You're a shameless flirt, Jamie."

His brother hung his head and groaned.

Looking around, Kate smiled at her other three children. "You all know what I'm saying. Maybe cut your brother some slack. After all, it's not just all the heavy lifting he does at the pub. Carrying around that giant ego of his has got to be exhausting."

There was a round of laughter and then it got quiet for a few minutes while everyone ate.

"So, Liam," his mother said after finishing her lunch, "how much more do you have to do today?"

Glancing around, he tried to gauge where they were at. "I think we got almost all the boxes in, so I'll need to unpack." He looked around again. "Although, I think Ryleigh's kind of been on top of that."

"I have," she called out in response. "Most of the kitchen is done and I hung up all of your stuff in the bedroom closet." Walking back into the kitchen and throwing out the remnants of her salad, she gave their mother the side-eye before continuing. "I unpacked the bathroom and linens too, so other than these last few boxes that Jamie brought in and random décor stuff, you're good to go."

"Holy crap, Ry," he said in amazement. "Thanks. I had no idea you got so much done."

She grinned. "Please. I love organizing stuff, so this was fun for me."

"Such a weirdo," he teased even as he pulled her in for a hug and kissed the top of her head. "Thanks." Then he looked at his mother. "There are a few more pieces of furniture out in the truck, but then it all comes down to getting boxes broken down, hanging curtains and pictures, connecting all the electronics..."

"Moving day is always exhausting," she replied before walking over to the box she had brought in with her. "Your father will stop by later on and help with anything else you need. I'm going to bring these sandwiches over to Will and Arianna and get back to the pub." Walking around, she kissed each of her kids. "I'll be sure to send dinner with him."

"Thanks, Mom!"

She paused and turned around with a smile. "Oh, and maybe a couple of pumpkins for the front porch to go with the ghost! It's so cute that you started to decorate for Halloween on top of everything you're already doing!" And with a wave, she was gone.

"Son of a bitch," he muttered.

"What's the matter?" Ryleigh asked.

Logically, he knew it was absurd to be this annoyed by an inflatable decoration, and yet...

"Excuse me for a minute," he said as he stalked out the front door. When he reached the ghost, Liam grabbed hold of it and yanked it along behind him as he stormed across the property to his new neighbors' home.

Picking up the tie that should have anchored the monstrosity to something, he decided to pick his own thing to attach it to. There were six-foot-tall lollipops on either side of the front walkway and he tied the offensive balloon to one of them before walking up and knocking on the front door.

"No need to get nasty," he quietly reminded himself. "Simply introduce yourself and let them know their ghost... wanders. That's it. Shake their hands and be on your way."

After a minute, he knocked again.

And a minute after that, he knocked one more time before looking around and noticing there weren't any cars in the driveway.

Muttering a curse, he walked back across the yard and made a beeline for the moving truck where his brothers were picking up his dresser and instantly went to give them a hand.

Maybe it was for the best that the neighbors weren't home. He wasn't really feeling particularly friendly and there were a million things he needed to do to get settled in. Perhaps in another few days he'd feel more like his normal self and could have a civil conversation with them.

So yeah. This was all for the best.

As long as the damn ghost stayed off his front lawn.

"Hmm...how on earth did you get over here, Boo?" Pausing in her tracks, Tessa Sullivan looked at where her smiling ghost was tied to one of the giant lollipops flanking her front walkway. Her arms were full of groceries, her purse, and her dog, so with a small shrug, she kept walking. Knowing the position of the ghost would have to wait, she let herself into the house and happily made her way to the kitchen.

"Obviously Boo was on the move again," she said as she put Phoebe, her pet teacup Pomeranian, on the floor and began unloading her groceries. "I thought I secured him pretty well this morning."

Moving around the kitchen, she put her fresh veggies in the refrigerator and made a mental note to make some soup with them at some point over the next few days. Glancing out her kitchen window, she saw the moving truck in the driveway next door and frowned. The Fosters had been the perfect neighbors—elderly and sweet, and they enjoyed decorating for the holidays just as much as she did. So far no one knew who the new people were and Tessa craned her neck to try to see anyone.

After a solid minute and no movement, she relaxed and looked down at Phoebe. "I hope they're nice," she said softly before putting away her reusable shopping bags and wiping down the counters. "Maybe once the truck is gone, I should bring over a welcome basket. What do you think? Doesn't that sound like fun?"

Of course the dog wasn't going to respond, but she found it comforting to talk to her anyhow.

Her phone chimed and she smiled when she realized what time it was.

Taking the phone from her purse, Tessa went and got comfortable on the sofa before swiping the screen.

"Hey, you," she said softly. "It's been quite a day." With a small sigh, she went on. "Phoebe had a vet appointment this morning and she's fine, everything's okay, but you know how much it bothers me when they take her back for her shots. To pass the time, I went next door to the farmers market and grabbed a bouquet of sunflowers—because you know how they always make me smile—and some fantastic veggies. I'm torn between making a cream of vegetable soup or something in a broth." She shrugged. "All the Halloween decorations are out and the weather is positively gorgeous today—fifty-five degrees and sunny." With a happy hum, she smiled at the screen. "When I got home, however, Boo was tied to one of the lollipops and I have no idea how he got there. I mean, obviously one of the neighbors did it, but I have no idea who."

Phoebe whined from her spot on the floor beside the

sofa and Tessa reached down and scooped her up. Giving her a small hug, she placed Phoebe in her lap.

"The new neighbors are moving in today," she said after a moment. "The truck is in the driveway but I haven't seen anyone yet. I know there's been a handyman coming and going almost every night last week. Personally, I can't imagine what they're doing to the house. The Fosters were always great about their renovations and they did all that work before putting the house on the market, so...I have no idea what these new people could find fault with that they'd want to change."

Another shrug.

"I'm going to make a welcome basket and bring it over once the truck is gone. I baked cookies earlier and figured I could throw in some herbal teas, some neighborhood information, and maybe the sunflowers." Pausing, she frowned. "Although I'd love to keep them for myself, but I guess it might be nice to share them, right? Spread the love?" Laughing, she reached out and gently touched the screen. "I miss you, Trev. Every single day." Tears stung her eyes and she willed them away. "I'll talk to you tomorrow."

She stared at the picture for several moments and—just like every other day—she wished things were different. Wished that life wasn't so unfair and this wonderful man hadn't been taken from this world so damn soon.

With a sniffle, Tessa swiped the screen and then put the phone down and promptly picked Phoebe up. Snuggling the tiny dog, she whispered, "It's not fair."

This was her daily routine. Every day at three o'clock, she spent a few minutes talking to Trevor and telling him about her day. It was a promise she'd made to him two years ago when he was in hospice care. They'd talked about all the things he was going to miss, and one of them was hearing about her day.

Honestly, Tessa had laughed at that because she didn't exactly live an exciting life. She was an elementary school music teacher and even though it gave her so much joy, it was hard to imagine anyone else feeling that way simply by listening to her talk about it. But Trevor had told her how much her words meant to him because her love of her job was infectious. So...here she was, still talking to him about it.

Her family was constantly telling her how it wasn't healthy, that she needed to move on. Part of her knew they were right, but she felt like it wasn't the kind of thing other people could decide for her. In her heart, she'd know when she was ready.

And it wasn't today.

Closing her eyes, she leaned back against the cushions and tried to think happy thoughts. It was something Trevor always used to say to her, "Just think happy thoughts, Tessa, and soon you'll feel better."

It sounded good in theory, but some days were harder than others.

Some days it felt like it took Herculean strength to simply get out of bed, smile, and prove to the world that she was okay.

Moving to Laurel Bay after Trevor died had been her way of getting a fresh start while also putting a little distance between her and her family. That seemed like the healthy option at the time. Her family had been harping on her for the decisions she made before his death and it became a daily struggle to survive both the loss and the criticism. So, she put her faith in a recommendation from her cousin Jenna and visited Laurel Bay.

It had checked all her boxes and she happily sold her home in Charleston and made the move north. It was far enough away that her parents and sisters couldn't just drop by unannounced—although they tried a few times—but it was close enough that they could visit each other with some ease.

After those few unannounced visits, they'd all come to an agreement that Tessa would come home and visit more often so they wouldn't worry. She agreed but also wanted to remind them of how she wouldn't have had to move if they hadn't hovered and complained about how she was living her life. She was thirty years old, for crying out loud. There was no reason for the constant interference and certainly no right for them to tell her how to grieve.

Once that was settled, things calmed down and for almost two years, life was pretty much perfect. Her teaching job was very fulfilling, this house was exactly what she wanted, and her little neighborhood in the tiny town was beyond charming.

Then the Fosters announced they were moving, the school announced budget cuts that meant her winter chorus concert was going to be a little less magical, and now she had no idea if the people moving in next door were friends or foes.

She desperately prayed they were friends.

Feeling a wave of sadness starting to wash over her, Tessa quickly sat up and forced herself to think of something good—something happy.

Standing, she picked up her phone and pulled up one of her favorite playlists of Disney songs and hit play. Within a matter of seconds, "The Gospel Truth" from Hercules began playing and she immediately burst into song with it. Placing Phoebe down on the floor, Tessa did a little dance on her way back to the kitchen and began putting together a small welcome basket to take next door.

As she put a frilly bow on the plate of cookies, the music changed to "Under the Sea" and she kept singing. Next, she pulled a vase down from one of her cabinets and considered keeping the bouquet of sunflowers for herself again.

"Nope. It's better to spread the joy with new friends." Putting the vase back, she put a matching bow on the bouquet and arranged them and the cookies into one of the many baskets she had. Then she put some packs of assorted herbal teas in there and then the helpful folder of local restaurants and places of interest that she kept on hand for when friends or family came to visit. Perhaps these new people were familiar with the area, but maybe they weren't. Either way, it went into the basket along with a sticky note that had her name and number on it, in case they had any questions.

Stepping back, she smiled at her handiwork. Feeling pleased, she walked over to the window and noticed someone was sitting in the driver's seat of the moving truck. A minute later, it slowly pulled away from the house and she took that as her cue to go over and introduce herself. She was sure they'd be tired and might appreciate a late afternoon treat.

Phoebe danced around her feet and Tessa instantly scooped her up. "Yes, you can come with me," she cooed.

Within minutes, she had the basket and her dog in her arms. With a pep in her step, she walked out the door and paused on her porch. Even though it could probably wait, she desperately wanted to get Boo back in his proper place so anyone driving by could marvel at her festive yard.

"Wait here," she told Phoebe as she placed her on the

porch swing with the basket and went to handle her wayward ghost.

It took a solid five minutes to get him secured again, and Tessa walked out to the sidewalk and smiled. It looked so much better and she felt good about taking care of it now rather than putting it off until later.

Like she was clearly doing about going next door and meeting the new neighbors.

"Okay, this is ridiculous," she muttered as she collected the basket and Phoebe again. "Meeting new people is always fun and a great way to maybe find a new friend. And who doesn't enjoy having more friends, huh?"

Big talk for a woman using a four-pound dog as a shield...

"For all I know, my new best friend is on the other side of that door. All I have to do is smile and knock and...who knows? This could be my destiny, right?"

Phoebe yawned broadly in response.

"Fine. Be that way. But I am going to look at this as a good thing. A great thing!"

Only...she wasn't sure who she was trying to convince—herself or Phoebe.

Ugh...trying to get my dog's approval has got to be a sign that I'm losing my mind...

Stepping up onto the front porch, Tessa let out a long breath, raised her hand, and rang the bell.

Was her heart beating a little fast? Maybe.

Was she considering turning around and trying again tomorrow? Possibly.

"Think happy thoughts," she whispered. "Just think happy thoughts."

Putting herself out there more and more was something Trevor always encouraged her to do, but it never got easier.

It helped when the people she introduced herself to were kind and welcoming. True, none of them had ever turned into her best friend, but...that doesn't mean it couldn't happen this time.

She heard movement behind the door as someone called out, "I'll be right there!"

It was on the tip of her tongue to say she could come back later. After all, maybe they were busy unpacking or up on a ladder...

She'd feel terrible if they hurt themselves in their haste to answer the door.

And before she could second guess herself, that's exactly what she did. "No worries! I'll come back later!" She took one step back and then another. "Bye!"

She was about to turn away when she heard the doorknob turn.

Drat! So close...

Moving forward again, she smiled and was all set to welcome them to the neighborhood.

The door opened and all the words died in her throat.

Well, almost all the words.

"Oh crap. It's you."

Chapter Two

Liam blinked as he tried to comprehend what he was seeing and why this woman was frowning at him.

Then he remembered.

Three months ago, he was in a wedding party and was partnered with her. She was an overly cheerful, super happy kind of person and it annoyed the hell out of him. For that entire weekend, she raved how everything was great, everything was beautiful, everything was super fantastic. It was exhausting. He couldn't fathom how someone could be that damn happy all the time.

She doesn't look so happy now...

Forcing himself to smile, he cleared his throat and stepped out onto the porch. "Um...Tracy, right?"

Her frown deepened.

"Tessa," she corrected and thrust the basket into his arms. "Welcome to the neighborhood." Then she turned and walked away.

For a moment, he was too stunned to speak. He caught a whiff of chocolate and noticed there were cookies in the basket, along with some tea and pamphlets and flowers. Who did this kind of thing?

That's when his manners kicked in and he went after her.

"Hey, uh...wait a sec," he called out as he caught up with her on the lawn. Luckily, she stopped and waited for him. Once he was facing her, he wasn't exactly sure what to say except, "How did you know I lived here?"

"I didn't," she said stiffly.

She was shorter than he remembered and as he studied her, he realized she was probably in heels that whole weekend. Right now, her dark hair was long and loose whereas she'd worn it up for all the wedding festivities.

She was also prettier than he remembered too.

Huh...

Her dark eyes were shooting daggers at him though, so...

"I live next door," she said after a moment. "I was coming over to introduce myself to my new neighbors. Any chance you're just the handyman and there's a nice, friendly family inside?"

"Excuse me?"

Shaking her head, she said, "Never mind. Wishful thinking. Anyway...welcome to the neighborhood. Keep the basket." When she turned to walk away again, it occurred to him that she clearly had a problem with him.

Moving in front of her, he blocked her path. "I'm a little confused here. Did I do something to offend you?"

Her eyes went wide. "You're joking, right?"

Crossing his arms awkwardly over his chest while still holding the basket, he shook his head. "I don't joke. Ask anyone."

"Oh, I don't need to. I fully believe that," she murmured.

The next thing Liam noticed was how she was holding her left arm awkwardly. That was something he didn't remember from the wedding, but he wasn't sure if it would be rude to mention it.

"Look, I'm sorry for whatever I did at the wedding," he said. "I don't remember us having any kind of confrontation, but since we're obviously going to be neighbors..." Turning slightly, he motioned toward his house. "Maybe you'd like to come in and we can start fresh?"

There. That was a nice gesture, wasn't it?

"No thank you," she said before stepping around him and walking toward the nightmare yard with all the decorations.

"Wait...you live *there*?" he asked in disbelief.

Tessa stopped again and looked at him. "Yes. Why?"

"Because your ghost was in my yard."

"And?"

Now it was his eyes that went wide. "And...don't you think that's all a bit much? I mean...it's a little tacky to cram your yard with so much crap. It's kind of ridiculous."

Her spine stiffened. "*Crap*? You think my yard is full of *crap*?" she asked incredulously. "I'll have you know the neighborhood kids *love* coming here to trick-or-treat. *Love* it. And last year, the local paper did a feature story on my yard as well as the local news station! I was on TV and praised for making this such a fun and festive yard!" Then she took a step back and let out a small snort. "Although I shouldn't be surprised. You're the kind of person who likes to suck the joy out of everything."

Was she for real?

"I do *not* suck the joy out of everything," he countered angrily. "Just because I don't view everything as being

19

perfect and magical doesn't mean I don't appreciate the fun in things."

Her only response was another snort.

It didn't matter that Liam was raised to be respectful to people, Tessa essentially threw the first verbal punch the second he opened the door to her.

"You know what? Think whatever you want, but the next time your ghost wanders over onto my property, I'm popping him," he said smugly.

"Wow," she murmured before walking away.

Liam was fine with it until he realized he was basically proving her point.

Dammit.

"Okay, I won't pop it," he said loudly. "Just...keep your stuff out of my yard. Please."

Tessa paused at the steps to her porch before strolling back toward him. "Thank you for adding the please," she said. "And don't worry. I made sure that Boo is extra secured."

"Boo?"

She nodded. "The ghost."

It was hard not to let out his own snort this time, but he controlled himself. "Cute."

"So do you hate all holidays or just Halloween?"

"I don't hate any holidays," he replied. "I just think the number of decorations is a little...much."

What he wanted to say was that her decorations bordered on obnoxious, but again, he controlled himself.

"Well, you're entitled to your opinion," she said casually. "Like I said, everyone enjoys them so..."

There didn't seem to be anything left to say—at least on this topic—but that still left him looking like a jerk for not acknowledging the basket she'd given him.

"Listen, um...thanks for the welcome basket. It looked like there were some cookies in there and..."

"Chocolate chip," she told him. "I baked them this morning and the flowers are from the local farmers market. I don't know where you're originally from, but I also included information about the town, like local restaurants and places of interest."

"I actually grew up here."

"Oh, well..."

"Still, I think it's a great idea...you know...the information. Very considerate."

That seemed to make her relax a bit. "Thanks." Studying him for a moment, she then asked, "So, where did you move from?"

"I was in the Marines for a little over ten years and only recently retired. I'd been renting an apartment downtown for years for when I would come home on leave. Now that I'm back for good, I figured it was time to buy a house."

She nodded.

"So...I don't think we've ever properly been introduced," he said. "The whole wedding weekend was a bit chaotic since I was a last-minute groomsman. I'm Liam Donovan." Holding out his hand to her, he was surprised when she didn't immediately respond.

"Donovan? Like Donovan's Pub?"

"Yeah! That's my parents' place. It's been in our family for like...four generations. I take it you've eaten there before?"

"Definitely! Their burgers are amazing!" Her smile was sweet and a refreshing change from all the frowning she'd been doing. "I go in there at least once a week. Is your mom Kate?"

He nodded.

"She's a sweetheart. And is Ronan your dad?"

"No, he's my uncle. My dad is Shane. He's usually in the kitchen, but he hangs out behind the bar with Uncle Ronan when things are slow."

"I've met him too. They're all very friendly." She paused, but her smile stayed. "Is Jamie your brother?"

Liam felt his own smile falter as his mother's earlier words about Jamie came to mind.

"There isn't a night that goes by that you're not flirting with one girl or another. You're the town Casanova and everyone knows it."

"Uh...yeah. Jamie's my youngest brother."

"So there are more?"

"There are actually five of us," he explained. "I'm the oldest, then there's Patrick, then my sister Ryleigh..."

"She's an amazing cook," Tessa interrupted.

"That she is. She takes after our mom," he agreed. "Then there's Jamie and the youngest is Arianna."

"She's the one who just got engaged, right?"

Chuckling, he asked, "How did you know?"

"Small town," she said with a small laugh of her own. "It's one of the things I love most about it—everyone knows everyone. It's nice."

"I don't know if I've ever thought about it quite like that, but...I'm sure everyone else might know your full name."

Blushing, she laughed again, and this time, she shook his hand. "Oh, I'm Tessa Sullivan. Sorry." When he released her hand, he noticed that her left arm stayed at that awkward angle.

"Hey, um...I don't mean to be rude, but...is there something wrong with your arm?" he asked carefully.

"My arm?" Looking down at it she laughed softly before meeting his gaze. "No. Why?"

"Because you're holding it funny." Inwardly, he groaned at how tactless he was being.

"I'm not holding it funny for no reason," she explained, amusement lacing her tone. "It's the easiest way to hold Phoebe."

"Phoebe?"

Nodding, she said, "Yes, my dog."

Then she held up a ball of fur that could not possibly be an actual animal. It was just a bunch of white with three black dots.

"That's a *dog*?" he asked and almost cringed at how sarcastic he sounded, but...come on! There was no way that thing was real.

If anything, Tessa cradled the dog even closer and whispered to it soothingly, something about not listening to the mean man. Liam didn't even attempt to hide the eye roll.

"You have to admit that it's a little unusual to have an animal that small. Is it a puppy?"

"First of all, Phoebe is a she," she said emphatically. "And she's three years old. But this is as big as she'll ever get. She's a teacup Pomeranian."

"I had a guinea pig that was bigger than that," he said, leaning in to get a better look at the dog. "Can it even bark?"

With a weary sigh, she gave him a patient look. "Yes, she's real, and yes, she can bark." After a brief pause, she said, "Look, Liam, I think it's best if we sort of stop right here. It's obvious that you think very little of me and the way I live my life, and to be honest, I'm not too fond of... well...you. So let's chalk this up to unfortunate circumstances that we ended up as neighbors and simply limit our interactions to waving from a distance and the occasional head nod, okay?"

It sounded simple, but...

It also made him feel like a total jerk.

"I'm sure we don't have to reduce ourselves to that," he reasoned. "Why don't we go back over to my house and we'll start over?"

She didn't even pretend to think about it.

"No, but thanks. I've got things to do. I really just wanted to bring over the basket and...well...you know."

There was no point in trying to convince her because she was right. They did seem to irritate each other, and it sucked that they were now going to be living next door to each other. It was probably best to cut their losses and just move on with their lives.

Behind him, Liam heard a car door slam shut and when he glanced over his shoulder, he saw his mother walking toward him with a big smile on her face.

Oh, no...

"Oh my goodness! Tessa! You're Liam's neighbor? This is wonderful!" She walked over and gave Tessa a hug. "Is this Phoebe? Look how precious she is! Liam! Did you see this? Isn't she the cutest little thing?"

"Um..."

"Tessa, come over to Liam's and have something to eat. Shane and I brought dinner and there's more than enough food to feed almost the entire block," his mother went on. "You were going to tell me about plans for the Christmas musical..."

She led Tessa away, but not before he caught her eye. It was clear she had no idea how to say no to his mother.

"Liam! Your father needs a hand! Go help him!"

And apparently, neither did he.

* * *

24

Two hours later, Tessa eyed the front door longingly.

No matter how many times she'd tried to leave, Kate Donovan found a reason for her to stay.

More than once she'd caught Liam looking at her with amusement, and all it did was make her want to stomp over and just kick him in the shin or something.

Of all the people for her to have living beside her...

Seriously, Universe? What the heck?

Three months ago, they met at her cousin Jenna's wedding. She had been so excited about the weekend in Myrtle Beach and even more excited to see Jenna finally marrying the man of her dreams. Unfortunately, she got paired up with Liam at the last minute because the groomsman she was originally supposed to walk with had fallen and broken his leg. It shouldn't have been a big deal, but Liam seemed to constantly be annoyed by everything she did and said and more than once she caught him rolling his eyes.

Like a jerk.

By the time the wedding reception was in full swing and they no longer had any bridal party duties, she had breathed a huge sigh of relief. Like it wasn't hard enough to smile all the dang time and be as upbeat as humanly possible, but to then have to deal with a guy who seemed to thrive on being stoic all the live-long day was just too much. It was *all* too much. Tessa enjoyed giving people the benefit of the doubt when they were less than friendly, but that weekend she had written Liam off as a miserable human being with no redemptive qualities.

That was something that still held true, no matter how charming his family was.

"Hey! We brought dessert!" someone called out as they walked in the door.

Tessa had never seen this couple before and if she had to guess, this would be Arianna and her new fiancé, Will.

A minute later, Kate confirmed that when she introduced them.

"Ari! This is Tessa," Kate said excitedly. "She's the music teacher I was telling you about. She's got the voice of an angel and the cutest little dog you've ever seen! And now she lives right next door to Liam! What a small world, right?"

Before Tessa could say anything, Kate had Phoebe in her hand and was holding her up to show Arianna.

"Oh my goodness! Look at this tiny baby," Arianna said softly before smiling at Tessa. "Is it okay if I hold her?"

"Of course. Phoebe loves to be snuggled and is a big fan of all this attention."

Unlike her owner...

For the next several minutes, Tessa answered all kinds of questions about what it was like to own a teacup dog. It happened all the time because they were a novelty and people were naturally curious. Plus, in this particular situation, it was a safe topic. She'd already endured an almost painfully awkward dinner with Liam, his parents, and his brother Patrick. Ryleigh Donovan arrived about thirty minutes ago and was currently organizing the bedroom closet while Liam, his father, and Patrick hung lights in the screened-in back porch.

"She is so sweet," Arianna said as she handed Phoebe back to her. "I think I'd take her everywhere with me!"

"I can't imagine they'd like that at the radiology lab," Will commented.

"Are you kidding? They'd love her and it would be amazing for our patients to have the distraction of this little love." Her eyes went wide. "Did you ever think of letting her be a therapy dog?"

"Not really," Tessa replied. "I'll admit I do bring her around to cheer people up, but that's just friends and family. When I go home to Charleston, I bring her to the assisted living facility my Nana lives in. All the residents love it when we come to visit."

"What does your husband think of her?" Arianna asked. "I imagine some guys don't mind having a tiny dog for a pet, but some might not find it manly."

"Oh, um…"

"Tessa's a widow," Kate said quietly, and Arianna gasped.

"I'm so sorry," she said. "I didn't know. I saw the ring on your finger and…"

Tessa looked down at her hand with a sad smile before doing her best to assure Arianna that it was fine. "It's okay. Really. There's no way you could have known."

"Still, that was awfully thoughtless of me to just blurt something like that out."

"Jeez, Arianna," Liam said with a small laugh as he walked back into the kitchen. "What did you do now?"

Tessa was about to say it was nothing, but his mother went and repeated the entire conversation.

All of it.

His eyes went a little wide when he looked at her. "You're a widow?"

She inwardly groaned and simply nodded.

"You didn't know?" Kate asked. "The two of you spent that entire weekend in Myrtle Beach at Nick and Jenna's wedding. Didn't you talk?"

"Um…"

"It's fine, Kate," Tessa quickly interjected. "It's not something I enjoy talking about, so…"

He stepped closer to the table; his expression was somber. "I'm really sorry, Tessa," he said gruffly. "I had no idea."

Then he was saved from having to say anything else when Jamie showed up. It seemed like everyone was talking at once and it was more than a little overwhelming.

"So, is your house the one with all the fantastic Halloween decorations?" Arianna asked.

"It is! Although, your brother is not a fan," Tessa said murmured.

"Ignore him," Kate chimed in. "He's a little too serious for his own good. I'm going to bring some pumpkins over tomorrow and put them on his front porch so he doesn't look like the neighborhood Scrooge."

"Can you be a Scrooge with Halloween?" Arianna pondered, and that led to an entire discussion of how the rest of the family enjoyed celebrating all the holidays.

"Liam's just a little more uptight about them because he was in the military for so long and couldn't celebrate," his mother concluded. "Maybe now that he's home he'll remember how we always went big on our decorations too. You see how the pub looks, right?"

It took almost another hour before she could make her escape. Most of the time had been spent between more questions about Phoebe and dodging Jamie's flirtatious advances.

By the time she was walking back into her own house, it felt like she'd been gone for days instead of mere hours.

Her own family was close and enjoyed spending time together, but the Donovans were loud and boisterous and seemed to know *way* too much about each other's lives.

"Okay, pretty girl, let's get you some dinner," she said when she placed the dog down on the floor. Together they went to the kitchen and Tessa poured the quarter cup of specialized food into Phoebe's bowl before putting it down and then giving her fresh water. All night the Donovans had wanted to give her table food, but she'd had to explain how dangerous that could be for tiny dogs.

Once that was done, Tessa walked into the living room and collapsed on the sofa and simply relished the silence. Being a teacher meant most of her days were spent surrounded by noise and some sense of chaos—especially as a music teacher. But spending time with the Donovans was noisy and chaotic on a whole other level. They talked loudly, laughed loudly, and most of the time, she wasn't sure if they were arguing or simply having conversations. And through it all, there was something else she noticed.

Liam Donovan was the quietest of the bunch.

Go figure.

Maybe that's because his face said it all.

Yeah, the disapproval, the annoyance, the condescension...it was all right there in every look, every expression.

And it just irritated her all the more.

The only redeeming thing she found was that it seemed to just be who he was and it wasn't like he had singled her out. The man clearly thought he was better than everyone and hopefully this would be the last and only time she was forced to hang out with him like that. Maybe she'd figure out his work schedule over the next week so she could be sure to avoid even having to wave or do the head nod thing.

"Ugh...why do people have to just be the worst sometimes?" she mumbled.

In the kitchen, Phoebe let out a little bark to let Tessa know she was ready to go out.

With a small groan, she got up and went to the back door. Scooping her up, Tessa turned on the outside lights before stepping out onto the porch. A teacup dog was too small to realistically put on a leash and walk, so every night they came out to the yard and Tessa would sit in one of her Adirondack chairs while Phoebe roamed the yard and did her business.

It was actually one of her favorite times of the day. The yard had been a labor of love when she moved into the house. It was her oasis. With the help of the privacy fence, Tessa had turned the backyard into a space that allowed her to enjoy and relax without a lot of noise and prying eyes.

Between the seating area under the pergola covered in twinkly lights and her attempt at an English garden with a bit of coastal flair, it was her happy place. She loved all the greenery and how peaceful it was, and Phoebe loved running around and getting her exercise out there. At one time Tessa had considered putting in a pool, but considering it was just her, it seemed like an unnecessary expense.

That's how she ended up with the hot tub.

Glancing over at it, she considered taking a nice, long soak to ease the tension the night had brought on.

"Hmm...and perhaps a nice glass of wine too," she said softly before picking Phoebe back up and bringing her inside.

Decision made, Tessa quickly changed into a one-piece swimsuit and poured herself a glass of wine before heading back outside. It took a few minutes to get everything right—taking the cover off of the tub, turning on her heat lamp, and getting the jets going—but once it was all done, she climbed in and let out a very happy sigh as she sank under the water.

For several minutes, it was perfect. She felt all the

tension leaving her body. Reaching for the wine, she took a sip and smiled.

"You should totally put a basketball hoop back here!"

Tessa didn't have to open her eyes or even glance toward Liam's house to know that was Jamie's voice.

"Or a pool! Yes! And not an above-ground one like Mom and Dad have, but a legit in-ground one with a diving board and slide! Think of how awesome that would be in the summer!"

"I was planning on doing an outdoor kitchen," Liam said.

Seriously, do these people never talk softly?

"You've got enough space to do both," Patrick said, joining the conversation. "You'd add a little value to the house and without an HOA, you don't have to get anyone's approval."

"That's one of the reasons I chose this house," Liam replied. "Although...I think an HOA would have put a stop to all those Halloween decorations next door."

"Dude, let it go," Jamie moaned. "They're just up for fun. Don't you remember how much we used to love going to the houses with the most decorations?"

He mumbled something in response and Tessa imagined he was annoyed that his brothers weren't agreeing with him.

"Maybe you should have moved to a retirement community," Patrick joked, and after that the voices faded and she heard a door close, signifying they'd gone back into the house.

Good riddance.

Still...his words got in her head a little bit.

Did her other neighbors have an issue with them? Were people annoyed or did they think she was tacky?

Halloween was a week away and maybe after it was over, she'd open up a dialogue with the neighbors she knew and liked to see if they thought she needed to tone things down.

In the meantime, she was going to push all thoughts of Liam Donovan and his grumpy attitude from her mind and think happy thoughts.

Chapter Three

Liam hadn't felt this tired in a long time.

And weirdly, it felt good.

Work on the fishing resort he and his buddy Will were building was coming along nicely. They were both big on being hands-on and several parts of the property construction they were handling themselves. He was filthy and more than a little hungry, and after he grabbed a quick shower, he was going to take a ride up to the pub and grab some dinner. All he needed to do was...

"What the hell...?" He was driving slowly past Tessa's house and she was dressed like Little Bo Peep. She had on a pink and white dress with big polka dots on the skirt, a bonnet, and was carrying a big blue staff in one hand and that ridiculous dog in the other. The woman was insane.

Slowly, he pulled into his driveway when the entire scene came together in his head.

Halloween.

O-kay. That made more sense. And the more he looked around, the more he noticed the number of kids and their parents walking along the sidewalks.

There was a trick-or-treating curfew in Laurel Bay and families were only allowed out to collect candy from five to eight p.m. He'd gotten the notice from the town about it and as he climbed from his truck, he realized he had completely forgotten what day it was and had zero candy to give out.

Muttering a curse, he kept his head down and let himself into the house, locking the door, and not turning on any lights until he got to his bedroom. He was sure that his entire family was going to mock him for forgetting what today was and for coming in for dinner to avoid dealing with trick-or-treaters.

Hell, not having to cook his own dinner and listening to the doorbell ring for the next three hours would be worth a little ribbing.

Moving around his room, Liam stripped and dumped his clothes in the hamper before walking naked into the bathroom. He could hear singing and children squealing with laughter outside—his master bathroom was on the side of the house that faced Tessa's—and there wasn't a doubt in his mind that families would linger at her property because of the crazy setup.

"Have at them," he mumbled, turning on the shower and giving the water a minute to heat up.

Stepping under the spray, he let out a low groan. It felt so good and he simply let the hot water beat down on him for several minutes while he did his best to clear his mind.

Only...he couldn't.

If anything, all he could think about was what was going on next door.

Dammit.

They had avoided each other for the entire week. Obviously they weren't going to be on the same schedule, but he figured at some point they'd be outside at the same time.

But they hadn't.

And the thing was, it wasn't one of those out of sight, out of mind situations. If anything, she'd been on his mind all damn week and it pissed him off.

A widow.

Yeah, that had come as a bit of a shock to him and he couldn't believe no one had mentioned it to him the weekend of the wedding. She was too young to be a widow. Of course, there wasn't ever a good age for that sort of thing to happen, but considering she was only a couple of years younger than him, he imagined it had to be beyond devastating. They were only just starting their lives and then...

He had no idea.

He'd lost a couple of buddies on his last deployment and they were both married. Liam remembered thinking of how they'd never gotten the chance to come home and start their families, but obviously it wasn't only military spouses who dealt with that. It could happen to anyone.

Even your neighbor.

With another curse, he grabbed his shampoo and quickly washed his hair before switching that out for his body wash and finishing up. This was no longer a relaxing shower and the sooner he was done, the sooner he could get dressed and go grab something to eat.

It didn't take long for him to dry off and get dressed, and as he walked through the darkened house, he knew he was mildly overreacting. Not everyone in the neighborhood was handing out candy and he was fairly certain no one was going to condemn him for going out instead of sitting home and answering the door.

But as he stepped out on his front porch, he realized he may have miscalculated everything.

There was an actual crowd in front of Tessa's house.

Parents and children were wandering around her front yard taking pictures and even from where he was standing, he could hear their praise of her display.

"So creative!"

"Always a treat!"

"She's so sweet to do this!"

"We need more people like this in the neighborhood!"

And yeah, with that last one he swore a group of parents turned to specifically give him the stink eye.

Great.

With his head down again, Liam quickly made his way to his truck and climbed in. Getting out of the driveway took a bit longer than usual because of the crowds of people all making their way to Tessa's house.

"Okay, but it's only once a year," he reminded himself. And if he planned it right, he could go out of town next October or work extra-long hours so he wouldn't have to live with the spectacle year after year.

By the time he pulled up to the pub a few minutes later, he felt a little better and was already thinking about the pot roast with mashed potatoes and gravy he was going to order. No one made a pot roast like his mother and after such a long day—long week!—he felt like it was a well-deserved thing to have some comfort food for dinner.

But when he walked into the pub, it was a mob scene.

A costumed mob scene.

Son of a...

"Liam!" Uncle Ronan called out from behind the bar. He was dressed as a vampire. Beside him, his brother Jamie smiled and waved. Tonight, he was dressed as a baseball player.

"I'm never going to live this down..."

"Wow, I guess you really are a Scrooge," Arianna said as

she walked over and kissed him on the cheek. Taking a step back she posed. "Can you guess who I am?"

Liam looked at her long red dress and wasn't sure, but when Will joined them wearing a medieval mercenary costume, he put two and two together. "Wesley and Buttercup," he said. "The Princess Bride."

"Yay! You guessed it!" she said excitedly, hooking her arm with Will's.

"You couldn't have given me a heads-up about this?" he asked his buddy. "We worked together all day—all week, actually—and not once did you mention dressing up for Halloween."

"Dude, it's Halloween. It's kind of a given about dressing up," Will replied with a small shrug. "And since your family apparently does this sort of thing every year, I just figured you were aware of it."

Yeah...now that he thought about it, he did remember this being a thing.

"You could tell people you're dressed like an uptight party-pooper," Arianna suggested with a sweet smile.

Before he could respond, Ryleigh walked over dressed as a Greek goddess. She took one look at him and smirked. "Man, you really just refuse to get into the holiday spirit. Don't let Mom see you or she'll..."

"Liam James Donovan!"

Too late.

Hanging his head, he knew there was nothing he could do but stand there and wait to get reprimanded. It didn't matter that he was thirty-two years old. Apparently age didn't matter in this family.

"Why would you show up here without a costume?" his mother demanded. "Look around! Everyone is wearing at least a hint of a costume! Even old Mr. Jacobs from the paint store put on a motorcycle jacket and sunglasses. Are you telling me you didn't have one thing you could wear to the party? Why even bother showing up if you weren't going to wear a costume?"

"Um...I sort of forgot about the party. I really was hoping to just grab some dinner. It's been a long week and I've been putting in a lot of hours and..."

"And yet Will managed to get himself into a costume."

"Yeah, well, I'm sure Ari had a little something to do with that."

She waved him off. "Go to the kitchen and make yourself a plate and eat back there."

"What?!"

"You heard me. You can eat in the kitchen because you look ridiculous. Now if you'll excuse me, I have costumed guests to serve."

As soon as she walked away, Liam looked to his siblings for help. "She's kidding, right?"

"I don't think so," Ryleigh said.

"Yeah, but..."

"Dude, where's your costume?" Patrick asked as he joined them.

Liam's eyes went wide. "You too?" he asked in disbelief and then noticed even he was in costume. "Han Solo? Really?"

With a shrug, Patrick straightened his vest. "What? You know how much I love Star Wars."

"Okay, but...you're just so strait-laced. I can't believe you dressed up."

"Um...first, I think you're confusing me with you. You're the strait-laced one. I've mellowed. Besides, it's Halloween. Everyone dresses up."

I'm in hell...

"You could have put on your old fatigues or something with no real effort," Will chimed in, and when Liam glared at him, he held his hands up in surrender. "I'm just saying..."

There was no way he was going home to change.

For starters, he didn't want to, but more importantly, he didn't want to battle the crowds of trick-or-treaters. So...he went and ate in the kitchen. Fortunately, his father was back there and they were able to have a nice conversation and hang out without being surrounded by costumed annoyances.

"We should do this more often, Dad. Just me and you," he said after eating a slice of apple pie. "How about we go fishing on Sunday?"

Shane grinned. "At the resort property?"

"Maybe. Or anywhere. We can take the boat out on the ocean and give that a try. I know I haven't done that in years."

"Sure. We'll make a day of it," his father said with a nod. "I'll bring the food, you bring drinks, and you'll have to be the one to tell your brothers if they find out we're going without them."

"No worries there."

Beside him, his father chuckled. "They giving you a hard time out there?"

"They give me a hard time everywhere since I've come home," he murmured and then realized he sounded a little whiny. "I mean...I get it. It's what we do to one another, but I just wish they'd take my side on something for once instead of constantly turning everything into an argument."

"Well...you've been gone a long time and they're trying to make up for it." He shrugged. "Plus, I think they're trying to get to know you again, but this time as a peer rather than the older brother. You're not kids anymore. You're all grown men. So...maybe take some time and do something, just the three of you."

It made sense.

"I will. Just...not Sunday."

Clapping him on the shoulder, his father agreed. "Deal." Then he stepped away to cook up a couple of burgers. "You should go back out there. Don't let anyone make you feel bad about not dressing up. Spend some time just enjoying a Friday night."

That was his cue and his father's roundabout way of saying he'd been hiding in the kitchen long enough. So... with a weary sigh, he walked back out to the dining room and saw it was still fairly packed.

It's a Friday night and Halloween; what did you expect?

Making his way around the room, he stopped and talked to a few familiar faces. It didn't take long for him to relax and no one else seemed to care that he wasn't in a costume. Accepting a beer from Uncle Ronan, he thanked him, but noticed him smirking at something across the room. Liam followed his gaze and wasn't exactly sure of what he was seeing.

Some guy was talking to Ryleigh and she looked more than a little uncomfortable. He was tall and his arms were covered in tattoos and it became more and more obvious that he was hitting on her.

"Should I go over there?" he asked his uncle. But before Ronan could respond, his sister had walked away, so...crisis averted.

"Ryker's harmless and your sister can handle herself. Trust me," Ronan said before turning away to take another drink order.

And that's when he realized his father's words were

right. They weren't kids anymore. For the last dozen years, he'd been away in the Marines and his siblings had grown up into adults who he didn't really know. The only thing he *did* know was that they clearly knew how to take care of themselves without any help from him.

You'd think he would have learned that after everything that happened with Arianna and Will, but...here he was.

And suddenly, he didn't feel like drinking anymore.

Hell, he didn't even feel like hanging out.

Putting his beer back down on the bar, Liam looked around and knew no one would really care if he left.

So he did.

"This is ingenious, Tessa! Thank you so much for all your hard work. This has been a real treat! And that sing-a-long you did earlier was precious! I'll send you the video."

Smiling, Tessa took a bite of her sugar cookie. "Thanks, Jeanie. I feel like the adults need a little something for themselves after taking the kids out and maybe the folks without kids need a way to celebrate too. So, having a little yard party for the neighbors just seemed like a great way for us to maybe have a little fun while the kids wind down with a movie."

She'd hung a white sheet against her front porch and rigged up a projector and currently had *Monsters, Inc.* playing for the kids so the adults could have their own little party.

She'd done it last year for the first time and it was a success, so she was thrilled that twice as many people showed up this year. Fortunately, it was a cool, clear night so no one was going to stay too long, but it was enough time to just hang out and catch up with everyone.

"Oh, look," Mike, Jeanie's husband, said in a mock whisper. "It's the new guy. Notice how he didn't even have candy for the kids tonight. Kind of a grinch if you ask me."

Tessa hid a smile even as she glanced in Liam's direction. He paused on his front walkway and she could tell he was curious about what was going on in her front yard. It was after curfew, after all.

The smart thing to do would be to ignore him and go back to talking to her friends, but when Mike questioned if anyone had met "the new guy," she knew she couldn't keep quiet.

"Um...I've met him," she said. "He grew up here in Laurel Bay, and..."

"Then it's even worse that he went out instead of taking the opportunity to meet his neighbors," Dave from across the street commented. "He knows that it's just a couple of hours once a year, and if he was interested in meeting people, this was a great way to do it."

A few others murmured in agreement and as much as it would have thrilled her to have more people not like Liam—or maybe have an angry mob not like him—she wasn't the kind of woman to encourage that sort of thing.

Dang it.

Raising her hand, she caught Liam's eye and waved him over.

It was too dark to tell if he was relieved or annoyed, but either way, he walked over. That's when she noticed he looked a little uncertain.

"Everyone," she called out. "This is Liam Donovan. He just moved in next door." Without looking at him, she continued. "He's just moved back to Laurel Bay after over ten years in the Marines and his family owns Donovan's Pub in town, so...you should come over and introduce yourselves and welcome him to the neighborhood."

"Tessa," he whispered, but she wasn't listening. Instead, she went and poured him a glass of cider and grabbed a couple of cookies and put them on a napkin for him. Wordlessly, she handed them to him and then stood back and simply observed.

Once introductions were done, she noticed people asked about his time in the service and some praised his parents' food at the pub.

Then the best thing happened.

People started pointing out how much they appreciated *her* and all she did to make the holiday even more festive.

"Tessa really knows how to bring the neighbors together..."

"Coming to Tessa's house was the highlight of the entire night..."

"No one does Halloween like Tessa does..."

"You're so lucky to have Tessa as a neighbor, Liam!"

"Tessa's a local celebrity! The newspaper ran another story on her decorations this year. Did you happen to see it?"

All she could do was smile and blush a little at the praise. Watching Liam smile and nod while not looking at her was its own form of entertainment.

"I know some people think it's overkill," she commented at one point, "but...I don't know...people seem to enjoy it."

"Whoever said it's overkill is crazy," Jeanie stated. "You are like a breath of fresh air in this neighborhood."

Everyone agreed.

Well, almost everyone.

Still, it gave her a smug sense of pride that Liam was

definitely outnumbered. He never said anything directly to her, and before she knew it, everyone was saying goodnight and offering to help her clean up.

Liam said goodnight to the group as a whole, but made no offer to help with anything.

Which was fine with her.

* * *

Halloween was over, but Tessa left the decorations up for a few extra days before diving into the task of taking them down.

Then she got to start decorating for Thanksgiving.

It wasn't nearly as fun, but she enjoyed the whole fall harvest theme. Her pumpkins didn't have faces on them, but she had a nice little display of them to put on her front porch, along with all the new plants she was going to purchase.

The week at school kept her busy and there was a lot of extra work going into the winter chorus concert. Every day when she came home, she felt a sense of exhaustion, but remembered it was all for a good cause.

On Friday afternoon, she sat on the sofa for her afternoon chat with Trevor.

"I'm telling you, the kids sound great, but the stage is going to be seriously lacking. I'm tempted to just go out and buy some stuff myself, but I know that's setting a bad precedent. Plus, I don't want the other teachers getting annoyed with me." She sighed. "But I am going to go to the farmers market in the morning to get a couple of pots of mums—hopefully in a few different colors—and whatever fun fall decorations I can find for the porch. I have my scarecrow from last year and I had grabbed some extra pumpkins last week, but hopefully there will be more stuff to choose from."

Phoebe whined up at her and Tessa bent over and scooped her up, giving her a little snuggle.

"I have a bunch of twinkly lights up in the big tree in the front yard, but I noticed there were a lot of bulbs out this week. I'm thinking of just getting a couple of new sets and starting fresh. It's such a pain but it looks so pretty when it's done, so...you know I'll do it," she said with a small laugh. "I got bigger bulbs on the lights in the backyard and they're on a timer. They're a lot less maintenance. Still... they're not as pretty as the twinkly ones. I'll have to pull out the ladder and work on it this weekend."

She considered hiring a handyman, but she enjoyed doing this sort of thing herself once in a while.

"Luckily the weather's going to be nice, so it won't be too much of a hardship." She sighed. "I wish you were here working on it with me. I know how fall was always your favorite season." As she always did, she gently touched the screen. "I miss you." And letting out a shaky breath, she let the screen go dark before putting the phone down.

It took her longer than it usually did to get back up, and instead of making herself the chicken piccata she had planned on, she decided to order Chinese food and have it delivered.

Tomorrow she'd be happy and perky and back to her old self, but tonight she wanted to just put on her jammies, turn off the lights, and watch some sort of documentary while eating her dinner on the couch.

So that's what she did.

By Saturday morning, however, she truly was feeling better.

The farmers market was crowded and there were so

many fantastic sights and smells that she didn't know where to look first. In less than an hour, she had purchased enough vegetables to feed the entire neighborhood, a couple of pints of soup, a fresh baguette, and enough mums to cover multiple porches. It took several trips to her car to get it all in, and by the time she arrived home, the thought of unloading it was more than a little daunting.

"But first...lunch."

Inside, she enjoyed one of the pints of soup and some fresh bread before taking Phoebe out into the backyard for a little exercise. As much as she would have loved to stay out there and relax, all the plants were waiting.

"There is definitely a soak in the hot tub in my future," she promised herself as she put Phoebe back in the house and headed straight out to her car.

It took an hour to get everything out and arranged on her porch exactly the way she wanted it. Of course, that included pulling out some of last year's decorations and incorporating them and putting some of the pots of mums on her back porch as well.

When everything was exactly to her liking, Tessa headed to her small shed and pulled out her ladder and carefully carried it out to the front yard. Hanging—or re-hanging—lights was her least favorite thing to do, but she hated the thought of paying someone when she was perfectly capable of doing it.

"Just...don't look down," she murmured as she climbed up and tacked the lights on the front porch first. These were easier to handle because they were in a straight line, so switching them out for the new set was a breeze. The ones in the big Sweetbay Magnolia tree were going to be a little trickier.

The tree itself was gorgeous and one of the reasons she

fell in love with her house, but its size definitely challenged her love of outdoor decorating.

Carefully, she moved the ladder into the yard and braced it against the tree. She'd done this at least four other times without incident, so she had no idea why she was freaking out about it today. Staring up at the tree, she took a minute to think things through. Out of the corner of her eye, she spotted Liam's truck driving by and knew he'd be pulling into his driveway and probably cursing her very existence.

"That's right, neighbor. I'm putting up new decorations, so...suck it." The giggle was out before she could stop it, and it made her feel a little like a badass to say that sort of thing semi-audibly, but it was all really just a stalling tactic before getting up on the ladder.

Tessa climbed up the first two rungs and jumped a bit at the sound of a car door slamming.

Liam's.

Jerk.

It didn't matter that there were plenty of other sounds coming from all over the neighborhood; she took it personally that he would make such a loud noise when she was clearly trying to concentrate on climbing into the tree.

Pushing all thoughts aside except for the task at hand, she climbed up to the second to last rung and began carefully unthreading the lights from the tree. It was slow going and the longer she worked at it, the more she realized that maybe it was too time-consuming for her and perhaps worth the money to pay someone else to handle. Still...she was already up in the tree, so she was going to finish what she started.

"Note so self, find a handyman..."

This strand of lights wasn't too long, but just when she

thought she had it all untangled, the end of it snagged on a branch. With a muttered curse, she stretched to give it a final tug, but all that did was make her lose her footing on the ladder.

A small cry escaped her lips as she found herself on her tippy-toes. It was either grab onto a branch or fall, and as she heard the ladder creak, she realized she was flailing and essentially kicking it away.

Dropping the lights, Tessa reached for the closest branch and scratched her arms in the process, causing her to cry out in pain. Upper body strength totally wasn't her thing and she had a feeling this was all going to end badly for her.

Desperately, she clawed at the branch and tried to pull herself upwards, but she couldn't get her footing. The ladder crashed to the ground and her whole body shook. Tears stung her eyes and this was the most afraid she could ever remember being. She might only be ten feet off the ground, but she had a feeling it wouldn't be a gentle fall if she simply let herself go.

"Help!" she cried out and prayed one of her neighbors could hear her because her voice was more of a hoarse whisper than an actual loud plea like she intended. When she tried to call out again, no sound came out and she knew she was going to fall. Her hands were slick and her sneakers didn't have good soles on them to get any kind of traction on the tree trunk.

"Tessa!" someone called out. "Let go! I've got you!"

"Liam?" she whispered, but was too afraid to turn her head to see if it was really him.

"Just let go! I'm right beneath you!"

"I'm scared! I'm just so..."

She lost her already tenuous grip on the branch and felt

herself falling. Another scream was out before she could stop it, and she was certain he couldn't catch her. It was too improbable. With her eyes slammed shut, she simply waited for the pain of hitting the hard ground and prayed she wouldn't break anything.

Suddenly, all the air rushed from her lungs as she felt herself surrounded by a pair of strong arms.

He caught me...

Her whole body was trembling and for a moment, Tessa wasn't sure if she was going to be sick or simply cry. Curling into Liam's solid frame, she let out a shaky breath and tried to compose herself.

Deep breaths...in...and out...

When she lifted her head to thank him, the first thing she noticed was the scowl on his face.

Uh-oh...

"Liam, I..."

"What the hell were you thinking? Do you have any idea how stupid this little stunt of yours was?"

Chapter Four

The words were out before he could stop them, and honestly, he wasn't sure he wanted to.

She'd taken ten years off his life when he looked over and saw the ladder fall and then her dangling from a branch.

Damn foolish woman...

Carefully, Liam put Tessa on her feet and saw her eyes brimming with tears.

That she quickly wiped away.

"Tessa, look um..."

She seemed to pull herself together as she squared her shoulders and met his gaze. "Thank you for catching me," she said stiffly. "I've been putting lights in this tree every season and every holiday for the last two years. This is the first time things went wrong." He watched as she swallowed hard. "I'm very thankful that you were close by and able to respond so quickly. Now, if you'll excuse me, I think I'll go inside and rest for a bit."

And without another word, she walked away and went right into her house and shut the door.

Loudly.

Leaving him standing in the middle of her yard, feeling like a world-class jackass.

Yeah, it was stupid for her to be up on a ladder all by herself with no one around to at least hold the damn thing, but that didn't mean he needed to yell at her. Hanging his head, he wondered what it was he was supposed to do now.

The obvious choice was to pick up the ladder and pull down the lights she had been trying to snag.

So he did.

Once the lights were on the ground, he spotted the new set she was more than likely going to replace them with.

So...he did that too.

Several things occurred to him as he worked; he was spending far too much of his time either thinking about this woman or watching her. There had been no reason for him to stay in his front yard as long as he had when he got home. If anything, there had been plenty of reasons for him to go inside and make himself lunch and return some calls and emails. But seeing her up on that ladder had given him pause and he'd lingered on his front walkway, watching her like a bit of a creeper.

Turned out it worked to her advantage, but...

Why the hell wasn't he in his own house eating lunch? Why was he hanging twinkly lights in her tree? Why was he thinking about her smile and how much she seemed to simply glow under all the praise she got last weekend? Or why did he wish all week long that he had a plateful of those delicious sugar cookies and some warm cider while sitting outside alone by his firepit? But basically, why was he thinking about her and her smile when he had a million other things that he needed to be thinking about?

Unfortunately, he didn't have any answers.

Folding up the ladder, he picked it up and placed it in front of her garage, along with the old set of lights. And as much as he'd love to pat himself on the back and congratulate himself on a job well done, he knew he needed to knock on the door and apologize.

And he really hated to apologize.

Raking his hands through his hair, he realized he hated procrastinating almost as much, so with nothing left to do, he walked up to the front door and knocked.

Tessa opened the door and stared at him blandly but didn't say a word.

Message received; she was wary.

Clearing his throat, Liam said, "Um...I put the ladder in front of your garage door."

She nodded.

"And I took down the old lights."

Another nod.

Damn, she was not going to make this easy on him at all.

"I also hung up the new ones," he said almost defensively. "They might not be as artistically arranged as you might have hung them, but...I did the best that I could." When she still didn't respond, he gave a curt nod and took a step back. "So...yeah. Next time you need help with something like that, just let me know."

Still nothing.

"And I'm glad you didn't get hurt." Then he realized he really didn't know that for sure. "You're not hurt, are you?"

"Other than some scratches on my arms and hands, I'm fine. Thank you for asking."

It was all he should have needed. He told her what he'd done, she assured him she was fine and...

Oh, right.

The apology.

"I shouldn't have snapped at you," he said after a moment. "I don't have any excuse and...I'm sorry."

She nodded again. "Thank you." Taking a step back, Tessa rested her hand on the front door and winced slightly. "I appreciate the help, so...I'll see you around."

The door was almost shut when he blurted out, "And I'm sorry about all the shit I said about the Halloween decorations. Obviously I was in the minority and I should have just kept my opinion to myself. So...yeah. Sorry."

She paused in the doorway and studied him hard for a moment, as if trying to figure out what to say.

Her response was the last thing he expected.

"Would you like to come in for some cider and cookies?"

Don't appear too anxious...

"Uh...sure," he said casually, impressing himself with how blasé he sounded. "That would be nice. Thanks."

Stepping aside, Tessa motioned for him to come in. He stepped inside and took in the cozy coastal decor. It all looked like something directly from a decorating magazine, and he had to admit he was impressed. Walking into the living room, he noted the oversized sofa with lots of throw pillows, a white-washed fireplace, and the built-ins around it. Walking over, he admired the craftsmanship.

"I want to do this at my place," he told her. "I feel like there should have been built-ins around the fireplace."

"It was one of my favorite things about this room," she was saying, but Liam was only half-listening because he spotted several framed photographs. Even without knowing anything about her past, he knew the man in the photos had to be her husband.

The one in the silver frame where Tessa was in a white sundress and the guy was in a suit looked like a wedding picture, and he couldn't seem to tear his gaze away.

Tessa must have noticed what he was staring at and quietly cleared her throat to get his attention. "If you think those are impressive, you should see the crown molding in the dining room and kitchen," she said, and as soon as he faced her, she turned and led him out of the room. "We can eat in the kitchen or we can go out back, if you'd like. I was just about to take Phoebe out."

He was curious about her yard—purely from a neighborly perspective. "Out back would be great. I'm trying to figure out what to do with my yard. The Fosters kept it in pristine shape, but it's pretty basic."

"He loved mowing that space," she told him. "I used to think it was adorable how much he looked forward to getting on his ride-on mower every Saturday."

"I'd really like to put in an outdoor kitchen. That was my initial thought when I first saw the property. But my brothers are trying to convince me to put in a pool." Shrugging, he watched as she put a bunch of cookies on a plate and then turned to pour cider into mugs. "Do you always keep it warming on the stove?" he asked.

"No, not always. After I came in earlier, I put some on and then sort of lost track of time," she said shyly. Turning, she looked at him. "I was mortified that you had to come and save me. I've never had something like that happen to me before. I'm not a fan of heights and it's a task I don't look forward to, but I've always gotten through it without any issues."

"You could always hire a handyman," he suggested and watched as she smiled.

And it lit up her entire face.

Then something strange happened…

Liam felt himself smiling with her and had a strange overall sense of lightness that he hadn't felt in…years.

"I was thinking the same thing before I went out there—and…several times this week—but it seemed like a waste of money when I could just do the job myself. Lesson learned."

Unable to help it, Liam stepped in closer. "Hey, don't be so down on yourself. Things like that can happen to anyone. It was just fortunate that you didn't get hurt."

She held out her arms and placed her hands palm side up and he saw all the cuts and scratches.

"Oh, Tessa…" His gaze met hers. "You really should put something on those." Reaching out, he gently touched the palm of her hand. "And you definitely should have them bandaged up. Do you have a first aid kit?"

"I cleaned them up when I came in—washed up and used peroxide and all that. I'm surprised you didn't hear me cursing all the way outside. It stung like fire."

Laughing softly, he continued to study her injuries.

At least, he told himself that's what he was doing and not simply enjoying the softness of her skin.

"I'm sure it did. Still, I know letting the air on them is good, but you should put some antibiotic cream on them and cover them up for a while too." Straightening, he looked around. "Why don't you get the first aid kit and I'll carry the cookies and cider outside? I can help you bandage up."

"Liam, you've already done so much…"

"It's not a big deal. I'd hate to think of you getting an infection." He felt something by his foot and looked down to find Phoebe sniffing his sneaker. "I'll carry her out too."

"I'm not sure you can balance two hot drinks, a plate of cookies, and Phoebe," she teased.

"Get me a tray and I'll make it work. Trust me. I've got excellent balance."

"As opposed to me, right?"

"Tessa..."

"Just kidding," she said with a laugh of her own and a few moments later, she had a tray on the island and was placing everything on it. Liam bent down and scooped up the dog and marveled at how she weighed next to nothing. "If you give me a minute, we can walk out together, and I can at least hold the door open."

"Deal."

And sure enough, that's what they did.

He stepped out her back door onto the deck and then paused in awe. "Holy crap. This is amazing back here."

She smiled at the compliment as she led him over to her seating area. "This is like my little sanctuary. Phoebe's really too small to take out on a leash, so we spend a lot of time back here. Plus, I don't know, it's kind of nice to have a bit of green space to call your own. It's peaceful." She let out a small sigh as she sat down and motioned for him to join her. "My mother always had the prettiest gardens when I was growing up and I had zero interest in learning how she did it. But then, a few years ago, I found that it was actually very relaxing and a little therapeutic. So when I bought this house, I tried gardening."

"Well, you've done an amazing job. Seriously, it's beautiful." Sitting in the cushioned seat beside her, Liam reached for the first aid kit and began pulling out the antibiotic cream and bandages, even as his mind wandered to think about if she took up gardening as a way of dealing with the loss of her husband.

It was none of his business and yet...he was curious.

Probably way more curious than he should be.

There was no way he would come right out and ask her, so he busied himself with getting her hands bandaged up along with a few spots on her arms too. When he was done, she thanked him and together they sat back with their cider and started to eat the cookies.

"I'm sure I already know the answer to this, but did you make the cookies yourself?" he asked.

"I did. Baking is something I've always enjoyed doing. I grew up baking with my grandmother on my father's side and it's just something that's always stayed with me. If there's a holiday or any kind of special occasion to be celebrated, I'm going to bake cookies." She took a sip of her cider. "I'm not great with cakes or pies, but cookies are always fun."

"My mother loves to bake pies," Liam said with a small laugh. "And when she gets in the mood, she'll make what seems like dozens of them."

"Well, with the pub, I'm sure she can always put them on the menu as a dessert special, right?"

"Definitely. She makes the absolute best apple pie." Grinning, he picked up another cookie. "Whenever I was deployed, I used to wish that she could send a pie, but..."

"Yeah, I'm sure it wouldn't be edible by the time it got to you."

"Exactly."

They sat in companionable silence for several minutes and Tessa seemed content to just nibble on her cookie and watch her dog.

And oddly, he wasn't hating it.

But his mind simply wouldn't shut up.

"So those built-ins," he began. "They look great and the

framed photos are a nice touch. Rather than filling them with a lot of clutter, it really just highlights the space."

She glanced at him and seemed to know exactly what he was doing.

"Liam, if you have something to ask, just ask it."

Damn.

With a bit of a sigh, he looked at her. "I guess I was just curious about...your marriage."

Beside him, she groaned softly. "That's what I was afraid of."

* * *

Tessa knew the instant Liam stopped and stared at her photos that this topic was going to come up and yet...she supposed it wasn't the worst thing in the world for her to talk about it.

"Trevor and I were best friends from the time we were in middle school. I tutored him in history and he helped me with math," she said before looking out at her garden. "We bonded over our love of Harry Potter books and our mutual dislike of Mr. Collins, our science teacher."

He nodded and waited for her to continue.

"By high school, everyone thought we were a couple, but...we were just really good friends. Although...guys hesitated to ask me out because they thought Trevor was my boyfriend." She shrugged. "And more than a few girls got annoyed with me because they had crushes on him, but I was always around." Looking over at him, she grinned. "It was actually a good test for who would make a good girlfriend for him."

Again, all he did was nod.

"Anyway, we chose the same college, and it was spring of our junior year when Trevor got sick." This time she let out a shaky breath because she remembered that day so clearly. "He came to watch the rehearsal for the musical I was performing in, and I could tell he didn't feel well. He was rubbing his head and shaking. I insisted he go to the doctor and before we knew it, he was in the ER having all kinds of scary tests. He made me promise not to call his parents until we knew he was going to be okay." Shaking her head, she said, "But he never was."

"Tessa, you don't have to..."

This time she looked over at him and smiled sadly. "It's okay. I should be able to talk about it." Taking a moment to sip some cider, she continued. "He had a brain tumor. Inoperable. Obviously we called his parents and things got crazy after that. I didn't want to finish college, but he insisted. As soon as I graduated, though, I was back in Charleston so I could be with him. After seeking second, third, and fourth opinions, we had to accept the truth."

Pausing, she took another sip of cider and watched as Phoebe pranced around the yard.

"Anyway, by that time, the doctors could tell how fast the tumor was growing and they gave him two years."

"Holy shit," Liam whispered.

"So we decided to try to cram as many things from his bucket list into those two years that we could. Trevor wanted me to start teaching, but...I couldn't. There was no way I could commit to a job when there was so much we wanted to do. So, I tutored and worked a bunch of random jobs—much to my parents' dismay—but I didn't care. In two years, I was going to have to say goodbye to my best friend. He wasn't going to get to live to see his 25th birthday."

Turning her head, she looked at him. "When you're faced with something like that, you realize what's important and what's not."

He nodded.

"Anyway, we did a lot as soon as we could because he was still feeling okay and the doctors said that could change at any time. So we took road trips, went to concerts, did some crazy stuff like zip lining in Colorado on the highest one in the U.S., went skydiving, swam with dolphins, rode horses on the beach, and rode in a hot-air balloon."

Beside her, he chuckled. "That's impressive. You're pretty brave."

"I faked it," she confided. "Climbing up on that ladder today required a bit of a pep talk, but...I mean, how crappy would it be to make him do those things alone? So I went and smiled and laughed and even though I was terrified most of the time, I did my best to never let it show."

"I'm sure he would've understood..."

"Oh, I know he would've, but...I didn't want him to do that. I wanted to be supportive. I wanted to show him how brave I could be, just like he was having to be brave." She shrugged. "I realize riding in a hot-air balloon isn't on the same level of facing your own mortality, but..."

"It wasn't a competition," he said, his voice a little low and gruff.

"Fifteen months later, he had a seizure," she said rather than address his comment. "That was like...it was the symptom we dreaded the most because it signified that things were progressing in a bad way. The doctors all said this was normal and he was put on some different medications to ease his discomfort, but...the countdown officially started that day."

Phoebe walked over and stood on her hind legs at Tessa's feet—her way of saying she was done playing and wanted to be held. Picking her up, she kissed the tiny dog on the head and knew she needed to finish the story.

"About a week later, Trevor said there was one last thing he wanted to cross off his bucket list."

"What was it?"

"To get married." A small laugh was out before she could stop it because, thinking back, she could still remember the shock she felt when he said it to her. "He had a ring and everything."

"Were you really surprised?" Liam asked carefully. "I mean, the two of you had been together for so long..."

Oh.

That.

Swallowing hard, Tessa paused, took another sip of her cider before putting the cup down. Twisting in her seat, she looked at Liam's confused face. "Trevor and I were never a couple. Ever. There was never that...that feeling, you know? We tried kissing a couple of times and always ended up laughing instead. So...yeah, I was surprised."

"Um..."

"I tried explaining how it wouldn't be the same—that the two of us getting married would be a waste of a bucket list task." She shrugged. "He disagreed."

"So the two of you...?"

She shook her head. "We loved each other very much, just...not romantically." Then she held up her left hand, wiggling her fingers. "And because I loved him that much, I married him."

His eyes went wide, but he said nothing.

"We got married, and I moved into his home with him.

61

He made me promise to let him stay home with hospice care for as long as humanly possible. I think he knew if his parents were in charge, they'd try to talk him into moving to a hospice center or the hospital and he didn't want that. So I was..." She paused as her voice caught. "I was his advocate. I slept by his side every night, we played games and sang songs and I made sure every day was filled with love and laughter."

"Damn, Tessa. How..."

"You just do it," she said softly. "When you love someone, you just do it. I knew I could cry and scream and get mad when he was gone, but while he was still living, I would be the happiest person on the planet."

"Wasn't it hard? I mean...to keep up the pretense..."

"It was exhausting," she admitted. "But...I did it." Tears stung her eyes, and she quickly brushed them away. "That last week, Trevor admitted that he knew—he could tell how much of a toll this was taking on me and made me promise that I would grieve when he was gone, but that I'd also remember to find the joy in every day. Those silly things we all take for granted—the things he would never get to do again—I promised to embrace them because I realized that tomorrow isn't promised to us."

Wiping away another wave of tears, she kissed Phoebe again as a distraction.

"After he was gone, my parents gave me a few weeks but then finally told me how much they disapproved of the way I put off my career and put my life on hold. They said Trevor would have understood. And again, I knew he would, but...I don't regret a single thing."

"Wow," he whispered.

"So now...I find the beauty in everything around me. I appreciate the mundane. I dance in the kitchen, I sing loudly, and I over-decorate at the holidays." She gave him a mischievous grin and winked. "And I don't expect everyone to understand or to approve, but loving Trevor was the best thing to ever happen to me. I mattered so much to him that he wanted to experience his last days in this world with me." Nodding, she stood. "Not many people experience a love like that. Not many people even understand it. But I do."

Picking up a cookie, she took a bite and walked back into the house. It was a little rude to just do it without saying a word, but she needed a few minutes to compose herself. Maybe he'd follow her inside, maybe he wouldn't. It didn't matter. Liam Donovan seemed like the kind of man who didn't take anything on face value; he needed facts. He needed to do the research and figure out how things work the way that they do and why.

Well, she'd just pretty much given him an instruction manual on herself so he could understand why she did the things she did.

And maybe moving forward, he'd keep his snark and disapproval to himself.

A few minutes later, he walked into her kitchen with an empty plate and their mugs. Tessa took hers from his hand and thanked him. She turned to get more cider, but his words stopped her.

"I think you're hiding," he said, sounding firm and as if his words were law.

"Excuse me?"

He nodded. "I think you're hiding behind this Pollyanna persona and avoiding life. Now, I realize I never met Trevor, but I doubt this is the way he wanted you to live. You need to move on, Tessa."

So much for him keeping his disapproval to himself...

Rather than argue—because this was the exact same thing her parents had been saying for almost two years—she gave him a serene smile. "I appreciate your concern, but, like you said, you never met Trevor, so you really can't say, and...it's none of your business."

He looked mildly taken aback by her words and if she thought he was going to back off, she was wrong.

"I'm not saying it's my concern, but I am saying that I don't believe he would want you walking around spouting sunshine that you really didn't feel. And even if he did, that's a heaping load of pressure to put on you."

"You're crazy. Trevor never put any pressure on me."

Studying her hard, he leaned against the kitchen island. "I can understand grieving, but you've taken it to an unhealthy level. Maybe go for counseling, maybe find a support group, but it's not healthy to still be living like this years later."

And that was it.

That was like hitting the launch button.

"Who the hell put you in charge of deciding how long someone is supposed to grieve?" she demanded. "Have you ever lost someone you cared about?"

"As a matter of fact, I have. I lost a few buddies during one of our deployments. I sat right there and watched them die," he countered. "You don't get to corner the market on grief, you know."

"Oh, I know, but I also believe grief is personal and no two people grieve the same. So spare me the pep talk or how it is you think I should be living." Turning away, she put her cup in the sink because she suddenly wasn't thirsty.

"Have you dated anyone since he died?"

Turning again, she looked at him in horror. *"What?!"*

"You heard me. Have you dated anyone since Trevor died?"

"What does that have to do with anything?"

Taking a step toward her, he explained. "I'm not saying you didn't love Trevor. But it wasn't a romantic love. Hell, it wasn't even a real marriage! I know I'm no expert in grief, but even I know there's a difference between the loss of a friend and the loss of a spouse. A real spouse."

"How dare..."

"I think you're hiding behind this bright and cheery persona because you're afraid of getting hurt again, and that is completely understandable. But what you really need to be asking yourself is if this is the life that would make Trevor proud. As your best friend, is this the life he imagined you living?" He took another step closer and his voice softened. "I don't think someone who loved you so much that you were the one person he wanted with him right until the end, would want to see you walking around smiling and being this uber-cheery person when that's not what you felt in your heart. You know if he were here that he'd be able to see right through this."

It shouldn't have mattered—anything that he said—but unfortunately, he was right. Trevor would see through this persona and yell at her for not being true to herself. She was a genuinely happy person—that much wasn't a lie—but she was also someone who enjoyed her privacy and could take comfort in a long, hard cry.

She was tired.

So damn tired.

Licking her lips, Tessa looked up at him and tried to smile. "Thank you."

He instantly looked suspicious. "For...?"

"You're right. He would see through this...this person

I've morphed into. And he would hate it." She cursed the sting of fresh tears. "I genuinely am a happy person who always looks for the best in everything, but...sometimes I feel like I go above and beyond and...I can't help it. That's what the world needs sometimes."

"But at what cost to you?"

Good question.

The sigh was out before she could stop it. "If it's all the same to you, I'm really not up for being under the microscope anymore today." She held up her bandaged hands. "As it is, I'm feeling a little like the walking wounded and all this talk is just...I just can't." With as much grace as she could muster, she said, "I appreciate everything you did today, Liam. Everything. So...thank you. But I think I'm going to crash on the couch for a little while and then figure out what kind of takeout I'm ordering since I won't be cooking with these hands tonight."

He nodded and together they made their way toward the front door. It was weird to think that she'd just sort of bared her soul to the one person who'd basically been nothing but a huge negative in her life. Even long after Jenna and Nick's wedding, she thought about him and would cringe at all the negative energy he brought with him. They'd seen each other a few weeks after the wedding and even then, he'd been a downer.

But today, he redeemed himself a little.

Not that she thought it would last, but still, it was nice to see another side of him.

At the door, Tessa smiled at him. "Thanks again and I guess I'll see you around." She had mixed feelings on whether or not she wanted to change the status quo between them. It was nice to just have to smile and wave occasionally—less chance of them griping at each other.

They had turned a corner today, but again, she wasn't sure it was a permanent thing.

Liam stared down at her like he was trying to think of something to say—which was weird because Liam always seemed to have something to say. But when he spoke, it was the last thing she ever expected him to say.

"Have dinner with me tonight."

Chapter Five

Liam looked around his kitchen and frowned. It was a perfectly fine kitchen, but after seeing Tessa's, it felt like it was lacking something.

Character.

Personality.

Just like the rest of his house.

Raking his hands through his hair, he let out a long breath. "Okay, I'm getting way too freaked out over the color of my backsplash and lack of crap to decorate the space." Groaning, he walked out of the kitchen and went to the living room.

Big mistake.

Now he was disappointed in a second space when just this morning, he was perfectly fine with his entire house.

Clearly going over to Tessa's was a mistake.

Except...it wasn't.

She would have gotten hurt if she'd fallen from the tree —not terribly hurt, but hurt just the same. And then everything that happened after that was just...unexpected.

She'd married a friend to fulfill a dying wish. He

wanted to ask what kind of person did that, but he already had the answer.

He just didn't agree with it.

To him, it seemed like maybe that last act of friendship was keeping her locked in this pattern of make believe and not really dealing with life.

"Then again, what the hell do I know? I can count on one hand the number of times we've actually spoken, so..."

Part of him wanted to pick up the phone and call his friend Nick and maybe get some insight, but that seemed a little extreme and sort of like invading Tessa's privacy.

And he did not want to be that kind of creeper.

Still...maybe inviting her over was a bad idea. At the time, it seemed like the thing to do. When they weren't arguing with each other, he found she was really kind of nice—especially when she wasn't in one of her super cheery moods and spouting about how wonderful everything was.

It wasn't like Liam hated the world or that he was overly pessimistic; he was just a realist. Sometimes things weren't great or fantastic or beautiful. That's just the way life was.

But Tessa's beautiful...

Okay, where the hell did that come from?

Sure, Tessa was attractive in a girl-next-door kind of way, but beautiful? No.

Yes.

Groaning, he paced around the house and there wasn't one thing out of place.

Mainly because he didn't have anything extra to be out of place.

No throw pillows, no afghans or decorative throws, no knick-knacks...everything he had served a purpose and was functional.

The damn place practically looked sterile.

It was almost like he was still living in the barracks.

He'd been working on the house since the day he closed on it. He'd taken down wallpaper, painted walls, installed some new trim around the windows, ripped up the carpet that was practically all throughout the main floor, and put up some new light fixtures. The house had been seriously outdated and in need of some upgrades. It occurred to him that decorating hadn't really been a priority.

The next project was going to be the master bathroom, then new appliances in the kitchen, knocking down the wall between the dining room and kitchen, and then the backyard. It was all planned out. But between the house and the fishing resort, Liam felt like he was being stretched a little thin.

There was a construction crew doing the bulk of the work at the resort, but he was still on site every day overseeing things and, with Will working beside him, they were ensuring that nothing went awry.

That's when the strangest thought hit him.

One of the things he most looked forward to when he retired from the Marines was slowing down his pace a bit. But as soon as he'd gotten home, he hit the ground running and bought a home, broke ground on a new business, and hadn't so much as taken one full day for himself in well over a month.

Liam felt that once he came home, he'd start dating and could finally have a social life and a possible romantic one and yet...he hadn't gone out with anyone since hooking up with one of the bridesmaids at Nick and Jenna's wedding three months ago.

I'm pathetic.

Was that why he was inviting Tessa over? Somewhere

in the back of his mind, was he looking at her in a potential dating way?

Um...no.

Maybe.

Okay, he wouldn't exactly say no if it came up in conversation.

Which he doubted it would.

The doorbell rang and he suddenly felt nervous and unsure and so unlike himself that it bordered on the bizarre. He was fearless, dammit. There was no reason for him to be feeling like this over some Chinese takeout with his neighbor.

Neighbor, not a woman he would consider dating.

But as soon as he opened the door, he wondered just how much he was lying to himself.

Looking up at him with those big brown eyes, Tessa smiled and handed him a plate of cookies. "I brought dessert," she said with a smile. "If I'd had more time and my hands felt better, I would have made more, but you seemed to like them and I thought it would be enough. I have ice cream that I can go and grab from my freezer and..."

"Tessa?"

"Hmm?"

"This is perfect," he assured her as he took the plate from her hands. "Thank you, but you really didn't need to bring anything." Stepping aside he motioned for her to come in.

"I have to admit, I've been curious about what you've been doing to the place. I was close with the Fosters and spent a lot of time here."

"You were here on move-in day..."

"I know, but everything was a bit chaotic and your

family distracted me from really seeing what you'd been doing with the place."

Closing the door, Liam moved beside her. "So? What do you think so far?"

She paused and looked around, and he knew immediately that she wasn't impressed.

"I mentioned earlier how I'm thinking of adding the built-ins around the fireplace," he explained, "and I'm thinking of refinishing the floors. Can you believe they had all this hardwood under the carpet? I mean…why cover it?"

Making a non-committal sound, she stepped further into the room before wandering around a bit.

"You really kind of stripped the place," she commented after a minute. "I realize the importance of putting your own stamp on a home, but what was wrong with what was here?"

Rather than answer right away, Liam put the plate of cookies on the kitchen table before joining her again. "It was all seriously outdated and felt like my grandparents' house." With a shrug, he added, "The house has great bones. It just needs to be brought up to date." He described all of his plans that he still needed to implement and when he was done, he felt pretty proud of himself. "Can I get you something to drink? I've got beer, water, wine…"

"Just water, please," she said before following him into the kitchen. "What happened to the island?"

Chuckling, he got her a glass and filled it with water and ice. "That thing was on its last legs and basically an eyesore. Did you know it wasn't even a built in? It was on wheels! It was kind of a safety hazard too."

She frowned. "I thought it was charming because it could be moved if you needed the space, but that's just me," she murmured before taking a sip of her water.

Since they clearly weren't seeing eye to eye on his improvements, he thought it best to change the subject. "So, I was thinking of ordering Chinese food. Is that okay with you?"

Thankfully, she smiled. "Ooh...that's my favorite. If I'm going to get takeout, nine times out of ten, that's what I get."

Relief washed over him. "I enjoy it too. Mostly when I get takeout, I grab it from the pub, but after that, my go-to is pizza."

"That's a good option too. If you'd rather get a pizza..."

"No. No, Chinese food is fine. Tell me what you like and I'll place the order and have it delivered."

It took several minutes for them to review the menu while talking about their likes and dislikes, and by the time Liam placed the order, he felt like he knew everything he needed to know about Tessa's taste in food.

Well, Chinese food.

"Would you like to go out to the yard? I can show you what I'm planning on doing."

All she did was nod.

Stepping outside, Liam launched into his description of where he was going to put the outdoor kitchen, how he planned on building a pergola, how he'll tear up the concrete patio and install new pavers, which bushes and shrubs he was going to pull, and where he'd put the pool when the time came."

"Wow. That all sounds ambitious," she said without the least hint of enthusiasm.

"I might add another seating area over there in the far corner," he added.

"But...what about the oak tree? It's in great shape and it's the perfect tree for a treehouse."

That made him laugh. "A treehouse? I think I'm a little too old for that."

Rolling her eyes, she let out a small laugh too. "Not for you," she said in a mildly condescending tone. "For the future. You know, when you have kids."

"Yeah, um...I don't think that's going to happen for a while. Why should I keep a tree just for the possibility that one day I might have kids? Who knows if I'll still be living here? And besides, maybe they won't like treehouses."

"Every kid loves a treehouse, Liam," she reasoned. "It's like having your own fort. You can't tell me you didn't want a space like that when you were a kid. I know I did."

"I did, but like I said, what if I never have kids? Shouldn't I get to use the yard in a way that works for me?"

She shrugged. "Sure. It's your place."

And there was something in her tone that screamed disapproval.

Again.

Doing his best to ignore it, he explained in greater detail more of his plans until he was sure their food would be arriving. "Come on," he said. "Let's go inside. The food should be here any minute."

Wordlessly, she followed.

But within a matter of minutes, she was questioning his choice in light fixtures, his color choices, and commenting that the house looked like a typical bachelor pad.

"I just moved in two weeks ago," he argued lightly. "In time, it will look more lived-in and will feel like a home."

"But it already did feel like a home," she countered. "The Fosters lived here for twenty-years and it worked perfectly for them."

"Yes, but that's the difference. It worked for *them*. I don't have the same taste. I'll never use a formal dining room, so taking the wall down makes sense. I paid for the house and I shouldn't have to keep it as a shrine to the former owners."

"I didn't say to keep it as a shrine..."

"No, but you're implying that I shouldn't change anything." Pausing, he frowned as everything suddenly made sense. "Oh...I get it."

"Get what?"

"This is about you not liking change and not wanting to move on with your life," he said simply.

"That's not what I'm saying, and the two things don't have anything to do with one another."

He was about to explain his theory when the doorbell rang.

Literally saved by the bell...

Within minutes, Liam had their food set out on the table and he was holding the chair out for Tessa.

Because his mother raised him to have manners.

They made small talk about the food and the local restaurants and she asked a ton of questions about what it was like growing up owning a pub.

"We all worked there from the time we could walk," he said with a small laugh. "Mom always brought us in and we'd either wipe down tables, take out the trash, refill the ketchup bottles..." He shrugged. "It was just something we always did."

"So you never had to look for an after-school job, huh?"

"Never," he said with a grin. "Although, I really wished I could work anywhere else but there."

"How come?"

"Just to try something different and have an identity away from Donovan's Pub." Another shrug. "What about you? Did you have any exciting jobs in high school?"

She laughed softly and Liam found he liked the sound of it.

"I did a lot of babysitting and worked as a nanny during the summers," she explained. "That's really what started my love of teaching."

"You're a teacher?" Wait...didn't his mother mention that the day he moved in?

Nodding, she said, "Music teacher. I teach at Laurel Bay Elementary."

"Wow! That's very cool."

"I enjoy it and the kids are great. Working with them has really helped pull me out of a funk more than once. It's hard to be depressed when you're singing happy songs."

Taking a moment to finish a forkful of food, he remembered their earlier conversation. She didn't like change, she struggled with depression...

"Look, I hate to harp on this, but...have you looked into...you know...therapy?"

Tessa gave him an odd look. "For what?"

"You know...depression."

Rolling her eyes, she reached for a fried wonton. "Liam, I'm not depressed."

"But you just said..."

"I just meant..." Pausing, she sighed. "I went for grief counseling after Trevor died and sometimes I get in a funk because I miss him. It's completely natural and then...I move on. I have to."

"Which brings me back to what we were talking about before the food arrived," he said, because clearly he was like a dog with a bone. "I think that maybe this whole inability to deal with change is keeping you from moving on with your life."

* * *

Tessa rarely lost her patience and she never argued when she was a guest in someone's home, but Liam Donovan pushed her over the edge.

Tossing her wonton down, she leaned back and glared at him. "What is it with you, huh? Do you get some sort of joy out of being a total jerk?"

His dark eyes went wide and his mouth moved, but nothing came out.

"Where do you get off psychoanalyzing me? Do you have a degree in psychology?"

"No, but..."

"Are you a psychiatrist?"

Frowning, he said, "No. But..."

"So you just feel it's okay to throw your completely unfounded opinion out there just because my life looks different from yours, is that it?"

Pushing his plate aside, Liam glared hard at her. "It's not that your life looks different from mine, Tessa. It's that I'm a fairly good judge of people and it's obvious that you've got some...you know...issues."

Mimicking his move and pushing her own dish aside, she met his glare head on. "So what if I do?" she asked loudly. "No one's asking you to do the things I do! I don't think it's a crime to have emotions or be sentimental! It's not hurting anyone if I'm sad one day and need to just be alone! And it's definitely not a cause for therapy because I happen to like the charm of an old house!"

"That's not what..."

She stood up. "It's exactly what you're saying." Mumbling a mild curse, Tessa walked out of the kitchen, grabbing her purse as she went. "I knew we should have stuck to our original plan of just waving from a distance. There's no point in even trying to be civil to someone like you." She was just a few feet from the door when Liam caught up to her and stepped in her path. Coming up short, she let out a huff. "I'm going home."

"Okay, okay, okay...I was out of line," he said quickly. "It's just...I'm the oldest of five kids. I'm used to watching after everyone, identifying if there's a problem, and then solving it. It worked that way in the service too."

It explained a little more about him, but she was unwilling to say it was a valid excuse for him to be rude.

"Whatever," she murmured and tried to step around him.

He blocked her.

"Liam..."

The next thing she knew, his hands were gently grasping her shoulders. "I realize we don't know each other that well, but from everything you've told me, it seems like you're sort of...stuck."

Tessa was fairly certain her jaw was on the floor. Her heart was racing and she prayed she wouldn't burst into tears.

The thing was...he wasn't wrong.

She knew she was a little stuck in the past; her family mentioned it a time or two or twenty. Still...no one understood! If she knew how to move on, she would! There was just something comfortable about this place she was at. Leaving it was scary and she honestly didn't know if she could survive opening her heart again to the kind of pain that losing Trevor brought.

"You don't know anything about me," she said, hating the slight tremble in her voice. His hands were still on her shoulders and as much as she wished he'd let her go, the other part of her—the part that was clearly crazy—was enjoying the contact. It had been so long since a man had touched her and here it was twice in one day that Liam Donovan had.

And she still wasn't hating it.

Ugh...maybe I do need therapy.

Unaware of her inner dialogue, Liam went on. "Have you dated anyone since Trevor died?"

"We've already covered this and..."

"Just...hear me out. I get that you were married, but...it wasn't a traditional marriage. You said so yourself."

"I never said that!" she argued, and now she did twist out of his grasp. "What is wrong with you? Why would you even think it's okay to talk to me about such a sensitive subject?"

"I can't help but think that if you put yourself back out there, maybe you'd be happier!" he challenged. "Don't you ever get lonely? Don't you ever just want someone who is physically there and not just a memory?"

"How dare you!"

"I just think..."

"No," she interrupted. "You don't think. You just blurt stuff out that has nothing to do with you. Maybe your siblings don't mind it, or maybe they're used to it. Heck, it was probably the same while you were in the Marines. But I'm not one of your fellow soldiers and I'm not one of your siblings! I don't want to discuss this with you anymore. I'd like to leave, please."

And she hated that even when she was this upset, she was still polite.

Dang it.

Fortunately, he listened and took a step back. Tessa

went to walk out but felt like she had one more thing left to say.

"You know, it's obvious that you've never truly loved anyone. Because if you did, you would know that going out on a date with another person doesn't change anything. Sometimes it makes things worse. So before you go and give anyone else some bad advice, maybe stick to things that you actually know about."

Her hand was on the front doorknob when he stopped her again.

"You realize you're just proving me right, don't you?" he said evenly and as much as she wanted to ignore him and go, her curiosity got the better of her.

"Excuse me?"

"You're running away. I said something that you don't like—perhaps I struck a nerve—and rather than discuss it, you got up and ran." Sliding his hands into his trouser pockets, he shrugged. "I didn't take you for the type to walk away when things didn't go your way."

Was he for real?

And what was worse…she took the bait.

Turning, Tessa faced him. "Okay, Ace. You want to talk? We'll talk." Crossing her arms and cocking her hip, she prayed she looked casual. The truth was that she felt ill, but there was no way she was going to let him get the last word like this. "According to your logic, dating someone new should make all the grief go away."

Rolling his eyes, Liam shook his head. "No, that's not what I said. What I said was that dating someone would help you move on. Hell, I'm not saying you have to get seriously involved with someone. Just a casual date or…or…even sleeping with someone could possibly do it for you."

Rage built up in her like nothing she'd ever felt before.

"Sex? That's your answer? *Sex?*" she asked incredulously. "That's incredibly shallow, Liam, and what little respect I had for you is gone."

This time, she was definitely going. Her hand grasped the doorknob again and...

"I think you're scared," he taunted. "I think you're afraid to be with another man because it will prove that all the things you've been feeling aren't what you've built them up to be." He took a step toward her. "You'll always love Trevor—as a friend. And you'll always have feelings for him —as a friend. But romantically and sexually? I think you've added that in there for some twisted reason and you won't allow yourself to get involved with another man because you'll realize you've been wasting your time and..."

Before another word could come out of his mouth, Tessa tossed her purse to the floor and launched herself at him. One hand reached up and anchored into his hair as she went up on her tiptoes and pressed her lips to his. It was supposed to be just a quick, harmless little kiss.

She was going to prove a point, dammit.

She was going to show him that a date or a kiss didn't flip a switch on how you felt about someone.

Except...she was wrong.

Uh-oh...

Liam's arm immediately banded around her waist as he pulled her in close right before he took control of the kiss. Clearly she hadn't thought this through because she figured he'd let her do her little test and either push her away or sort of not engage. But the way his tongue was gently coaxing hers and the fact that he was holding her even tighter said that he was not only fully engaging, but maybe even enjoying this.

Just like I am...

Tessa's free arm wrapped around him, and it was impossible to get any closer. She could feel every hard inch of him.

Every.

Hard.

Inch.

Oh my...

As much as she wanted to clear her mind and simply feel all the things this kiss was making her feel, she couldn't seem to shut it off. Never had a kiss felt so intimate—so carnal. And never had a single kiss ever made her want to throw caution to the wind and do something reckless.

Like ask a thoroughly annoying almost-stranger to have sex up against his front door.

It had been so long since she'd been kissed that she hadn't even really thought about it—but she had a feeling it was going to be all that she thought about now. And as much as she wanted to be annoyed about it, she couldn't. Not when the kiss just kept going on and on and on.

Her lungs felt tight and certain girly parts were feeling all tingly and achy in a way they hadn't in years and yet all she wanted was for Liam to keep kissing her while she just rubbed herself all over him.

It would be shameless and brazen and far more sexually aggressive than she'd ever been and...

That's when reality hit her like a bucket of water to the face.

This isn't who I am...

As much as she hated to, Tessa slowly pulled back. Her eyelids felt heavy, but she forced herself to look at him and keep her composure as much as humanly possible.

When she got home, she knew she'd overanalyze every

second of the last few minutes, but for now, the key was to look as unaffected as she could muster.

Unable to help herself, she quickly licked her lips before bending over and scooping up her purse. Then she made the mistake of looking right at him.

And almost stripped herself down and begged him to do whatever he pleased with her.

His hair was mussed up, his breath was ragged, his eyes were dark with desire, and he looked just as turned on as she felt.

Damn him.

Gently, she cleared her throat. "So, um...yeah, sorry. No switch has been flipped. Thanks for dinner and I'll see you around." It was amazing how calm she sounded when her heart was beating so loud she could barely hear herself speak.

Without a backward glance, she walked out the door, across the lawn, and into her house.

And promptly took a cold shower.

Chapter Six

"*Ow!* Son of a bitch!" Tossing the hammer aside with a loud curse, Liam shook his hand and prayed he didn't break his finger.

"Dude, what is going on with you?" Will asked. "You've been a walking disaster all day."

It was Monday afternoon and as much as he wanted to argue with his friend that he was wrong, the fact was that he wasn't. All day, Liam had been making mistakes and most of them ended up injuring him in one way or another.

"If you keep this up, the general contractor is going to throw you off the job because you're a safety hazard."

"We're the general contractors," he murmured as he straightened.

"Yeah, and I'm going to throw your ass off the job for the day," Will countered sternly. "Seriously, I don't know what's on your mind, but your focus isn't here and we can't afford for you to do something that hurts you or someone else. It's already after four, just...call it a day."

"It's unnecessary. I'm just having an off day."

"Liam, I've known you for a long time and you've never been this off. If there's something on your mind..."

Damn straight there was something on his mind.

Or rather, someone.

Tessa.

Where the hell did she get off kissing him like that and just walking away? He'd been turned on for days and it had taken an act of iron will not to go knocking on her door and demanding to know what she was thinking.

Um...that I provoked her and maybe she was just taking my advice?

Yeah, okay, that thought had occurred to him, but he never expected her to do such a thing.

But since she did, he'd been fantasizing about her coming back and doing it again and again and again. And in each scenario, she was dressed in less and less.

If anyone would have told him he'd be tempted by his uber-cheery neighbor, he would have told them they were crazy.

And yet, here he was.

Tempted and slowly losing his mind.

"Um...Liam?"

Sighing loudly, he glanced at Will. "It's nothing. Can't a guy just have a bad day? Does it have to mean something's wrong? Maybe I didn't get enough sleep last night!"

"Did you get enough sleep last night?" Will asked with mild amusement.

Sadly, he hadn't gotten a good night's sleep because he had rather detailed, erotic dreams about Tessa.

"Okay, clearly you don't want to talk about this, but can I make a suggestion?" Will asked a moment later.

"Sure..."

"Go home, take a shower, and go out. Call up a woman

or maybe go to the pub and meet one. Just...you're clearly in a funk and even though we haven't talked about this, I don't think you've gone out and...you know...been with anyone in a while."

Rolling his eyes, Liam fought the urge to laugh.

Only...it wasn't funny.

Sadly, it was quite possibly the most honest observation.

"Maybe you're right," he forced himself to say, raking a hand through his hair. "And thanks, Will." Before he could second-guess himself, Liam gathered his tools and cleaned up. "I'll see you tomorrow."

"Take tomorrow if you need to," his friend called after him. "I won't mind."

"We'll see." Ten minutes later, he was in his truck and heading home.

It had been months since he'd been with a woman and while he knew it was partially the issue, it wasn't lack of sex that had him off his game. In the service, sometimes he'd gone a full year without sleeping with a woman. Right now, he definitely wouldn't mind crawling between the sheets and getting naked and sweaty with someone.

Tessa.

"Yeah, this has got to be dealt with," he mumbled. It had only been two days and yet he'd thought about the kiss— thought about *her*—almost continuously since. "It shouldn't be like this. I shouldn't feel like this."

Liam was always the one in control of his emotions. Maybe it had to do with the fact that he was the firstborn and had to set the example for his siblings, or maybe it was his military training. Either way, he did not enjoy this sudden...awareness—the need for one person in particular.

The drive home took only a few minutes and as he drove past Tessa's house, he almost missed his driveway and pulled onto the lawn when he spotted her watering the plants on her front porch.

He knew the instant she noticed his arrival because her movements suddenly sped up—like she was trying to wrap things up quickly before he could come over and talk to her. Well, he wasn't going to let anything deter him. He wanted answers, and he wanted them now.

Hopping down from his truck, he slammed the door and made his way across his front yard toward her. She straightened and met his gaze. Today she had on a pair of dark jeans and a maroon sweater. Her dark hair was loose and even from across the yard, he could tell that her lips were glossy.

Swallowing hard, he closed the distance between them. When they were mere feet apart, he stopped short.

And had no idea what to say.

Tessa eyed him warily and, after a moment, she turned to shut the hose off before facing him again. "Was there something I could do for you, Liam?"

Now that was a loaded question.

"As a matter of fact, there is."

She arched a dark brow at him in response.

"What the hell were you thinking on Saturday?" he asked.

"You'll have to be more specific," she casually replied.

Inwardly groaning, he stared down at her. "The kiss, Tessa. Why would you do that?"

With a shrug, she walked up the two steps to her porch before looking at him again. "I was testing your theory. You made it sound like going out on a date and kissing someone would miraculously change my life. I figured I could count the semi-dinner we had and the conversation as a date, so then I thought I'd try the kiss. You know...

since you were so confident that would be the answer to all my problems."

This time, the groan was outward and full of annoyance. "That wasn't what I said."

"Oh, I realize I'm taking some minor creative liberty with it, but it's essentially the same thing." Another shrug. "I was curious."

"That's it? You were curious?" he repeated incredulously.

"Mm-hmm. I'll admit I've never done anything like that—you know, initiating a kiss that way—but there's a first time for everything."

He waited for her to elaborate but she didn't, and it was infuriating as hell.

"And?" he prompted impatiently.

"And what? I believe I told you my thoughts on my way out the door. Why? Did you think there was more?"

Her smile was sweet and serene, and it annoyed him even more.

"So you're telling me you felt absolutely nothing?"

She nodded.

"Bullshit."

Her eyes went wide. "Excuse me?"

Taking one giant step up onto the porch, he stood in front of her. "I said bullshit. I think you were really into that kiss and just don't want to admit it because you don't want to prove me right."

He almost smiled when she paled slightly.

"I'm not saying it was a bad kiss, Liam. It's nothing personal. It just didn't have the magical healing properties you seemed to think it should. No offense."

"No one said it would have *magical* healing...jeez, Tessa, I swear you make this stuff up just to aggravate me!"

Grinning, she shrugged again. "I'm sorry this is bothering you. I never intended to upset you this much. But you'll have to excuse me. I just got home a little while ago and I have things I need to do."

When she pulled the screen door open, Liam reached for it and held it that way. "You didn't upset me," he lied. "I just wanted to know if you had time to think about it afterwards and if it maybe, um..."

"Maybe what?"

Ugh...how did he word this?

"Did it have you looking at things differently?" he asked diplomatically. "Did you maybe go into work today and consider asking out one of your coworkers? Or...or is there someone in town that you would consider going out with?"

Why was he goading her like this? The last thing he wanted was to think of her being interested in another man, but he doubted she'd admit to suddenly being attracted to him.

No matter how much he would love to hear that.

She seemed to consider him for a long moment. "You know...there is someone I was a little attracted to..."

Swallowing hard again, he nodded.

"Before the kiss, mind you," she quickly corrected. "But...I don't know. I don't think I could ask him out."

"Why not?"

Her soft sigh was the first response. "Liam, no offense, but...this really doesn't concern you. I appreciate your interest and how you thought you were helping, but I'm not comfortable being the one asking a man out. And besides, it's been a long time since I've been...you know...intimate with anyone. Heck, you were my first kiss in years, so..."

It was stupid how much that pleased him.

"If it makes you feel any better, it was a great kiss," he

told her, and watched as her cheeks turned the prettiest shade of pink. Taking a step closer until they were both in the house and the screen door gently shut behind him, he nodded. "It's true. Whoever this guy is, I bet he wouldn't mind if you kissed him like that."

She was shaking her head before he finished the sentence.

"That's sweet of you to say, but...it will be awhile before I'm comfortable doing anything like that with anyone. It's been too long and I'm out of practice..."

"It's like riding a bike," he said with a boyish grin. "Trust me. You're a natural."

"Liam..."

Okay, he knew exactly what he was doing and exactly what he wanted.

He was just too afraid to ask.

Doing his best to sound casual, he said, "You could totally practice on...you know...me." Clearing his throat, he continued, "Obviously we've already done it once so it wouldn't be weird and you know that neither of us is going to take it for anything more since whenever we're together we're arguing about something..."

Her back seemed to stiffen a little and he thought maybe he'd gone too far.

"Wait...you want me to kiss you again?" she asked, the confusion on her face obvious.

"Just for practice," he quickly reminded her. "You can consider me your safe space. No one has to know and..."

"What do you get out of this? Clearly I annoy you, so why would you even want to do this?"

Because I can't stop thinking of you and maybe this will help me come to my senses...

"I feel bad for all the grief I've given you, and you

shared something that was deeply personal with me. I should have been more supportive, so...now I think this is a way that I can be."

That sounded logical, right?

The face she was making said otherwise.

"I appreciate the offer, Liam, but..." She glanced away as Phoebe came prancing into the room. With the grace of a dancer, Tessa bent down and scooped the tiny dog up before straightening and snuggling her. "There's my good girl. I promised we'd go out back and play, right?"

Maybe that was his cue to leave, but he wasn't ready to just yet.

"I meant to ask you," he began before she could show him the door, "who did the work in your yard? The pergola and all that? I'm guessing you did some of it yourself, but did you hire a landscaping company?"

Smiling, she shook her head. "My family and I did it all together. My mom is a total whiz with gardens and my dad and both my brothers-in-law are super handy, so they did all the building. Amazingly enough, we got it done in two weekends. It wasn't quite as full as it is now. I've been adding to it ever since, but it was a fun project for all of us to do together."

Yeah, he knew his family would help him when the time came, but he figured there might be more to her story so he could stay longer.

"Would you mind if I looked at it again? After our talk Saturday night, I've been thinking about your suggestions—especially regarding the tree. Maybe if I don't take it down, I can do some sort of garden thing like what you have. I don't know anything about flowers, but..."

Tessa's eyes lit up with pure delight. "Sure! Come on back! Phoebe needs to go out so she can do her thing while we walk around. I know a lot about different kinds of flowers and what works best in this region and climate and I can help you make your yard as beautiful as it can be!"

There was that perkiness that usually bugged him, but right now, he kind of liked her enthusiasm.

Just like he was liking her.

And he had no idea what it all meant.

* * *

Tessa walked out the back door ahead of Liam and had to fight the urge to simply burst into song. It was her go-to response when she was happy and right now, it was hard to even keep her feet on the ground.

It was thrilling to know she wasn't the only one affected by their kiss. She already knew she'd been playing it on a continuous loop in her own head, but no matter how he was trying to pull this whole thing off, he wasn't simply trying to be a good neighbor or make up for being a jerk to her so many times.

He wanted to kiss her too.

Yay!

Of course she'd never admit that out loud because... well...she just wouldn't. If she seemed too eager to take him up on his offer, he'd probably think there was something wrong with her. But there was also the fact that a small part of her was hesitant. The man she referred to earlier when the two of them were out front—the one she said she was attracted to—was Liam.

But...there was no way she'd get involved with Liam Donovan. They'd already proven how incompatible they were. Unfortunately, she had opened a Pandora's box with that kiss two days ago and now it was all she could think about.

Her plan had been to just keep herself super busy so she wouldn't have time to think about it, but so far that hadn't happened. If anything, she found herself doing activities that left her with nothing to do but think.

Earlier today, she had been looking over songs for the holiday chorus concert at school and it all had her thinking of Liam.

"Walking in a Winter Wonderland": Thoughts of walking with him in the snow and then kissing to keep warm.

"Baby, It's Cold Outside": Thoughts of all the ways she'd love for them to keep each other warm and they all involved kissing.

And that wasn't including the contemporary classic Christmas songs like "All I Want for Christmas is You" or "Christmas, Baby, Please Come Home."

Every single song had her tangled up with Liam in one way or another and to have him here right now, proposing a little more kissing? Well...it was a miracle she hadn't thrown herself at him yet.

"So, um...what kind of garden were you thinking of?" she asked as they stepped out into her backyard. For the next several minutes, they walked around and Tessa described all the different flowers she had planted and why she chose them, but the entire time she was hyper-aware of Liam beside her. She had no idea if he was genuinely interested in anything she was saying, but she could feel his eyes on her.

"That is a lot of information," he said as they moved back toward her sitting area. "I don't think I'd have a problem doing the heavy labor or building anything, but all the planting stuff I'd probably need to hire a landscaper for."

They sat and she nodded. "It is a lot, I know, but the reward is so worth it." Motioning to her yard again, Tessa couldn't help but smile. "I know you're looking to have a little more of a recreational space with a pool and all, but I think you can still do a lot with the right shrubs and flowers. Plus...that tree is amazing." Leaning forward, she pointed at it. "I have to admit, I like the shade it gives the back corner of my yard too." Then she felt herself blush. "But um...that totally wasn't why I wanted you to keep it."

Smiling, Liam reached over and touched her arm and she felt it from her head to her toes.

I'm in trouble.

"Relax," he told her softly, and she wasn't sure if he was referring to her reaction to his touch or what she'd just said. "I already know you're not the diabolical type."

Okay, so...the tree.

"I just wanted to be sure you understood that," she replied as she slowly moved out of his grasp. "I think with a little help from a landscaper you could make your yard a genuine retreat."

Phoebe walked over and stood on her hind legs and gently scratched at Tessa's legs before getting picked up.

"Do you leave her home all day?" he asked, motioning to Phoebe.

"Sadly, I do. There was a time when I used to bring her to work with me, but she ended up being a major distraction for my students. Sometimes I still take her with me, but only if I know I'm going to be staying late. And even then, I come home after my last class and pick her up then. I don't have her with me the entire day." She scratched the pup's head. "She's good about being home alone and she never gets destructive. I just feel bad and worry that she's lonely."

"Do dogs get lonely? Seriously?"

And just like that, all the good feelings she was having toward him started to melt away.

"I think most living creatures—the ones with an actual heart—do. If I could, I'd take her with me every day or have someone stop in while I'm at school to check on her. As it is, I leave music playing just so she has a little noise in the background."

"Tessa, come on. That's a little crazy, don't you think?"

With a weary sigh, she pinched the bridge of her nose before looking at him. "And this is why there won't be any practice kissing," she said with a frown.

"What? Why?"

"Because I'm tired of defending everything I do to you. It's exhausting!"

When he didn't respond right away, she got mildly suspicious.

"What I mean is..."

"So if I didn't speak, then you'd kiss me?" he reasoned, and it wasn't really a question.

"I didn't say that."

But...she kind of did.

"Okay, I'll admit that I have a problem—I say what's on my mind. I don't mean for it to be confrontational, but that's how you always seem to take it."

"That's because whatever's on your mind tends to be that I'm doing something you think is crazy or ridiculous or...or..."

He reached out and touched her again and she realized the skin on his hands was a little rough and calloused and felt really good.

So good that she wanted to feel it on other parts of her body and not just her arm.

Ugh...I'm pathetic.

This time she fought the urge to pull away as she met his gaze.

Which was sexy as hell and full of heat.

Well...maybe one kiss wouldn't hurt...

"You're right," he said, interrupting her thoughts. "I guess some things you do seem...you know...like what you said, and that's not fair to you. I'm sure there are plenty of things that I do that you don't like and you keep them to yourself. Right?"

She nodded.

"So if I promise to think before I speak, then would you practice with me?"

Tessa's eyes narrowed. "Why is this so important to you? I mean, why do you even care if I move on with another man?"

His hand on her arm tightened somewhat, and she noticed a slight twitch in his jaw.

Interesting.

"Like I said, I just thought it was a way for me to make it up to you for being such a jerk," he said after a moment. "If you don't want to..."

"I didn't say that," she interrupted quickly.

A little too quickly, and he quirked a brow at her.

Shoot.

"I guess it can't really hurt..." she said and was amazed she wasn't struck by lightning. "And it's not like you're a bad kisser."

"Um...thanks?"

His reaction made her giggle and she couldn't believe they were sitting here talking about kissing each other again.

She'd never had a discussion like this in her entire life, and that it was all his idea was just a bit bizarre to her.

Slowly, she pulled her arm away and stood. "Would you like something to drink?" And before he could answer, Tessa was walking into the house. Fortunately, he followed, and once she put Phoebe down, she turned to face him.

He didn't want a drink.

The way he slowly advanced on her—like a predator stalking its prey—told her the only thing he wanted was her.

Yay, me!

At some point, Tessa moved toward him to close the distance sooner. She couldn't be sure who reached out first, but the next thing she knew, she was in his arms and completely surrounded by him.

And it was glorious.

She wanted to be embarrassed by the little hum of pleasure she made the moment Liam's lips pressed against hers, but she was far more interested in what was to come. His tongue slid along hers even as they both tilted their heads to get the best angle. His hand reached up and fisted in her hair as their lips did their best to devour each other. It was madness and wild and untamed and more passionate than anything Tessa had ever experienced in her entire life.

If this is what he kisses like, I can only imagine what he's like in bed...

It was crazy to even let that thought take hold.

Especially since this kiss was essentially the best thing to happen to her in a long time.

Possibly ever.

How she had gone so long without ever being kissed like this was beyond her and she had a feeling she'd be comparing every other kiss for the rest of her life to this.

What was becoming abundantly clear was that Liam

brought out strong emotions in her—primarily passion. Whether it was with anger or desire, it was always intense. She'd been living in her happy little world—her cheery bubble—where one day simply blended into the next with no real surprises and certainly no bumps.

Liam disrupted all of that, and it was as terrifying as it was exciting.

And who knew arguing could be such a turn-on? It was...it was...

Tessa instantly ended the kiss and took a horrified step back as her fingers shakily touched her lips. "Oh my God, I can't do this," she blurted out.

There was no mistaking the confusion on Liam's face, even as he stood frozen to the spot.

"You...you should go," she said, even as her entire body trembled and her voice shook. Although she wasn't sure if she was shaking for sexy reasons or out of nerves.

"What's going on?" he asked softly. "Did I do something wrong? Something you didn't like? Because..." When he took a step toward her, Tessa instantly took a step back as she held up a hand to stop him.

"The kiss was fine," she told him.

"Fine? Just fine?" he asked with wide-eyed disbelief. "Tessa, that kiss was off the charts and..."

"And I know that," she interrupted. "It's just...it's angry kissing. We provoke each other and then kiss and that's... it's..." Her shoulders sagged. "It's wrong, Liam. That's not good for anyone. And it's certainly not the kind of thing I should be practicing."

That seemed to relax him. With a nod, he gave her a weak smile. "That makes total sense. Kissing should not only be done out of anger."

Finally, they agreed on something.

Relief washed over her and it was wonderful to not have to defend herself to him.

"Kissing is all about enjoyment," he was saying, and something in his tone had her on alert. That walk was back —part stalking, part swagger—and his voice was low and gruff and almost hypnotizing. "With a little seduction thrown in." They were toe to toe again, and this time he reached up and caressed her cheek. "It should start out slow and then get to a point where you both just sink into it before it turns into what you and I have been doing."

Tessa felt her breath quicken along with her heartbeat. "Oh?" she whispered.

Nodding, his hand gently stroked her jaw and then along her throat. His eyes were so dark and as she watched him, she swore he was the most handsome and sexy man she'd ever met. Guys like him never paid attention to girls like her.

Well, until now.

It was a little like an out-of-body experience. Tessa licked her lips in anticipation and Liam's gaze instantly homed in on that one little action.

"Tessa?"

"Hmm?"

"I'd like to kiss you now," he said in a voice that made her knees go weak and all she could do was nod.

There was no frantic move to get closer. There was no rushing. It was like it was all happening in slow motion until she had no choice but to close her eyes and just...feel.

Oh...oh, this is so much better...

Without all the urgency, there was tenderness.

And without all the anger, there was a gentler feeling of desire.

Tessa had no idea if one was better than the other. All

she knew was that no matter how Liam Donovan came to kiss her, her entire body was completely on board. They swayed together before slowly working together to get over to her sofa. At that point, Liam took control and guided her down with him and cradled her in his lap.

It was the sexiest move he could have made.

His arms were loosely banded around her waist and hers rested on his shoulder while her hands gently raked through his silky hair. Every move, every stroke of his tongue was slow and languid and she knew she would happily stay like this for hours if he'd let her.

And it felt like he did.

By the time they broke apart, it was obvious a significant amount of time had passed. The sun was setting, the room was darker, and she felt completely boneless. "Wow," she whispered, resting her forehead against his. "That was a little unexpected."

"Was it?" he murmured, caressing her cheek again. "Because I think we both knew what we were doing."

Tessa felt herself blush. "I know, but...after the first two times, I just never expected it could be like...well...like we just did."

And she wanted to do it again, but the sound of his phone ringing ruined the moment.

She carefully moved out of his lap. "It's okay. You can answer it."

He apologized as he came to his feet and greeted whoever was calling. Two minutes later, he was back with a sad smile. "I hate to do this, but...I need to go."

Coming to her feet, she asked, "Is everything okay?"

"Yeah. My folks are doing some work on the pub and some things went wrong today so they've got an all hands on deck kind of situation going. I'm really sorry."

She held up a hand to stop him. "It's okay, Liam. It wasn't like we had plans or anything. This all just sort of...happened."

Although, she had been on the verge of inviting him to stay for dinner, but maybe some other time. And hopefully that would lead to more kissing.

She really hoped there'd be more kissing.

And as Liam leaned in and kissed her again, she knew there would be.

Chapter Seven

"Dude, redhead at the bar is checking you out hard," Jamie said as they moved a bunch of tables into the far corner of the pub.

"Um, yeah. Shouldn't we be doing all of this when we're closed? I feel like we're potentially going against some sort of health codes by working on the renovation with customers here."

Rolling his eyes, Jamie stacked one table on top of another. "We're closing at eight." Glancing at his watch, he said, "So, in another twenty minutes. If I were you, I'd go over and strike up a conversation with her and get her number for later."

Liam glanced over at the woman in question and felt...nothing.

She smiled at him, but he honestly had zero interest in her.

And he immediately knew why.

She wasn't Tessa.

Yeah, he'd completely misjudged that whole situation.

He'd meant to go there to kiss her again and just get it

out of his system—or to prove that he had remembered it wrong.

But that didn't happen and now he was more turned on than ever and he had no idea what to do about it.

"What's wrong with you?" Jamie asked with annoyance. "Why are you just standing there glaring at her?" He paused. "Great, now she's leaving." With a slight shove, he stepped around him. "I swear, it's like I'm the only Donovan male who knows how to treat a woman."

Before Liam could ask him to clarify that statement or to even argue with him. Jamie was walking across the floor toward the redhead and, of course, managed to make her smile and giggle.

Maybe he is the only Donovan who knows how to treat a woman...

"Is he seriously not helping because he's flirting with a customer again?" Patrick asked as he walked over with another table. "Seriously, I wish we had a hose in here because I'd totally turn it on him."

Honestly, it didn't bother Liam. He had too many other things on his mind than worrying about his little brother's love life. "Let him be. He's stuck here all the damn time. I think I'd be hitting on the female clientele too if this were my life."

"What's wrong with this life?"

Shrugging, Liam walked over and sat in one of the booths and waited for Patrick to follow. "Don't get me wrong, the pub is great and it can be fun working here. Hell, all through high school, I used to meet a lot of girls while working here on the weekends. It's just..." Sighing, he leaned back against the seat cushion. "I don't know how he stands it. Stuck inside all day, seeing the same people, hearing the same stories..."

Patrick studied him for a minute. "Okay, valid point. However, just because this isn't appealing to you doesn't mean it's not appealing. This was never something you were interested in. You wanted to see the world, you wanted adventure, you just wanted something different where you could be the guy in charge."

"It wasn't about being in charge..."

"Oh, it was totally about being in charge," his brother countered. "You've always had issues with anyone who doesn't think like you or do things the way you do them. It's annoying as hell and I'm not gonna lie to you, it was very freeing after you enlisted because we were all free to do our own thing without you being so damn judgy about it."

"I wasn't judgy..."

Nodding, Patrick leaned back and got comfortable. "You were unbearable," he stated. "You corrected all of us about things we weren't doing wrong; we just weren't doing it like you. It was like having three parents and it was annoying as hell." Then she shrugged. "I don't think you're even aware that you're doing it. And obviously you still are because I'm sure you're dying to lay into Loverboy over there about how he shouldn't be flirting with the customers."

Ugh, am I that predictable?

Then he remembered some of the things Tessa had said to him and realized it wasn't just that he was predictable, but he was a jerk about it as well.

Awesome.

"Are you sure you're not just jealous because obviously Jamie's getting laid and you're not?"

"Excuse me?" he snapped. "Who said I'm not getting laid?"

"Please, just like I know I'm not getting laid. We're both

here on a Monday night moving tables on short notice." Another shrug. "Besides, I drive by your place every night on my way home and your car is always there. By itself."

"Maybe I'm sleeping with someone in the neighborhood. Ever think of that?"

"*Are* you sleeping with someone in the neighborhood?" Patrick asked.

Clearly, he hesitated too long because his brother's grin was smug.

"Okay, fine. No, I'm not sleeping with anyone in the neighborhood and haven't gotten laid in months. I've been busy with the resort. I'm putting in long hours, working on the house, and there just aren't enough hours in the day."

Patrick motioned to the pub. "Plenty of women come in here and as you just witnessed, you could meet someone if you put in a little effort." He glanced over to where Jamie was still chatting with the redhead. "I thought she was checking you out."

"That's what Jamie said, but I sort of zoned out and he said I was glaring at her, so he swooped in."

"Yeah, you have to be fast around him because he has no problem doing shit like that. Were you even interested?"

He shook his head. "Not really."

Patrick turned and looked toward the bar again. "Really? She's pretty."

Not as pretty as Tessa.

It wasn't like he was the kind of guy who was big on sharing his feelings, but...maybe his brother could help him out.

"Can I ask you something?"

"Sure."

"Have you ever been attracted to someone who—mostly —made you...um...crazy?"

Grinning, Patrick rested an arm along the booth seat. "Crazy in a good way or in a bad way?"

"Bad way. Like...polar opposite in every way and normally aggravates the crap out of you," he explained.

"So you're into a woman who annoys you. Do I have that right?"

He nodded.

"Is she annoying to other people or is this just you being you?"

Groaning, he shook his head. "A few minutes ago, I would have said other people, but I have a feeling this is a me issue."

"Okay, so...one hurdle crossed." He paused for a moment. "Annoying...how?"

Now he knew he was going to sound like a jerk.

"She's just...super cheery. Like...all the time. The perpetual glass is half full, every cloud has a silver lining, always looking on the bright side..." He shook his head again. "She bakes cookies for the neighborhood, bursts into song just for the joy of singing, and has this ridiculously tiny dog that I can't even believe is real!" Raking a hand through his hair, he leaned forward, resting his arms on the table. "But here's the kicker: she married her best friend who was dying. It was something he wanted to do before he died— get married. And it's like she's stuck in this holding pattern! She hasn't dated since and it doesn't make sense since it wasn't a real marriage!"

He let out a long breath, feeling better just for finally being able to say all of that out loud.

When he looked over at Patrick, he was frowning. "What? What did I say?"

"You have a problem, Liam. Like a serious problem."

"I don't..."

106

"Oh, you do," he interrupted. "So you're annoyed because this woman is happy, kind to people, makes sacrifices for a dying friend, and just genuinely enjoys life. The dog thing I'm kind of with you on. Tiny dogs are just ridiculous."

"I know, right?"

"However, I can't believe you're actually giving this woman grief—either to her face or behind her back— because she's grieving for someone she cared about. I realize you and I aren't the most emotional guys, but damn. That's just heartless to be giving someone shit because they did something so selfless." The look he gave Liam was full of disgust. "Even I wouldn't do something like that."

"I realize I was wrong to say anything to her about it," he said defensively, "but things took an interesting turn and now I'm completely confused."

All his brother did was stare blandly at him.

Liam explained how he had essentially provoked her about dating again or at least kissing a guy and how she kissed the living daylights out of him.

Now Patrick looked amused.

Then he told him about their earlier kiss. "And the thing is, I keep telling myself I'm doing this for her benefit, like I'm the guy who's going to get her over this grief and push her to take back that part of her life."

"But...?"

Sighing, he shook his head. "I'm a selfish bastard. As soon as she kissed me, all I could think of was how there was no way I wanted her kissing anyone but me. Unfortunately, me and my big mouth are a major issue for her."

"You are kind of an ass..."

After giving his younger brother the finger, he groaned.

"Tessa isn't someone I should want to date. She's not my type and..."

"Wait...Tessa Sullivan? You're trying to hook up with sweet little Tessa Sullivan?" Patrick asked with wide-eyed amusement.

"How do you know Tessa?"

"Who knows Tessa?" Jamie asked as he slid into the booth beside Patrick. "Tessa Sullivan?"

Shit...

Patrick grinned at him. "Yeah, Liam's got the hots for the town music teacher."

"What?" Jamie asked with a hearty laugh. "Come on, seriously? That's just wrong."

"Why?" Liam demanded hotly. "Why is it so wrong?"

"It's like...Bo Peep and the Big Bad Wolf."

"No, no, no..." Patrick said. "You got that mixed up. It's like Little Red Riding Hood and the Big Bad Wolf." Then he laughed. "Wait, speaking of red, how'd you make out with the redhead?" Then he laughed harder. "And yeah, pun intended."

"I'm meeting her once we're done here, so as much as I'd love to sit here and know more about why Liam would even want to go after such a sweet girl, I've got a date to get to." Then he looked at Liam before reaching over and slugging him in the arm—hard. "She's not for you, bro. Move on."

Then he stood up and walked away.

"What the...?"

"Yeah, I've got to agree with Jamie on this one," Patrick said after a moment. "You kissed her a couple of times, but... let it go at that. She's far too sweet for you. Hell, if you hurt her, the entire town would be after you like an angry mob. If you need to hook up with someone..."

"No," he said miserably. "Just no." Sighing, he realized he had one more question. "Why do you think I'd hurt her? Maybe I'm exactly what she needs."

This time Patrick leaned forward; his expression was deadly serious. "Dude, trust me, the negative energy you tend to throw at people is definitely not what someone like Tessa needs."

And before Liam could defend himself, Patrick slid out of the booth and walked away.

Muttering a curse, he stood and was about to go after him and then realized it wasn't his brother he needed to talk to. It was Tessa.

Only...he couldn't.

He'd promised his father that he'd be here to help. Jamie was still flirting at the bar and Patrick had walked off, but there was still a lot that needed to get done, so...he was going to do it.

Because he was a man of his word.

Even if he was heartless.

Thursday afternoon, Tessa arrived home in a great mood. She'd sang along to the soundtrack from *Hamilton* and was just feeling light and happy. Tomorrow was a holiday, so she had a long weekend ahead of her and she was looking forward to it. She was going to hit the farmers market, do a little baking...and maybe go out walking in the park. The leaves were hanging on a little longer this year and the colors were magnificent. She and Trevor used to love this time of year, and he would always take some amazing pictures of the foliage. If she had planned it better, she would have opted to go to the mountains and do the drive along the Blue Ridge Parkway to take it all in.

And maybe learn to take some good pictures herself.

"There's always next year," she said as she climbed from the car. She'd stopped for groceries on the way home and was opening the trunk when she spotted Liam's truck pulling into his driveway.

They hadn't seen each other since Monday when they had their phenomenal make-out session.

Oh, God...did I just refer to that as a make-out session? What am I, fifteen?

Still, whatever it was, it was amazing and she had really hoped they would have done it again, but...maybe Liam had second thoughts.

Well, that's a depressing thought...

And because it didn't take much for that thought to take hold, she decided it had to be true and so she put all her focus on getting her shopping bags out of the trunk while singing "Don't Stop Me Now" by Queen. She'd heard it on the radio in the grocery store and it was stuck in her head, so she embraced it.

"Like a tiger defying the laws of gravity, I'm a racing car passing by like Lady Godiva..." she sang, right before turning and walking directly into Liam. With a scream, she jumped back and banged her head on the open trunk. His arms instantly wrapped around her to steady her.

"Jeez, Tessa! I'm sorry! Are you alright?"

Swallowing hard, she nodded. "You scared the heck out of me!"

The lopsided grin he gave her was adorable. "I didn't mean to do that and I tried to get your attention, but you were deep into your song and didn't hear me."

"Oh...yeah, I've been told I zone out when I sing."

"Your voice is amazing," he told her with a hint of awe. "I don't think I really noticed that before."

"I'm not sure I ever sang around you." Had she?

"Maybe, but still. You sing beautifully. I'm beyond impressed."

Tessa could feel her cheeks heat and she smiled up at him. "Thanks." Feeling calmer, she carefully stepped out of his embrace. "Would you mind closing the trunk for me? I've got frozen foods in these bags that need to get inside, and then I need to take Phoebe outside."

"Here, let me take these," he said as he took the bags from her hands.

She thanked him and pulled her keys back out of her purse to unlock the door. Liam followed her inside and went right to the kitchen while she gave Phoebe some love. It seemed weirdly natural for him to be there and by the time Tessa walked into the kitchen with the dog in her arms, Liam was putting the perishable foods away for her.

"You didn't need to do that," she gently chastised. "But I appreciate it."

"Glad I could help." He smiled and it made her reconsider her thoughts from only moments ago. Surely he wouldn't come over here and help her like this if he had second thoughts, would he?

Placing Phoebe down, she watched as the dog danced over by the back door. "I need to take her out."

He put the carton of milk in the refrigerator for her and then followed her out to the backyard. "So, how was school today?"

Unable to help herself, she giggled.

"What? What's so funny?"

"My mom used to ask me that all the time when I was

growing up," she said with another laugh. "Sorry. It's been a long time since anyone said that to me."

Fortunately, he laughed with her.

"What about you?" she asked. "How are things going at the resort?"

With a small groan, Liam sat down in the closest Adirondack chair. "I'm beginning to think we made a mistake."

Eyes wide, she sat down beside him. "Oh no! Why?"

"I don't think it's coming together the way I envisioned it. The first cabin is done and it looks a little more rustic than I thought it would. I mentioned it to Will and he got a little pissy with me. He said I'm just being too picky, and the project manager swears everything is exactly as it's supposed to be, but...I don't know. It just feels a little off to me."

"How come?"

Shaking his head, he looked at her with a small smile. "It's too much to explain. I'm sure it will be fine."

Out of the corner of her eye, she spotted Phoebe doing her business before looking back at Liam. "Can you take me to see it? Am I allowed on the site?"

For a moment, he simply stared at her. "You want to go to the job site?"

Nodding excitedly, she explained, "I really do! I'm a very visual person. So you can sit here and tell me about it and I'll be able to see it a bit in my mind, but it's so much better to go and walk the property so I can truly understand what you're worried about."

Then she waited for him to argue that he wasn't worried, but...he didn't.

"Do you have a sturdy pair of boots?" he asked.

"Yup!" she proudly replied. "I used to do a lot of hiking.

And I know to wear clothes that cover you properly—like jeans and a long-sleeved shirt. Does that mean we're gonna go? Like now?"

"Are you sure you really want to?"

Jumping to her feet, Tessa smiled down at him. "Give me five minutes!" She turned to walk away before looking at him again. "Can you watch Phoebe for me?"

"Um...sure?"

"Thanks!" Running inside, she was true to her word and quickly changed into a pair of her favorite old jeans, a hoodie, and her hiking boots. Tossing her hair up into a ponytail, and putting on a touch of lip gloss, she made her way back out to the yard where Liam and Phoebe were exactly where she'd left them. "Ready?"

He stood and grinned. "That was impressive. I wish my sisters were fast like that."

Walking across the yard, she picked up the dog and carried her back into the house. "Well, I can't say I'm always this prompt, but I know the sun's going to go down soon and I don't want to miss out."

They made small talk on the way over to Liam's truck, and once they were out of the driveway, Tessa listened to all of his concerns. The more he talked, the more she figured he was just a little overwhelmed with the whole project and maybe wasn't as visual as Will and the rest of the team.

Not something she was willing to bring up just yet.

The drive was short and when they pulled onto a dirt road, she thought maybe he was on to something. "So, um... this is it?"

He chuckled. "It's not much to look at, I know. Eventually we'll do some landscaping at the entrance and put up proper signage." He parked and muttered a curse.

"What's wrong?"

"Everyone's gone for the day," he murmured. "I swear, we're never going to get done at this rate."

There wasn't anything she could say to that, so she simply climbed from the truck and followed him to a single-wide trailer. "I guess this is the office, huh?"

Unlocking the door, Liam nodded. "Yeah. It's not bad and it's a great place to come and either warm up or cool down—depending on the weather." He walked across the space and grabbed two hard hats. "You'll need to wear this." Placing it on her head, he chuckled when it wouldn't sit properly.

"I think my ponytail is in the way. Hang on." Handing him the hat back, she made quick work of moving the band down a bit and went from a high ponytail to a low one. Taking the hat back, she put it on and smiled. "There! All good!"

"Yes, you are," he said, and Tessa was certain he was going to kiss her.

But he didn't.

Instead, he took her by the hand and led her out of the trailer, where they began walking along the cleared paths—which would more than likely get paved at some point. They were wide enough for construction vehicles, but it was fairly rough terrain.

"This whole area will have small cabins," he explained. "We're planning on a dozen of them and then further down by the lake will be campsites."

"How small are the cabins?"

"They're like those tiny houses that were all the rage for a while." He pointed to a structure down the path. "That's the model that we just finished earlier this week. Want to see it?"

"After we look at everything else. Show me what's bugging you overall about the property."

It took several minutes, but when he stopped talking, Liam also stopped in his tracks and studied her. The sun was going down and she knew they should head back to his truck, but she could tell he'd just had an epiphany of sorts.

"Do you know what I just realized?"

She shook her head.

"This is what I needed," he said, sounding incredibly pleased. "There's always so much going on that every conversation is chaotic. But being able to walk around and just talk without someone correcting me or interrupting me was incredibly helpful. Thank you for suggesting this!"

She was beyond pleased to be of help.

"Do we have time to see the cabin?" she asked. "I know it's getting dark, but..." Looking up through the trees, she realized it was also very cloudy.

"It has electricity and we have lights along the path— solar ones—so we'll be fine heading back to the truck."

"Sounds good." Together they walked toward the cabin and the closer they got, the more excited she became. "Oh, wow! This is amazing!"

"We didn't want anything too contemporary, but we also didn't want to go too rustic. I think this look works, but now I'm wondering if we should have gone with the traditional tiny house floor plan."

"What's the difference?"

"Ours have everything on one floor and the traditional ones all have a sleeping loft. I just felt like for the sake of housekeeping, a loft would be a pain to deal with."

"I think you are totally right. That could get to be annoying and then if anyone started slacking off, you might get a bad reputation. Plus, think of the smell if it didn't get cleaned." She shuddered and then screamed when lightning lit up the sky, followed by a boom of thunder. "Uh-oh…"

"Come on," he said, walking faster. "Rain wasn't in the forecast, so it will probably blow over quickly. We can hang out in the cabin for a few minutes."

Nodding, Tessa followed him and just as they were approaching the front path to the cabin, the skies opened up and they were soaked in a matter of seconds.

"Sorry!" Liam called out as he fumbled for his keys. She wanted to argue that the cabin didn't need to be locked up, but as soon as they stepped inside, she realized she was wrong.

"Oh my goodness," she whispered. "Look at this!" Everything looked so shiny and new that she didn't want to walk too far in with wet and muddy boots. Whipping her hat off, she placed it on the floor as she bent over to untie her boots. Beside her, Liam did the same. Straightening, she took a few steps further in and looked around in awe. "Liam, this is beautiful!"

"This is the one-bedroom model. We'll have two and three-bedroom ones too." Coming to stand beside her, he shrugged. "I don't know, it just feels…small and bland."

"It's perfectly cozy," she countered. The space was definitely small. There was a living room, kitchen combo, a bedroom, and a bathroom. But they decorated it to make it feel very welcoming. "Seriously, it's wonderful." Roaming into the bedroom, she looked around and took note of the quilt on the bed that looked handmade, the small pieces of furniture that had a rustic-chic vibe, and that nothing felt crammed.

When she turned, he was standing right there and suddenly the space felt very small.

Tessa's heart was hammering so loudly that she was certain he could hear it.

One strong hand reached up and cupped her cheek. "I thought about you all week," he murmured gruffly.

"You did?"

Nodding, he said, "I did. I wanted to call you and invite you to dinner, but...it never felt like the right time. And I figured you might not be interested in anything more than just...you know...practicing your kissing skills on me."

Practicing her kissing skills? Was that really even still a thing?

If she were the braver sort, she'd admit that she was fairly confident in her kissing ability now thanks to him, but there were other areas that she could use a little help in.

Namely, sex.

Could I be that bold?

Thunder shook the tiny house, loud enough that it made her jump and move even closer. When she looked into Liam's eyes, she had her answer.

She *could* be that bold.

At least...she hoped she could.

Resting her hand on Liam's chest, she softly told him, "I think I'm confident enough with kissing."

His expression fell slightly.

Pressing her entire body against his, she whispered, "But there are other things I'm out of practice on that I think you can help with."

"Whatever you want, Tessa. I'm yours."

Holy. Crap.

"Kiss me, Liam," she softly commanded.

The heated look in his eyes almost had her asking for more, but she knew they'd get to the good stuff. The rain was pouring down outside and they weren't going anywhere for a good long while.

His thumb gently caressed her lower lip. "Do you have any idea how beautiful you are?" he murmured as he began to lower his head.

Slowly, Tessa shook her head. People had often told her she was pretty in a girl-next-door kind of way, but no one had ever called her beautiful.

Until right this moment.

"It's true," he went on before placing tiny kisses along her jaw. "You are pure temptation." More kisses. "So sweet." More kisses. "So sexy."

Sexy? Me?

Before she could respond, Liam captured her lips in a kiss so deep, so carnal, that Tessa almost couldn't keep up.

But as she anchored her hands in his hair and held on, she was determined to be the woman he seemed to think she was.

Chapter Eight

Warning bells should have gone off in his head.

But they didn't.

All week he'd stayed away based on the conversation with his brothers, but in the end, Liam knew he'd regret it if he simply walked away from her. Coming to know her the way he was, there wasn't a doubt in his mind that she would take it personally and the last thing he wanted to do was cause her to doubt herself.

Which was why he was showing her just how damn tempting she was.

How desirable.

And how much he wanted her.

Even if he hadn't said the words yet, he was fairly certain she could feel just how turned on he was.

Carefully, he maneuvered them across the small room and was about to sit on the sofa with her, but Tessa surprised him by breaking the kiss and panting, "The bed."

He didn't need to be told twice.

The bedroom was less than five feet away, but the urge

to pick her up in his arms and carry her there was too strong to deny.

"Oh!" she whispered against his lips, but before he could utter a word, he was placing her on the mattress and covering her body with his.

And then he was kissing her.

Or she was kissing him.

Actually, they were devouring each other.

For so many years, Liam felt like he had to be in control of his emotions, but with Tessa, he felt like he could let that go. When it came to speaking his mind, he would most definitely need to reel that in, but with what they were doing right now? With passion? There was no controlling it. She was turning his world upside down more and more every day—driving him wild with a need he didn't realize he had.

Tessa's hands clutched his hair before smoothing down his back and then up over his shoulders. Her touch was everywhere, and it made him want to do the same to her.

Without breaking the kiss, Liam let one hand gently make its way under her sweatshirt so he could cup her breast. She moaned into his mouth as her back arched. Then she surprised him as she broke the kiss and said, "Wait."

Before he knew it, she reached down and tugged the sweatshirt up and over her head, tossing it to the floor, and left him staring down in shock.

As a matter of fact, he was sure his jaw was hanging open.

For a woman who seemed relatively conservative in just about everything, her taste in lingerie bordered on fantasy-inducing.

"Tessa, I..." But there weren't any words.

The bra was so sheer that it left nothing to the imagination. His hand felt rough and scratchy against it, and he quickly lifted it away.

Only to have Tessa put it back.

There was an impish grin on her face as she said, "It's okay. But we can take it off if it makes you feel better."

Um...yes please...

They worked together to remove it, and once it joined her sweatshirt on the floor, Liam went to lower his head because he couldn't wait to put his mouth on her breasts. She stopped him again.

"I think I'm at a slight disadvantage here," she said sweetly before one of her hands snaked under his shirt and smoothed over his abs and up to his chest.

Message received.

In a flash, his shirt was up and joined the rapidly growing pile of clothes on the floor. "Better?"

Her hand continued to move all over his chest, so Liam slowly lowered himself until it was trapped between them. Her beautiful eyes went wide right before he kissed her again.

Her skin was warm, her lips were soft, and the sounds she made were sexier than anything he had ever heard. It was obvious this attraction wasn't one-sided and as long as the storm raged outside, Liam was confident they they'd be just fine right here.

Sometime later—it could have been minutes; it could have been hours—but Tessa was naked and breathless in his arms and Liam was perfectly content for them to stay right where they were.

His fingers gently ran through her hair, and he turned

his head to place a kiss on her forehead. "I want you to know I didn't bring you here for this." It was important for him to clarify that so she didn't think he had ulterior motives.

Smiling sleepily up at him, she quietly replied, "I know." Then added, "But maybe it's why I wanted to come here."

Unable to help it, he chuckled. "Tessa, I'm not sure which one of us needs a filter, but I'm beginning to think it's you."

She shrugged. "Maybe. I think you bring out a side of me that knows I can say whatever I want and you'll be okay with it."

That was...surprising.

Pulling back a bit, he stared down at her. "Who could possibly have a problem with anything you say?"

Her eyes went wide before she laughed. "For starters, you seem to. But I was referring to other people in my life— my family, friends..."

Now she had truly piqued his curiosity.

"I don't understand. You're like...the happiest, most upbeat person I've ever met."

With a slight frown, Tessa pushed up on one elbow and looked at him. "Liam, you've openly admitted how much my upbeat things annoy you. Do you think you're the only one?"

"Um..."

"Okay, I think I worded all that wrong. With you, I know I can say whatever I want and even though we'll argue and disagree, we move on from it. My family and friends? Not so much."

"Damn, I had no idea..."

"Even before Trevor got sick, I was a very upbeat

person," she began, and Liam had to fight a wave of jealousy at the mention of her friend-slash-husband. "But when he got sick, everyone criticized me for being too upbeat. Like they expected me to show how devastated I was or to let Trevor see how upset it all made me and all I could think was...why? Why does he need to see that? He had enough to wrap his head around. Why did I need to add to that?"

All he did was nod.

"I've had people accuse me of not feeling enough, feeling too much, not accepting what was happening, being too accepting of what was happening..." Pausing, she groaned. "It was exhausting. There's no handbook on how to handle situations like this."

That he could totally understand.

"Anyway, the thing that most people don't get is that being positive doesn't mean that you love every single day. Or just because I am grateful for my life and the things that I have doesn't mean every moment is great." She sighed and rested her head back on his shoulder. "The thing is, Liam, some days are hard. Sometimes I still get sad and wish things could be different. You have to make a conscious effort to find the good each day and to search for the lesson in each and every struggle so you can grow from it." Another shrug. "I'm not stuck in my grief and Trevor didn't need to spend his last days worrying about me. Every day I choose to be happy and keep moving forward. But sometimes those steps are tiny and I'm the only one who can see them."

Guilt shamed him hard in that moment, and he hugged her close. "I'm sorry," he whispered against her forehead. "I'm so sorry. I never thought of it like that."

If anything, she snuggled even closer. "Most people don't. You don't know until you're the one going through it."

She kissed his chest. "A good friend of mine was estranged from her dad for years. If you ever brought him up, she'd tell you he was dead to her. A month before he died, he reached out because he knew he was dying." Letting out a long breath, she continued. "She spent a lot of that last month with him and when he died, she was devastated. And I mean, devastated. I didn't question it and I didn't tell her she was wrong for feeling the way she did. One day she looked at me and said how she never in a million years thought she'd feel such sadness. So..."

He understood what she was saying. "Two years ago, when I was deployed, we lost several guys in our company. It's something you go into any combat knowing is a possibility, but you hope and pray everyone goes home together. We had to learn to turn off the part of ourselves that grieves. Or, at least, I did. Because you have to go on. You're in the middle of a war and you have to keep moving forward. So I get that part of it—the moving forward—but it just feels different from how you do it." He hugged her again. "And just because it looked different didn't give me the right to criticize you."

"Liam?"

"Hmm?"

"I realize I'm out of practice with this sort of thing, but... this is absolutely the worst post-sex pillow talk I've ever heard of."

They each pulled back at the same time and laughed.

Hard.

"Okay, okay, you've got a point," he finally said. "Sorry."

Beside him, she hummed and snuggled back into his arms. "Do you think it's still raining out?"

Once they were both silent, they had their answer. The rain was pounding down on the roof. "If you need to get home to Phoebe, I can run up to the truck and then drive it down here and get you."

She happily sighed his name. "As much as I love that you'd do that, I wouldn't let you."

"Why not?"

"Because it's very muddy out there and if your truck got stuck in the mud, then we'd really be in trouble. Phoebe's fine with the rain, and she's used to be alone." Pausing, she placed a kiss on his shoulder and then his chest. "Besides, I'm not opposed to staying here for a bit longer."

He liked where this was going.

Slowly, she moved over him, covering him with those gloriously smooth and sexy limbs. "In fact," she went on, "I'd say it's probably very smart for us to stay here as long as possible."

Leaning in, she kissed his throat and then moved lower to kiss his chest. Liam reached up and gently fisted her hair. "I couldn't agree more. We'll stay here all night if we need to."

Tessa lifted her head slightly and smiled. "That sounds wonderful."

They didn't stay at the tiny house all night, but it was after nine by the time they got home. They had stopped and picked up a pizza along the way and were currently sitting in her kitchen eating.

It was nice having him here and she felt a strong wave of relief that he simply didn't walk her to her door and wish her a good night. She truly was out of practice with sex and dating, so she wasn't sure what exactly to expect once they got home.

Or what this all meant in general.

Kissing Liam was one thing and something Tessa felt confident she could handle with no real problem; sleeping with him certainly complicated things. She didn't regret it and would certainly do it again if he asked, but she wasn't sure if it meant they were dating or if he was doing this for the sake of helping her.

Although...she couldn't imagine going to such extremes for a friend.

Oh, really? Like you didn't marry a friend?

But she and Trevor had loved each other. They'd been best friends for years. Of course she would do something extreme to help him.

But Liam wasn't in love with her. Heck, she still wasn't sure he truly liked her, so...what was his motivation?

You mean other than guilt-free sex?

Oh, right.

That.

"With all this rain tonight, will the crews still be able to work tomorrow?" she asked as a way of keeping her confusing thoughts at bay.

He nodded. "It may limit some things, but not a lot. Considering we're dealing a lot with the landscape and that sort of thing, it makes clearing some areas easier. We need for the ground to be dry when we're building, but there's so much of both going on that there's always something to do. Of course, if it's raining in the morning, we'll probably take the day off."

"I have tomorrow off for the holiday. I'm a little psyched for a three-day weekend. On my way home I contemplated a trip to the mountains, but...I would have needed to plan better."

"Why? Why not just be spontaneous?"

"It's a six-hour drive. If I really wanted to do it right, I would have left right from school today so I could have gotten up early tomorrow and enjoyed a full day of exploring and enjoying the fall foliage."

"You could get up early tomorrow and get at least a half a day in…"

"It's okay. There are plenty of things I can do around the house and lesson plans to work on." She took a sip of her wine. "And baking. I plan on going to the farmers market and getting some supplies and baking this weekend."

"Cookies?"

"Always," she said with a wink. "But I was going to do an apple pie too. My mom's recipe is amazing and I know she'll make it for Thanksgiving, but there's never enough to go around, so I thought I'd make one for myself."

"My mom makes a great apple pie too. She serves it at the pub a lot."

Tessa nodded. "I've had it and it's delicious. I also love her pot roast." She hummed appreciatively. "Oh my goodness, some of the best winter meals I've ever eaten have been from the pub on those nights when I don't want to cook."

"Mine too," he teased.

"You're lucky to have access to it the way you do. I'm sure your parents are thrilled to have you home. Your siblings too."

He shrugged. "My folks, definitely. My siblings?" He chuckled. "That I'm not so sure about."

"Seriously? You don't get along with them?"

"I always thought I did, but since I've been back, our relationships aren't exactly how I remembered them."

"I'm not sure what that means."

Taking the last bite of his pizza, he took a moment

before explaining. "My baby sister, Arianna? She hid an important relationship from me and our entire family because of me."

"Why?"

"Will's my best friend and they knew I wouldn't approve, so..."

"Why wouldn't you approve? Is he a good guy?"

"Well, yeah. Will's the best, but he's a lot older than Ari, and apparently, I'm overprotective." He shook his head. "Will kept it from me for over a year because of how I'd react."

"Okay, but that's kind of understandable. There's nothing wrong with looking out for your sister."

"I'm just getting started."

"Oh."

"It actually hit me Halloween night," he began. "I went to the pub and everyone was there celebrating and...I didn't fit in. I hung out in the kitchen with my dad and I mentioned how different everything felt and he said how they're trying to get to know me again. I'd been gone for a long time—even though I always came home whenever I had leave time. He told me we're not kids anymore and how they're all trying to get to know me as a peer rather than the older brother."

"That makes sense."

"Then my uncle made a comment to me that really hit me hard," he said. "I watched some guy hitting on my sister Ryleigh. I was about to go over and intervene, but Uncle Ronan told me that she could handle herself." He shook his head. "And I realized he was right. I was so used to always stepping in and handling situations and fighting their battles for them, I don't know how to just be their brother. It's weird."

"Personally, I don't think it's weird. I think it makes total sense," she reasoned. "You left home as the big brother who—according to you—fought their battles and probably was bossy with them because there was a lot of responsibility put on you."

He didn't respond, but simply studied her.

"Now you're back and they're too old for you to be bossing around—although I'm sure you've tried—and you're trying to figure out this new role. It's got to be confusing for you."

"Um...it is," he said with a bit of wonder.

"I have two sisters and they're both older than me," she explained. "We're close, but since I'm the baby, they never quite saw me as an equal. They were both married by the time they were 22 and had babies by 25. So they had that in common and there I was, single and childless." She took another sip of her wine. "When Trevor got sick and we got married, I felt like I could finally talk to them like a peer rather than their little sister, and neither of them knew what to do with that. I got the whole 'it's not a real marriage' and 'you don't understand' thing thrown at me more times than I care to remember. But it wasn't until after he died that they saw how I didn't need to have a conventional marriage or children to be on the same level as them. I had grown up and my version of that differed from theirs."

"Tessa, I think your version of life differs from most people's," he said gently. "And I'm not saying that to be snarky or mean, it's just...I'm a little in awe of you. I've been deployed multiple times and seen things that give me nightmares, and I'm realizing you might not have walked my identical path, but you've lived just as much as I have."

Tears stung her eyes because most people never saw

that about her. They don't realize the depth of her experiences or they minimize it.

Reaching across the table, she squeezed his hands. "Thank you." But she didn't let her touch linger because—again—she still had no idea what it was they were doing. Instead, she stood and began cleaning up. Liam stayed seated while he finished his wine and they were both somewhat lost in their own thoughts.

It was now after ten and her normal routine had her taking Phoebe out one last time before coming inside, getting into her jammies, and either reading or watching TV until she was ready to go to sleep. Even though she didn't have to be up early for school, she was kind of tired after such an exciting afternoon and evening. Liam had worn her out and she wouldn't mind crawling into bed a little early tonight. Maybe...

In the blink of an eye, his arm was around her waist and Tessa was falling into his lap. "Oh my goodness!"

"I was sitting here thinking about a dozen different topics for us to talk about because I didn't want to go home yet," he admitted before leaning in and running his tongue along the shell of her ear.

Tessa couldn't help but shiver with pleasure because it felt so good. She tilted her head to give him better access. "I don't believe I was kicking you out..."

"Not yet," he whispered against her skin. "But I didn't want to take that chance."

There was no way she couldn't smile at that, because it was so honest and she had a feeling they had maybe been in that situation a time or two before. And because she was becoming more comfortable with him in so many ways, she felt like maybe she could tease him about it.

"Well, to be fair, it only comes to that when you talk too much."

His chuckle was low and deep and a little rumbly and for a moment she felt like Red Riding Hood in the arms of the Big Bad Wolf.

"Then I guess I'd better use my mouth for other things," he murmured before tilting her head so he could kiss her.

Yeah. This was so much better than teasing banter, she thought.

Curling into him, Tessa's arms went around his shoulders as she pressed herself closer. Liam's arms tightened around her as his hands moved leisurely up and down her back.

And he had great hands.

They were large and slightly calloused and felt absolutely magnificent on her skin.

But sounded slightly scratchy on her shirt.

One way to rectify that…

Liam's eyes went wide with confusion as Tessa broke the kiss and pulled back. Smiling sweetly, she casually maneuvered herself so she could pull the sweatshirt off and dropped it to the floor.

Where Phoebe promptly came over and made a bed out of it.

His hungry gaze raked over her. "Not that I'm complaining, but…"

"I was thinking about how amazing your hands feel on my skin and the sweatshirt was in the way," she replied. "I can put it back on if you'd like."

Instead of saying anything right away, his hand reached up and gently caressed her breast. "This bra is the sexiest thing I've ever seen." One finger slowly scratched over her nipple. "It's so sheer and hides nothing." Then he looked up at her with a seductive grin. "I love seeing what my touch does to you."

Tessa raked one hand through his dark hair. "What a coincidence—I happen to love what your touch does to me."

His expression turned serious. "I don't know how we got here and at some point we're going to have to talk about it, but I want you to know that I...um...what I mean is, I'm really glad..." He muttered a curse.

"Liam?"

"Hmm?"

"Talk to me," she whispered, cupping his stubbled jaw.

"You just told me that bad things happen when I talk to too much," he said, amusement lacing his tone, and she couldn't help but laugh softly.

"I'm not saying we have to have a deep conversation, but there's obviously something you need to say."

Then his eyes met hers and she read so much there—the question, the passion, the turmoil, the indecision—and she wasn't sure she was going to like what came next.

"Thank you," he said solemnly after a long moment.

That...was totally unexpected.

"Thank you?"

He nodded.

"For...?"

Oh God...please don't let this be a 'thanks for letting me sleep with you' or something weird like that...

"For being you," he said, resting his forehead against hers. "You had no reason to give me a second or third or fourth chance at being a good neighbor or friend. But you still did and it's just one of the things that makes you amazing."

A week ago, she had a feeling it was something he

would have mocked her about, but she was glad to see he was changing.

No, that wasn't the right word. Changing makes it sound like there was something wrong with him, and she hated to think that way. Instead, she'd say he was learning and growing and that made her feel better.

Her hand continued to play in his hair, and she knew now wasn't the time to get into any of her thoughts with him. So instead, she said, "I'm really glad you're here, Liam. And I'm glad we're here like this."

Lifting his head, he studied her. "I'm torn between picking you up and carrying you to bed or carrying you out to the hot tub, stripping you down, and seeing what kind of mischief we can get into out there."

"Ooh...naked in the hot tub? I've never done that..."

And suddenly, she very much wanted to.

"How about this?" she suggested. "Let's go outside and explore this whole hot tub idea and then you can carry me inside to bed and see what kind of mischief we can create there."

His smile was downright lethal. "A woman with a plan. I love it."

He stood with her in his arms and Tessa let out a laugh. "I didn't really mean you had to carry me everywhere. I am perfectly capable of walking."

"I know, but this is way more fun," he said, kissing her soundly before they ever moved away from the kitchen table.

Sighing with contentment, she rested her head on his shoulder as he walked to the back door. When he paused and seemed uncertain, she thought for sure he was having second thoughts.

"Liam?"

"Is she going to be okay in here or do we need to bring her out with us?" He motioned to Phoebe and her heart nearly burst at how considerate he was being.

"She'll be just fine," she assured him, kissing him softly. "Thank you."

"For...?" he teased, mimicking her tone from minutes ago.

"For being so wonderful."

Now it was his turn to laugh. "I don't think anyone's ever referred to me as being wonderful."

But Tessa wasn't laughing with him. With her hand on his jaw, she forced him to look at her. "Then they're not seeing what I'm seeing, because you are. You may try to come off as being in charge or being the guy in control, but that's only because you were put into that role from the time you were young. When you look beyond that one tiny layer of yourself, there's so much more there. And I'm enjoying discovering all that makes you who you are, Liam Donovan."

He swallowed hard before carrying her out to the yard and placing her on the edge of the hot tub. Stepping between her legs, he kissed her with a ferocity that should have scared her, but she knew exactly why he reacted that way.

So she soothed him.

Encouraged him.

Loved him.

But more importantly...she accepted him for exactly who he was.

Chapter Nine

A week later, Liam walked into Tessa's house and the entire place smelled like all the best parts of fall.

Someone's baking...

They'd gotten into the habit this past week where he came over after he got home from work. She told him he didn't have to knock or ring the bell, that he could just come in. It didn't seem like a big deal, but he kind of liked how she trusted him.

He also liked the way she normally greeted him.

For someone who said it had been a long time since she'd been intimate with a man, she was most definitely making up for lost time and Liam was more than happy to be the one she did that with.

With each day he was discovering something new about her—something that was completely at odds with the woman he initially met. She was still ridiculously cheery and overly optimistic, but there was a bit of wildness to her that she only showed when they were alone. A lot of the time, Tessa was the one to initiate sex and he loved all the ways she would seduce him.

Not that it took much. All she had to do was look at him and he was ready to strip her down and make love to her.

The night in the hot tub seemed to be the turning point.

Well, that entire afternoon and evening had changed things between them. Once they crossed the line to lovers, Liam knew nothing would ever be the same, but the hot tub seemed to unleash a little part of her she had been repressing.

Now he looked forward to seeing what part of Tessa she was going to reveal to him each day.

He found her in the kitchen where she was pulling a couple of pans out of the oven. Thanksgiving was only a few days away, and he knew she was getting ready. He hated how she was going to South Carolina to be with her family while he was staying here with his. As much as he loved a big Donovan holiday dinner, this year he would have enjoyed letting Tessa experience one too. Only...

They weren't dating.

At least, he didn't think they were.

Hell, whenever he tried to talk to Tessa about it, she changed the subject and he was getting a bit of a complex.

Was it possible that he was more into her than she was into him? Could she be sticking to his original plan, that this was all just about him helping her get comfortable dating again?

Oh God...is she...using me?

For sex?

Groaning inwardly, he told himself that would be poetic justice. He'd finally found a woman he wanted to date and he'd put himself in a position where she didn't take him seriously. It would totally serve him right for pushing her into re-discovering the sexual side of herself. Maybe now she realized that she could have all the pleasurable fun that she wanted without having any deep entanglements.

For years, that had been the dream—hell, for most guys, it was the dream—but Liam was feeling like he was ready for something more than casual, something more fulfilling.

So then, what am I doing here?

"Hey, you," she said softly, smiling at him as she took the oven mitts off. Her hips swayed as she walked around the kitchen island toward him, and when she reached him and wrapped herself around him, she looked very pleased with herself. "I made an apple butter pound cake that I'm going to put caramel frosting on." Then she kissed him thoroughly before smiling again. "I remember you saying how much you loved caramel."

She was out of his arms before he could say a word, and his stomach growled louder than he was prepared for.

"I'm experimenting with some new recipes," she told him. "My mom makes all the usual stuff and I wanted to maybe add my own personal touch to Thanksgiving this year."

Nodding, he walked over and watched as she stirred something up in a bowl. "What's that?"

Dipping her finger into the mixture, she then held it up to him. "Taste."

Slowly, Liam leaned in and sucked her finger into his mouth. He heard her soft intake of breath and watched as her eyes got a little dazed. Licking his way up and down her finger, two things hit him. First, that was the caramel frosting and it was freaking delicious, and second, he wanted her right here, right now, in the middle of her kitchen.

"I'm not sure which tastes better, you or that frosting," he said gruffly. "I hope you made extra because I'd love to put it to use right now." Glancing around, he looked for a clear spot on the island, but there wasn't one. Tessa surprised him by pushing a bunch of bowls and pans into the sink before hopping up onto the counter.

"Was this what you were hoping for?" she asked breathlessly. Her chest was heaving and she was nibbling her bottom lip and it was crazy how they did this to each other with such little effort.

Frosting, for fuck's sake. He was practically brought to his knees with need over caramel frosting.

Well, that and pretty much everything about Tessa.

He'd say he was in trouble, but he was enjoying himself far too much.

They were kissing, clothes were either being flung to the floor or being shifted, and all he could think of when he was deep inside of her was how this was pure bliss. She was temptation personified, and he was the luckiest damn bastard to be able to have her like this.

It was fast and furious and over faster than he wanted, but as he rested his head on her shoulder and tried to catch his breath, something else hit him.

Maybe this was all they did—maybe this was why she didn't take him seriously—because he never tried to take her out.

They stayed in all the time. Not once did he ask to take her out to dinner or a movie or...anything. Maybe she thought this was strictly about sex—or friends with benefits —because that's all they had done.

Well, that stopped right now.

Kissing her shoulder and then her cheek, Liam pulled back and smiled at her. "Damn, Tessa. That was incredible."

"I guess you really liked the frosting," she said with a

wink as she slowly unwrapped herself from him. He helped her down from the counter and they took a few minutes to get dressed again. But when she went to move away from him, he grabbed her hand and gently pulled her toward him.

"Hey," he began softly. "How about we get cleaned up and go out somewhere to eat?"

"Um...what?"

Okay, that wasn't quite the response he was hoping for, but he wasn't deterred.

"Yeah, I was thinking we could go out someplace. What are you in the mood for? I know we've gotten Italian from Vincenzo's, but there's a place down in Magnolia that has a great menu." Taking a minute to think, he then suggested, "Or we can go for seafood or Mexican or...hell, we can even go to the pub if you'd like."

"You think we should go to the pub? Really?"

He shrugged. "Why not? If that's what you're in the mood for..."

"It's not that, Liam. It's just..."

"What?"

"Well...it could be weird," she said slowly. "I mean... some of your family will obviously be there. Are you prepared to have them questioning you about us?"

And this was his opening. Giving her a small tug, he grinned when her breasts were pressed against his chest. "Who says they're going to question us?"

The look she gave him spoke volumes. "Liam, please. I obviously know your family and your mother has always been vocal about wanting her kids to settle down. You don't think us going in there together is going to start some specu- lation that we're dating?" Then she laughed a little and stepped out of his grasp. "I mean, I think they'd realize pretty quickly that we're not, but I just don't want you to get upset with them."

Wait a minute...was she serious?

"Um...what exactly are you trying to say? What would be so wrong with them thinking that we're dating?"

Letting out a breath, she began loading dishes into the dishwasher and cleaning up after her baking endeavor. "Liam, be reasonable. You and I are as opposite as night and day, and I'm sure you complained about me to them a time or two."

He had, but...

"That was before I got to know you," he said defensively. "And there's nothing wrong with you. You're beautiful and talented and friendly...I mean, why wouldn't we date?"

She chuckled again and he was getting more than a little annoyed with it.

"We're friends, Liam," she said after a moment. "Good friends." Pausing, she looked up at him. "I get that we've got some...blurred lines here, but you're just helping me out, right? You're not likely to fall in love with me!" Another laugh. "Eventually, I'll be confident enough to give dating a try again." Her shoulders sagged a bit and she seemed to sober. "I have loved every moment of this last week, and I just don't want you to get uncomfortable if people think something more is going on."

Honestly, he had no idea what to say to any of that.

"Are you saying you wouldn't be uncomfortable if anyone came over and made that assumption?" he asked and yeah, he was even more defensive than he was a moment ago.

Tessa's eyes went a little wide at his tone, but she

shrugged. "Like I said, you and I know what's going on, so we'd just set them straight. Not a big deal."

And for the first time in a long time, Liam was eager to be around his family.

If anything, he was going to use their nosy, interfering ways to his advantage.

Tessa might not think they had anything more than this friends-with-benefits situation, but Liam was determined to start a campaign proving to her that they could be so much more.

"You're right," he said casually. "I'm sure it won't be a big deal. Besides, I really could go for either some pot roast or the beef stew in the bread bowl. Have you tried that yet?"

Shaking her head, she closed the dishwasher. "I haven't, but that sounds amazing! Do they bake the bowls themselves?"

"Honestly, I have no idea. You'll have to ask my mom." Looking at his watch, he saw it was after six. "I'm gonna run next door and wash up."

She eyed him curiously. "Didn't you do that before you came over?"

"Um...I did, but then we just did what we did and..."

"Ah. Gotcha. I'm going to go and do the same. So what do you say? A half hour?"

"That should work." Leaning in, he kissed her and turned to walk away, but she stopped him.

"Or..." she began.

"Or...?"

"We could wash up here together and then go," she suggested. "I've got plenty of soap and my shower—as you know—definitely fits two."

If he were a stronger man, he'd be a gentleman and decline.

Samantha Chase

But…being a gentleman was the furthest thing from his mind as she gave him a sultry look.

The little vixen.

"Sweetheart, if you think I'm ever going to say no to getting you naked and soapy, you're crazy," he said with a grin. "Lead the way."

* * *

Something was up.

It was almost like Liam was purposely trying to provoke his family into thinking they were dating.

From the moment they walked through the doors of the pub, his hand held hers or his arm was around her, and he had her practically plastered to his side.

Not that she was minding it, but it was all very different from what they had discussed earlier.

You mean when your pants should have been on fire from all the lying?

Okay, fine. Yes.

Technically, she was being less than truthful with him on a few subjects.

Namely, how she felt about this turn in their relationship and how she viewed it.

Yes, she had gone into this new physical part of things truly believing she could keep herself in check and treat it all casually.

That was the first lie she told herself.

Then, after sleeping with Liam the first time, Tessa swore she wasn't going to let herself fall for him.

That was lie number two.

As the week went on, she'd had many conversations with herself where she got firm and said that she would be

142

fine if this was all they had and Liam eventually moved on.

That was the biggest lie of them all.

He hadn't argued with her earlier about where things stood, but as they sat in the corner booth of the pub with several of his family members, she found she was more than a little confused.

"So, Tessa, are you going home for Thanksgiving?" Mrs. Donovan asked as she put an order of corn fritters on the table.

"Um...I am. I was just doing some baking today and testing out some new dessert recipes," she said before Liam interrupted.

"Mom, Tessa made this amazing apple butter pound cake with homemade caramel icing. It was to die for!"

She wanted to remind him how he never tasted the cake and only had the icing, but...

"Ooh...that sounds good. Do you ever make cheesecake? I recently found a recipe for a gingerbread cheesecake," his mother explained. "I'm thinking of trying it, but none of my kids eat cheesecake."

Tessa looked over at Liam in shock. "You don't like cheesecake?"

He shrugged. "Not really. I prefer an actual cake or cookie. The sugar cookies you brought to my house that night were delicious."

She felt herself blush and caught Mrs. Donovan's knowing smile.

"Ryleigh likes cheesecake," Liam reminded his mother. "Maybe test it out with her?"

"She gets mad when I make her eat desserts," she said wearily.

"Why?"

"Probably because then I tell her she's putting on a little weight and won't ever find a nice man to settle down with." She shrugged. "Who's to say?"

"Mom," Liam said with a chuckle before serving both of them some of the fritters. "Hey, can we get some sour cream with these?"

"You can't find your way to the kitchen?" his mother snapped, and Tessa was shocked when he slid from the booth without a word.

Uh-oh...

"So? You and Liam, huh?" she said with a big smile.

"Oh, no...no. *No*," she said a little more firmly. "We are just friends. Living next door to each other, we've gotten to know each other and were talking about some of our favorite dishes that you make. When he mentioned your beef stew and bread bowls, I was curious."

The older woman's expression fell slightly. "Hmm... but...Liam's a nice man, right? He's been polite and respectful?"

Tessa didn't want to touch that question with a ten-foot pole, so she simply nodded.

"I know you and I don't know each other very well, Tessa, but...I know it's been a long time since your husband passed. May he rest in peace," she added solemnly. "But maybe it's time for you to start dating. Liam is..."

"Liam is not interested in me," she quickly interjected. "Trust me. I'm far too cheery for him. He's told me that a dozen times."

"My son could use some cheery in his life. I think all his years in the Marines, he saw too much—too much death and destruction. I think it's been hard for him to be back home and trying to find his place."

"The resort project is going well and he has his house..."

"On a professional level, he's fine. But he's too serious and he...I don't know, he's not the same boy he was when he first enlisted."

"Of course he's not," she gently replied. "He's a grown man now. We all change as we age. Maybe he's more serious because he appreciates how fragile life is now. It's got to be hard to come home after so many years and not really know his siblings as intimately as he would have if he never left. It's an adjustment going back to civilian life and maybe that's why he threw himself into this business venture so quickly—so he wouldn't have time to sit and dwell on those things."

Mrs. Donovan studied her hard for several moments. "You understand him," she said quietly before she nodded. "That is a true gift when a woman understands a man. It took me a long time to fully understand my husband. I loved him from the time I was a young girl, but understand him?" She shook her head. "It took us being married and living together and having children before I truly felt like I knew him. But listening to you talk about Liam..." Her hand went to her heart. "You would be good for him."

I think so too, but...

Liam slid back into the booth with a bowl of sour cream, another beer, and a plate of something deep fried. Grinning, he put everything down. "My father makes these amazing taco bites. When I saw he was prepping some, I grabbed the ones that were finished."

"Liam!" both she and his mother admonished at the same time before starting to laugh.

"What? Ryleigh handed me the plate and Dad said it was fine," he argued lightly before holding up one of the bites to Tessa's lips. "Trust me, once you taste this, you'll know why I snagged them."

And he was right.

"Oh, wow," she said around a mouthful of food. "Those are delicious!"

"My Shane is a phenomenal cook," she said with a smile. "All my kids know how to cook. Well, except Arianna, but she's learning."

"Only because I refused to keep secretly cooking for her," Ryleigh commented as she slid into the booth too. "Hey, Tessa! What did you think of the taco bites?"

"They're delicious," she said with a smile. "Not that I'm surprised. Everything I've ever had here has been amazing."

Both Ryleigh and Mrs. Donovan smiled with pride.

"So, what brings you two in for dinner tonight?" Ryleigh asked.

"We're on a..." Liam began, but Tessa cut him off.

"I was super curious about the bread bowls! Do you bake them here on site?" she quickly asked.

"Definitely not," Ryleigh said with a small laugh. "The bakery over on Fourth makes them for us. Our kitchen can't handle baking anything like that on top of everything else."

"That's why we're upgrading," Jamie said as he placed fresh drinks on the table. "And why does everyone get a break to sit down but me?"

"Join us!" his mother said as she slid in closer to Tessa, forcing her to press up intimately against Liam.

"I didn't know we were having a family dinner," Jamie commented with a grin at her and Liam.

"It's not," Liam said through clenched teeth. "Tessa and I just wanted to grab a quiet dinner together."

"And you brought her here?" Jamie laughed. "Dude, just how bad are you at dating?"

Tessa heard him groan and carefully reached under the table to playfully squeeze his thigh. Unfortunately, he sensed her move and his hand instantly covered hers, holding her in place.

Which was dangerously close to...well...

"Patrick was supposed to stop by too," Ryleigh said with amusement. "Maybe we should call Arianna and Will and really make it a family meal!"

"Aren't we all going to be together on Thursday?" Liam reminded them. "Thanksgiving? Any of this ringing any bells?"

"Will Tessa be joining us?" Ryleigh asked.

"Oh, um...no," she replied. "I'm going home to see my family for the weekend."

"It's a shame they couldn't come here and then we could have a massive Thanksgiving dinner!" Jamie threw out there. "Think about it, we could do it here so there'd be plenty of room, everyone could even be in the kitchen at the same time. It really would solve so many problems. What do you think, Tessa? Would your family be up for a change of venue?"

"Um..."

"That's enough, Jamie," Liam said wearily. "Tessa's family isn't coming to hang out at the pub with us." Then he looked at her. "Or do you think...?"

Unable to help herself, she frowned at him as if willing him to put a stop to this whole conversation. It took a moment, but he seemed to take the hint.

Facing his family, he smiled easily. "Thanksgiving will go on as planned." Looking at his mother, he asked. "Who else is joining us?"

"Well, it will be the eight of us and Ronan, both sets of grandparents, and the Murphys."

Jamie groaned loudly. "Seriously? The Murphys? Why? Don't they have any other friends they can hang out with?"

"What's wrong with the Murphys?" his mother asked. "They've been our friends since all you kids were little." Reaching over, she smacked the back of his head. "What's wrong with you?"

Tessa caught the look of amusement between Ryleigh and Liam and knew there was a story there. But before she could ask, Patrick joined them.

"Hey! Did I miss the text that we were all having dinner together?"

Tessa chuckled and Liam leaned in until his breath was warm on her ear. "This was the worst idea I've ever had. Please tell me you're not upset."

When she turned her head, their noses brushed, but neither pulled back. For a moment, she swore they were the only two people in the room. "I'm fine," she whispered. "It's kind of fun." Then she smiled at him and he seemed to relax, but...they were definitely going to have a conversation about this when they went home. His family was great and she truly liked them; what she didn't like was that he deliberately put them in a situation that he said he didn't want them to be in.

Yeah, they were definitely going to have a conversation.

"Okay, okay," Mrs. Donovan said as she nudged Jamie from the booth and then slid out herself. "This is not a family dinner and we've intruded on Liam and Tessa's meal enough. Everyone go away and find your own spot to eat." Looking over her shoulder, she winked at the two of them. "Enjoy the rest of your meal, and I promise to keep your siblings away from you."

Jamie waved on his way back to the bar, Ryleigh smiled and said she hoped to see Tessa again soon, and Patrick and Liam were having some weird wordless conversation that was beyond bizarre.

"Good to see you, Tessa," he said a minute later before glaring at Liam one more time as he walked away.

"Everything okay?" she asked.

"Yeah, why?"

"That looked...intense. Are you mad at your brother for something?"

He shook his head and put the last corn fritter on his plate. "No, but I think he's a little peeved with me."

"How come?"

Shaking his head again, he said, "It's not important." Cutting the fritter in half, he put one piece on her plate. "What did you think of these?"

She knew a diversion when she heard it, but she wasn't about to argue with him here. "Like I said, everything I've had here has been amazing."

Within minutes, Ryleigh brought their dinners out and wished them a good night. "I probably should have gone back there and done that myself."

"You mean grabbed our plates?"

He nodded. "I know I'm going to catch a lot of shit for making them wait on us."

"I'm not sure what to say to that," she said with a small laugh. "But I will say that this looks and smells delicious too!" The stew was piping hot and was filled with huge chunks of beef, baby carrots, onions, peas, and potatoes. It was the ultimate comfort meal on a cool fall evening.

They ate and talked about how the resort was coming along and then they shared stories about their typical family Thanksgivings.

"Why does Jamie hate the Murphys?" she asked.

"They have a daughter two years younger than him, but she is brilliant and graduated with his class. She's been calling Jamie out on his BS since they were teens and I can say without a doubt that she is the only female who isn't impressed with my baby brother's charms. Thanksgiving will be like dinner and a show because they can't seem to stay away from each other."

"Are you sure they're not into each other? Otherwise, wouldn't they be keeping their distance?"

He shook his head. "No, it's like a weird competition where Jamie spends the entire day—no matter what the holiday or occasion—trying to prove to her why she's wrong about him."

"Like I said, then maybe he's into her?"

Another head shake. "No, it just pisses him off that she doesn't fawn all over him like most women do. It's both comical and embarrassing."

"Sounds interesting, that's for sure."

When they were done eating, Liam asked if she wanted dessert and she shook her head. "I've got that apple butter cake back at my place, if you're interested."

The heated look he gave her told her he remembered where the frosting for that cake had led them earlier. "I'm very interested. Come on. I'll take these plates back to the kitchen and then we'll go."

Nodding, Tessa slid from the booth and watched him walk away.

"Hey," Ryleigh said quietly as she sidled up next to her. "I know it's none of my business, but I just want to say that if there's anything going on between you and Liam, well...it would be great for him. I've been worried about him since he came home but...he doesn't really like to listen to anyone giving him advice and he has zero tolerance if he thinks we're coddling him, but...he could really use someone to coddle him a little. He's done so much for everyone else that it would be nice to know that someone was looking after him."

Her words stopped abruptly when Liam stepped out of the kitchen.

"So I'm glad you enjoyed the stew, and you can get the bread bowls from the bakery almost any time," she said, almost comically loud as her brother approached. "Good to see you both and Liam, I'll see you Thursday!" And then she was gone.

"You ready?" Liam asked.

"Sure."

The ride back was quick and quiet, and they pulled into Liam's driveway since he was the one who drove. He took her hand as they walked across the yard to her place. She often wondered if he'd rather they go to her house, but she knew he would never suggest it because she had Phoebe to consider.

As soon as they stepped inside, he was the one who scooped the dog up and headed for the back door. "Why don't you take care of the cake and I'll make sure she does her business?"

"Thanks." She watched as she walked out the door and marveled at how...normal this all felt. Like it was completely natural for them to come home together and for him to take the dog out while she served up their dessert.

Maybe it feels natural because that's just the way it is. There's nothing weird about this...

Only...she thought there would be. The thought of some other man being in her home—a man who wasn't Trevor—always seemed strange to her. It was why she hadn't dated in so long, because she couldn't imagine anyone else being that close to her. But Liam had sort of come into her life in the most unconventional way and...stayed.

Sighing quietly, she whispered, "I don't know what to do, Trev. Are my feelings real or am I just projecting them because I'm lonely?"

As usual, there wasn't a response, but...there never was.

The frosting wasn't quite cooperating, so she had to heat it up for just a few seconds in the microwave. Eventually she got it to the proper consistency, just as Liam was walking back in with Phoebe.

"I think she sniffed every blade of grass in the yard," he said with a laugh before sitting down at the kitchen island. "Anything I can help with?"

"Nope. I think it's ready." Slicing the cake, she plated a piece for him and then one for herself. Sliding his plate over, Tessa stayed standing opposite him. "So...I wasn't sure if I should bring this up..."

Looking up at her, she could see the concern on his face. "What's going on?"

"I guess I'm a little confused, that's all."

"About?"

"Well...it seems like you *wanted* your family to think we were dating."

"Did I?"

The short bark of laughter was out before she could stop it. "Liam, come on! You were holding my hand, had your arm around me, and joined in when they wanted to invite my family to Thanksgiving! That's hardly something you'd do with a friend."

"Agree to disagree," he said before taking a bite of cake. "Oh, wow...I already knew the frosting was killer, but with the cake? Holy shit, is that good."

"Thanks," she murmured before taking a bite for herself and...okay, wow. That was much better than she thought it would be. "I just don't understand. When we left here

152

earlier, I thought we were on the same page about not giving them the wrong impression, but…"

"Okay, I'll admit that maybe I wasn't thinking. Between the sex in the kitchen and then in the shower…" He gave her a lopsided grin. "You can't blame me for wanting to be more than a little attentive to you. Hell, I almost considered changing plans altogether and ordering takeout so we wouldn't have to get dressed and leave!"

"Really?" she asked, wanting to believe him, but still not feeling like he was being one hundred percent honest.

"Really." Standing, Liam walked around to her side of the island and slid his arms around her waist. "Tessa, I love spending time with you, just the two of us. But I honestly thought you might want to…um…you know…get used to going out places with a guy. Obviously going to the pub wasn't the right thing to do, so maybe next time, we pick someplace where there aren't a bunch of Donovans waiting to swoop in and join us." He placed a kiss on the tip of her nose. "What do you say?"

Now it felt like it made more sense.

Even though it depressed her a bit.

He was still all about just trying to help her get back into the dating world.

If only he knew that the only man she wanted to date was him.

Chapter Ten

"Okay, enough. You glared at me over the mashed potatoes, threw a dinner roll at me, and purposely dropped my slice of pumpkin pie. Can you maybe try being an adult and talk to me?"

Rolling his eyes, Patrick turned and walked out onto their parents' back deck, forcing Liam to follow. Closing the sliding door behind him, he stepped out into the freezing air and mentally cursed as he could see his breath in front of his face.

"Well?"

Turning, his brother faced him. "What is wrong with you? There are probably dozens of women here in Laurel Bay who would love to date you! Why Tessa? Why would you go bring your twisted, negative view of the world into hers? I mean...I don't get it!"

"Why are you taking this so damn personally, huh?" Liam demanded angrily. "Believe it or not, I heard what you said that day and I took it all into consideration, but the bottom line is this is between me and Tessa, not you!"

Patrick paced, raking a hand through his dark hair.

"Guys like you and me are far too intense, Liam. Trust me. We see things in black or white and we're driven with laser focus," he said heatedly. "Right now, you're starting a whole phase of your life and you made sure you came home and made a big damn fuss about it! Are you telling me you have any clue about how to balance that with a relationship? Do you honestly think you can give Tessa what she needs? Or... or do you think she'll just be fine with the few crumbs of your time that you toss her way whenever it's convenient for you?"

"What...?" Pausing, Liam took a moment to collect his jumbled thoughts because there seemed to be a lot more going on than he was aware of. "Do have feelings for Tessa? Is that what this is about?"

His brother stopped in his tracks. "You mean other than basic, common respect for her as a human being? No. This is about genuine concern because I know you."

"So your issue is fully with me," he stated.

"Basically." And the stance he took appeared like he was ready to fight.

Bring it...

"Then let's hear it, little brother. What is it you think is so wrong with me?" Then he braced himself for whatever was about to come his way.

"You're a control freak," Patrick began. "You always have to be right. You criticize everyone who doesn't do things the way you do. You're constantly telling all of us what to do and how to live our lives!"

"Need I remind you I've been gone for like twelve years?" he asked incredulously. "Any of this shit you're obviously still pissed about is from when we were kids, Patrick! Would you like me to hold you accountable right here in the present for the way you behaved and the things you said when you were a damn kid? I mean, if you're going to be pissed at me, at least make it because of who I am right now!"

"That's just it, Liam. I don't know you right now! You spent the last twelve years in the military, and when you came home, everything was a fucking group activity! And when it wasn't, you were out with friends! Do you even know who I am or what I'm doing with my life or why?"

"You're hell-bent on world domination!" he shot back. "You're buying up properties here in Laurel Bay and either flipping them to sell or renting them out and being the property manager! As for why, the short answer is because you can and you're good at it. But if I had to dig deeper into the psychological reason you chose this career path, I'd say it's because we never left this damn town and were too poor to ever own anything. We didn't travel much, but there's a comfort in being here. It's home. It's just been neglected for too long." Pausing, he let out a long breath. "Maybe you feel neglected too because—like me—you got lost in the shuffle of having a bunch of younger siblings. Maybe you wished someone had given you a little more attention so you could better yourself and that's why you can relate to the town."

He turned away and hated himself for blurting all that shit out but he turned back around and continued.

"No matter what the reason, Pat, I'm damn proud of you for what you're doing. Do I think you work too hard? Absolutely! Do I wish you could see just how successful you are and relax a bit? Hell yes! But I don't look at it as a character flaw. I'm not standing here looking at you as being damaged because of the way you choose to live your life. So maybe I'm not the one who's closed minded here."

The string of curses his brother let out actually made him blush.

Which told him he'd definitely struck a nerve.

"Bravo," Patrick said sarcastically. "I didn't realize you also added psychologist to your perfect resume!"

"Now, just a minute…"

"No! You got to say your peace; now it's my turn."

"Again? Because, um…I thought you already did when you told me all the things that were wrong with me when we stepped out here into the freezing cold."

"Here's the thing, Liam, if you're so good at figuring people out, ask yourself this: do you think you're good enough for Tessa? Do you think someone who's been through what she has genuinely needs a guy like you picking apart her faults—or what *you* deem as faults?" He let out a loud, weary breath. "People like her—people who are upbeat and positive—they need other people who are upbeat and positive. And if there's one thing I *do* know about you, is that upbeat isn't in your vocabulary. You're basically one of those glass-half-empty people. Think about that."

And without another word, he walked back into the house, leaving Liam standing there, freezing his ass off and feeling thoroughly confused.

Walking over to the railing, he leaned down and hung his head. "Shit."

He had no idea how long he'd been out there, but when Arianna popped her head out the door and called his name, he had a feeling it had been a while.

"What are you doing out there? It's freezing!" she said with a laugh, stepping outside as she slid her coat on. "Will and I are getting ready to leave. You okay?"

An hour ago or even a few minutes ago, he would have said yes. But now he wasn't so sure.

"Can I ask you something?"

"Of course!"

"Am I a terrible brother?"

She looked up at him with total bewilderment. "Um..."

"I'm serious, Ari. Apparently, I'm the reason you and Will couldn't be together for so long. I mean...I think we've all gotten past that, but..."

"Okay, hold up," she said, pulling her coat in close around her. "Yes, you were the reason Will pulled away instead of dating me, but that was on him. Although...he probably wouldn't have felt that way if you weren't so vocal about how much you wanted to strangle any guy who dared to date one of your sisters."

"Ari..."

"Wait, wait, wait...look, I get it. It's what older brothers are supposed to do. It's annoying as hell and there was a time when I genuinely hated you for it, but...it also meant that you cared," she told him. "I know you're cool with me and Will now, but I do sometimes wonder if you would have relaxed the way you did if you didn't know him. Like... what are you going to be like when Ryleigh gets serious with a guy?"

He didn't even want to think about that right now because his brain already hurt too much.

"So what's going on? Are you really still worried that I'm mad at you? Because I thought we'd all moved on. I know you like to give Will a hard time every once in a while, but we all know you're just teasing, so...what's up?"

As much as he enjoyed being a private person, he needed to talk to someone. And if anyone in this entire family had the right to have an issue with him in the here and now, it was Arianna. So he told her about his relationship with Tessa and the way Patrick reacted to it.

"Now do you see why I'm asking?"

"Okay, first of all, wow."

"Yeah, I know. Tessa's not at all like..."

"Not, Tessa, you doofus! Patrick! I can't believe he would say all that crap! And who is he to be passing judgement on anyone?"

"Um..."

She held up a hand to stop him. "First, he's completely closed off from all of us, even though he lives right here. We never know what's going on in his life because he's super secretive about it. Hell, I needed a place to live for a year and he's in real estate and wouldn't help, so...if anyone has issues, it's him." Then she smiled. "Liam, you were the oldest of five kids. You had to grow up faster than all of us and then you chose a career that is all about being in control, following the rules, and being a leader." She shrugged. "I think that's what you've done for all of us."

Some of the tension started to ease. "Thanks, Ari."

"However..."

And...it was back.

"I think Tessa's awesome and there is no doubt she's your polar opposite."

"O-kay..."

"I know sometimes people say opposites attract, but I'm just not sure this is the right relationship for you. I'm sorry," she said quietly.

"Can I ask why?"

She shrugged again. "I kind of agree with Pat on this a little. Not in the angry way he feels about it, but..."

Shit.

"I'm saying this with love, okay?"

He nodded.

"I don't see you being able to handle Tessa's...perpetual cheeriness for too long. It's going to get on your nerves because you're far too practical and you've been through some really dark stuff. Not everyone looks at life through rose-colored glasses and she does. Those of us who don't—myself included—tend to get annoyed by people like that. And you will too." She sighed. "The thing is, Liam...don't be the guy who dims her light." Pausing, she snorted. "Ugh...that sounded awful, didn't it?"

"Just a little," he murmured miserably.

"You get what I'm saying. Maybe someday you'll relax a bit and have a more...sunny view of the world. But right now? I don't see this being a good thing for her." Stepping in close, she got up on her toes and kissed his cheek. "Go inside and get warm. It's too cold to be out here for so long."

She turned to go back inside when he said, "What about me?"

Arianna turned and looked at him curiously. "What?"

"What about me?" he repeated gruffly. "What if I need her light, her sunniness, her rose-colored glasses? What if that's what I need to change who I am?"

Her shoulders sagged. "Oh, sweetie, there's nothing wrong with who you are. You just need some time to decompress after serving in the military. You need time to figure out who you are and what makes you happy. If the two of you had met a year or two from now, I'd think it was great. But...I don't know..." She sighed again. "This is more than a fling, huh?"

He shrugged. "I don't know. It could be."

Her expression saddened. "Then that's your answer."

"What is?"

"If you don't know for sure, then maybe you need to back away until you are. Less chance of anyone getting hurt. Including you."

Hanging his head, he nodded grimly because she was right.

"Are you going to be okay?" she asked softly. "Should I get Will?"

"No. It's okay. I'll be fine. I've just got a lot of thinking to do."

Liam watched his baby sister walk back into the house and wondered how he went from being the brother with all the answers to being the one who needed them.

Saturday afternoon, Tessa loaded up her car and started counting down how long it would take for her to get home. She loved spending Thanksgiving with her family and had a great time, but...for some reason, they were annoying her.

A lot.

"Have you started dating anyone yet?"

"Don't you think it's time you stopped grieving?"

"You know it was very selfish of Trevor to convince you to marry him..."

None of it was new, but normally she was fine with simply letting them talk.

Not this weekend.

This weekend she had pushed back a bit and gave them almost the exact same speech she had given Liam a few weeks ago right before they kissed for the first time. She hated arguing and she hated having to defend Trevor when he wasn't there to defend himself. But more than that, she was tired of having this discussion every time she came home to visit. So, she'd walked out the door five minutes ago after saying, "I don't think I'll be home for Christmas this year. I know you all think you're helping, but you're not. If anything, you're keeping me in the past. Not Trevor."

Yeah, it wasn't her greatest exiting line, but it was mostly true.

So many times she had felt like her life was great—and it was—and then she'd come home and have to deal with the same barrage of questions that put her back in that place. It was like they didn't know how to deal with her as the person she currently was and preferred to see her as the woman she was a few years ago.

Either way, she was done explaining herself.

And she didn't tell them about Liam either.

Mainly because she wasn't sure what was going on with them and the last thing she wanted was to get their hopes up and then have them disappointed the next time she came home if things didn't work out.

Which...the jury was still out on that one.

After their dinner at the pub and dessert back at her place, Liam had stayed the night. They had made love and maybe it was just her own imagination, but...it felt different —more intimate than any other time before.

It was probably just wishful thinking.

Still, they spent every night together—sharing dinner, talking, laughing, and making love. The man had pretty much ruined her for sex with anyone else. She craved him like she craved chocolate when she was PMS-ing.

Damn him.

And just when she thought maybe it was just sex, he went and did something incredibly sweet. Thursday morning, she had to get up early because it was almost a five-hour drive down to Charleston. Liam had gotten up with her, made her coffee, and put it in a travel mug before loading the car for her. Then he'd taken care of Phoebe and made sure she was all ready for the trip before putting her in the car too.

They had been standing in her driveway with the sun barely up, and he'd kissed her until they were breathless.

"I wish you weren't going," he said softly. "Or that maybe...I was going with you."

Her heart had melted right there on the spot.

"I figured you needed to be here with your family since it's your first big holiday since coming home."

He'd nodded solemnly, but...she felt like there was more to it. Unfortunately, she'd had to get on the road because she needed to be with her family.

I should have stayed home and enjoyed Thanksgiving with the Donovans. I'll bet he had a much more relaxing time than I did...

She put Phoebe down in the grass one last time before they got in the car and was waiting for her to do her business when her mother came and stood beside her.

Great.

"Here's something most people don't tell you about being a parent," her mother said as she watched Phoebe prance around in the grass. "The worrying never ends. Neither does the overwhelming urge to want to make things right for your kids." Sighing, she looked at Tessa. "I never realized how all that worrying and fussing might be detrimental to you." Reaching out, she pushed the hair away from Tessa's face. "You're actually quite strong and doing great things, and we all need to focus on that rather than the past. When you're ready to...well...you know...then you will."

"What about Beth and Casey? Do they feel the same way?"

"Oh, sweetie, what difference does it make? They don't

understand because they married young and they want you to experience all the things that they did. The truth is, you were always your own person. Don't try to fit into anyone else's mold." Pausing, she smiled sadly. "And I'm sorry if I tried to force you into that too."

"Thanks, Mom." And because she wanted to, she hugged her. "I love you and I need you to trust me when I say I'm okay."

Cupping her daughter's face, she smiled. "I do, Tess. And you want to know how I know you're doing well?"

"How?"

"This is the happiest I've seen you in years," she said softly, giving Tessa's cheeks a slight squeeze. "And I mean even before Trevor got sick. Whatever is going on in your life, it's agreeing with you. Don't let me or your sisters take that away." She hugged her. "Don't let anyone take that away."

"Thanks, Mom."

Feeling a lot lighter than she had minutes ago, Tessa scooped up Phoebe and put her in her carrier before climbing into the car. After going through her little checklist to make sure she had all her necessities, she waved to her mother and pulled away. Her phone was plugged in and as soon as her playlist kicked on, she was more than ready to sing at the top of her lungs.

She didn't sing a lot when Liam was over because they were either talking, kissing, or eating, and she found that she missed doing it.

Not that he'd stop her, but she also couldn't imagine him singing along the way Trevor used to.

"Okay, note to self, stop comparing the two because they aren't the slightest bit the same."

And that gave her pause.

Of course it didn't matter; Trevor was her best friend, but there had never been any romantic feelings for each other. It would make sense that someone completely different would attract her.

"And you don't get much different than Liam," she murmured before sighing happily.

There had been a definite change in him since their initial meeting at the wedding, but he was still incredibly serious and focused and driven. None of those were bad traits, but it seemed to take him a while each day to just unwind and relax and not think about work. Tessa loved hearing about all the building going on and his plans for the next phase and what he and Will were looking to do next, but...it was almost like he didn't know how to talk or think about anything else but work. Sometimes she just let him talk because he obviously needed it, but other times she had to get creative in how she changed the subject.

Sex and food were great motivators.

Before she could really focus on that, one of her favorite Whitney Houston songs came on and after that, all her attention went to the road and singing.

Mile after mile, song after song, her spirits lifted and her soul felt lighter than it had all weekend. By the time she saw the "Welcome to North Carolina" sign, however, she was more than ready to be home.

But then the most perfect song came on, one that summed up her life at the moment, and it gave her the final push to keep going. Disney songs were always fun to sing just because. But "I Won't Say (I'm In Love)" from Hercules had her smiling so hard her face hurt.

"Who d'you think you're kidding? He's the earth and heaven to you..." she sang and then danced a little in the driver's seat.

165

By the time the finale came and she was saying, *"At least out loud, I won't say I'm in love,"* Tessa knew it was true.

She was in love with Liam Donovan.

They were going to have to talk about it eventually. It scared her to even think about it because...she'd never had to do something like this. Her dating life was rather uneventful before Trevor got sick, but she had dated enough men to know she never had to be the one who said they were in love.

Because you've never been in love, dummy.

Yeah. That.

Dang it.

There were guys she'd really liked, but...none of them ever made her heart feel the way Liam does.

"Uptown Funk" was playing and it was something she normally loved to sing to, but suddenly, all she could think of was being rejected. What if Liam had truly only been trying to help her out and now she was going to blather on and on about how she was in love with him? And then she'd have to live right next door to him feeling like a total idiot because she couldn't handle a casual relationship!

There was a tightening in her chest, and she was fairly certain she was having a heart attack. "Oh God..."

Of course, there was a chance—albeit a small one—that maybe he felt something for her too, something more than friendship. It didn't mean he was ready to propose or anything, but maybe he'd be open to changing their status to one of a dating couple.

"It could happen," she murmured. "Maybe."

But if it didn't...

She could clearly imagine him walking to his truck and

completely ignoring her if she was out in her yard. Or seeing him at the pub and pretending she wasn't there.

And the worst?

Sitting alone in her yard and hearing him out in his fabulous backyard with its swimming pool while he fooled around with a woman he actually wanted to date.

So I guess I'll be moving next.

Ugh...it was the curse of being artistic and creative. She had a very vivid imagination. And now, with an hour of driving left, all she could think about was one crazy scenario after another where she told Liam she loved him and he said he didn't and all the awkward ways they'd bump into each other in town.

"Okay, so this sucks," she mumbled, and by the time she pulled into her driveway, she was completely brokenhearted and angry at the same time.

The original plan for the weekend was for her to come home on Sunday, so there was no way for Liam to know she'd be pulling up now. His truck was in his driveway, but she wasn't going to call or text or even go and knock on his door.

Their imaginary breakup was still too fresh in her mind.

I seriously have issues.

The first thing she did was get Phoebe out and let her run around the front yard while Tessa pulled her carrier out of the car. She had barely put it down on the front porch when she spotted Liam jogging toward her with a smile on his face.

It really wasn't fair that he was so handsome and yet so unattainable.

Dang it, dang it, dang it!

"Hey!" he said when he reached her and then kissed her

until she barely remembered her own name. "You're back early."

"Yeah, um...it wasn't the best visit with my family, so I decided to come home." Carefully stepping out of his embrace, Tessa headed back to the car to unload it.

Liam jogged over to her. "Go let Phoebe in and I'll get this stuff, okay?"

She was too tired to argue, so she simply nodded and walked away. It took all of three minutes for him to have everything in the house and her car locked up, and before she knew it, he was sitting at her kitchen island watching her.

"Is everything okay?"

No.

"I don't really want to talk about it," she said evasively. "I'm going to have a glass of wine. You want one?"

"Um, sure."

After pouring them each a glass, Tessa handed Liam his. "What about you? How was your Thanksgiving?"

"Yeah, I don't really want to talk about that either," he murmured before taking a sip of his wine.

Tessa did the same and when she put her glass down, she looked right at him and said, "My family ticked me off with their constant harping about my life and how I'm not moving on the way they think I should. Much like you said to me not that long ago."

She hadn't planned on sharing this—or starting a fight—but her words and tone said otherwise.

"Tessa, we went over this. I apologized for all of that. I had no business saying anything to you about how you live. Hell, you're probably the most together person I know."

"Clearly I'm not, otherwise we wouldn't be doing...you

know...the things we've been doing," she challenged and felt a small sense of satisfaction when his eyes narrowed.

Carefully pushing the wine aside, Liam's expression turned a little fierce. "And what are we doing?"

"Sex. Sleeping together. You know, to help me ease back into dating and all that crap."

He got to his feet, his eyes never leaving hers. "I don't understand what's happening right now. When you left Thursday morning, everything was fine. Now you're back and apparently mad at me for something and I have no idea what." Then he muttered a curse, stepping away from the island. "And you know what? My family pissed me off too about how I'm living my life, so maybe instead of getting all kinds of snarky with me, maybe we should talk about this since we're both dealing with the same crap!"

"Liam, I..."

He paced for a moment before facing her. "Do you not want me here, Tessa?" he demanded.

"I didn't say that! I..."

"Yes or no? Do you want me here? Did I misread something these last few weeks?"

"Um..."

It was on the tip of her tongue to say yes. Yes, he had misread something, and now she was crazy about him and had no idea what to do about it! But that would open the door for any of the scenarios she'd been playing in her mind on the way home and, honestly, she just wasn't ready for that yet.

"I'll go," he was saying as he walked out of the kitchen, and that's when Tessa realized she'd been in her own head a little too long.

"Liam! Wait!" He was already at the front door when

she caught up with him. "Hey!" she snapped. "No one asked you to leave."

"And no one asked me to stay, either."

Sighing with frustration, she reached for his hand. "I needed a minute to think, okay? It was a rough weekend, a long drive, and then...this! *Gah!* I should be allowed a moment to gather my thoughts in my own home!"

Eyes wide, he stared back at her. "What was there to think about? I asked if you wanted me here. It shouldn't have required that much thinking time."

"You know what, Liam? I honestly wasn't sure if I wanted you here. There. Are you satisfied? Maybe a lot of what I argued about with my family had to do with you and how I have no idea what this even is that we're doing! I'm not a casual sex kind of person and I know I said I could be when this all started, but maybe I'm changing my mind! Is that allowed? Am I allowed to think about that? Huh?"

"Tessa..."

But she was on a roll now and it seemed like her mouth and her brain were on a break.

Moving away from him, she did her own pacing around the living room. "Move on! Stop grieving! You made a mistake! You're not living right! On and on and on and now I'm looking at you—at us—and wondering if this was a mistake too!"

Her eyes stung with tears and she wanted to curse them, but clearly she had more to say.

"I want to come home and sing and I want to go out and meet other people and not have to be all weirded out about what they'll think or what they'll assume! I'm just sick and tired of having my life constantly put under a microscope to where *I'm* even criticizing the way I'm living!"

Tears fell in earnest now, and Liam walked over and wrapped her in his arms.

"Shh...it's okay," he whispered, holding her close. "It's okay. I'm sorry. I overreacted. I guess I was still a little on edge from Thursday and I didn't mean to take it out on you." He held her tighter. "The last thing I want to do is upset you and if this is all too much for you, then I'll go."

Pulling back slightly, she looked up at him. "Do you want to go?"

"Tessa, not five minutes ago I asked you this exact same thing."

Swallowing hard, she made a decision.

It might not be the wisest, but it was what she wanted most right now.

"I don't want you to go, Liam. There's so much about my life that I'm unsure of, but I know that I want you here with me tonight. Please. Don't go."

Then he was kissing her and lifting her up and carrying her to bed and for a little while longer, she allowed herself to live the fantasy.

She knew it wouldn't last, so she had to just enjoy it for now.

Chapter Eleven

The week kicked off with freezing temperatures, which meant some of the work on the resort was at a standstill, and Tessa was working extra hours on the school holiday concert. It meant their schedules were off a bit, and Liam was trying to figure out what to do with his time.

He was sitting in the construction trailer Wednesday afternoon when Will walked in. "Hey."

"Hey. Did the lumber delivery get here?"

"I actually made arrangements with a warehouse down in Wilmington," he said as he sat at his desk.

"For what?"

"We're going to assemble some of the cabins off-site. I'm renting warehouse space so we don't lose a lot of time because of the weather."

Frowning, he asked, "Did we talk about this? I don't remember us having a conversation about it."

Will shrugged. "I made an executive decision."

"But...people build in the winter all the time. And I don't imagine a warehouse would be much warmer."

"It's not just the temperature; it's the precipitation. It

means a bit of an expense, but we won't be losing time. Ultimately, it will all even out, but I hate sitting still when we were finally hitting a good pace."

Raking a hand through his hair, he nodded. "I guess."

Will stood and made himself a cup of coffee and one for Liam before he sat down and passed the mug to him. "So, you and Patrick. Want to talk about it?"

"No."

Chuckling, he said, "Fair enough." After taking a sip of his drink, he grinned. "So, you and Tessa. Want to talk about it?"

"You mean my sister didn't tell you everything?"

"Of course your sister told me everything, but you know she has a flair for dramatics and went off on twenty-seven different tangents. I wanted to hear it all from you."

"I don't think I can handle one more person telling me I'm too serious and depressing and unworthy of love," he murmured before picking up his mug.

"So dramatics run in the family. Good to know," Will teased with a laugh. "C'mon, Liam, you did not just say that to me! No one said you're unworthy of love."

"Maybe not in so many words, but that's the bottom line. Tessa's like...she's this princess or paragon of happiness and up on some pedestal surrounded by sunshine and unicorns, and I'm this nasty, stinky ogre who's trying to defile her. It's pretty damn insulting."

"Um, no. That was insulting to princesses, unicorns, and ogres. You're taking this all wrong."

"I don't see how."

"Naturally." Pausing, Will took another sip of his coffee. "Do you remember when you used to freak out about the guys your sisters were dating?"

Liam just glared at him.

173

"Dude, you knew me. You knew me well, and you still gave me shit about dating your sister. You thought I was a great friend, a great soldier, and I was someone you trusted enough to go into business with. But put me with your sister and suddenly I was...wait...what did you call it? A nasty, stinky ogre who was trying to defile her." He grinned. "I kind of like that."

"You're an ass."

"No, I'm your friend," he said seriously. "And not to be a dick, but how does it feel to have the tables turned on you? You're a great guy who obviously cares about your family and you look out for the people who mean something to you, and it's not enough. Well, newsflash, sometimes it's not enough and you have to actually work at it. Sometimes you have to prove people wrong. So if Tessa means something to you, prove your family or whoever else is giving you shit wrong!" He shook his head. "You're a lot of things, Liam, but a quitter isn't one of them."

"I'm not quitting..."

"Not yet. But you're certainly not doing anything to change their minds."

"I told Patrick..."

"You argued with him," Will interrupted. "Two different things. You weren't going to change his mind on Thanksgiving. You couldn't. But everything you do from this point forward could."

They were silent for several minutes before Liam admitted his worst fear. "I don't know how," he said gruffly. "I honestly...I don't know how to be the man she deserves. I can't change a lifetime of habits or my entire personality just to match hers."

"I don't think anyone's expecting that. It wouldn't be real. What about...?" Then he seemed to catch himself.

"What? What about...?"

"Why don't the four of us go out one night? A double date?"

Ugh...how did he explain this?

"Um...because Tessa doesn't really think we're dating."

Will sighed loudly. "Okay, now this I've got to hear."

"I thought you said Arianna told you everything!"

"Clearly something was lost in translation because this is brand new information."

So, Liam briefly explained the initial reason for everything they were doing. "The thing is...I didn't expect this. Didn't expect her. Getting involved with someone was the last thing on my mind. But now that we've been spending time together, it's all I want and I know I'm being a damn coward by not telling her that." Groaning, he said, "I'm afraid to spook her; I'm worried that I've helped her build up her confidence and she'll want to go out and experience the world—or other guys—and then where will I be?"

"I'm not trying to harp on it, but I had to let Arianna go for an entire year. Don't you think I worried about that kind of stuff too? You've just got to have a little faith that it will work out." Then he chuckled. "And try not to piss her off because you have no filter."

"I'm working on it," he grumbled. "I guess I'm afraid to rock the boat—you know, putting a label on what we're doing can change things."

"So maybe don't put a label on it. Is Tessa pushing for that?"

"No, but..." The sigh was out before he could help it. "I can't have these kinds of deep feelings for her this soon, right? I mean...a few weeks ago, she annoyed the shit out of me. It can't turn around that fast. It's not possible. No one falls that fast."

"Dude, I fell in love with your sister in less than a day," Will stated. "When you know, you know."

"I didn't say I was in love with Tessa."

"No. Not yet. But I think that's also part of the problem. You're overanalyzing everything—which is typical of you and not necessarily a bad thing—but you're also fighting what you're feeling. It's like you're trying to talk yourself out of feeling what you really do."

"And you know what pisses me off the most?"

"That everyone's not falling in line and saying 'Sir, yes, Sir!'?" Will teased.

"Now you're definitely being a dick." Standing, he walked over to the window and looked out at their property. "Nothing has ever scared me. Ever. I've always willingly taken on challenges, I went into every deployment confident in our platoon and with our strategies, and any relationship I ever had, I was cocksure that I was the one in control with no chance of having my heart broken." Looking back at Will, he frowned. "And ever since we came home, I'm second-guessing myself at every turn, and it scares the hell out of me."

"You're human. We all feel like that sometimes."

"But that's just it, it's not sometimes. It's been like every moment since we got home. I look out at this resort and think we're making a mistake, every interaction with my family feels like an attack where I'm fighting battles for unknown reasons, and then this whole thing with Tessa..." He sat back down and put his head in his hands.

"Maybe that's why you're a little...um...overly defensive?" Will suggested. "I kind of think it's more like you're a man without an identity. You came home and even though your family is still your family, they've changed and you didn't notice it over the years. The dynamics have changed. Now they've got opinions..."

"They've always had opinions. They're just louder now."

Chuckling, Will shook his head. "You know what I'm saying. You didn't come home and instantly step back into the big brother, third parent role you had when you left at eighteen. So then you have to wonder just who exactly you're supposed to be. As for the resort, believe me, I've had more than my share of second-guessing this whole thing."

"Really?"

He nodded. "Absolutely! I'm sure your sister is tired of hearing me obsess about it all the damn time."

"What are you worried about?"

Will let out a long breath. "Everything! Is this the right area for this kind of resort? Is it going to make any money? Is there even a market for this? I know you did a lot of research, but it's still daunting, Liam. Neither of us has any experience with this and we've invested a lot of time, money, and energy here. I'm looking to buy a home and marry Arianna. What if this fails? Will I be able to do that?"

"My sister would marry you if you had to live in one of those damn tiny cabins and you know it."

"Yeah, but I don't want her to have to do that. I know how independent she is and how much she really doesn't need anyone taking care of her, but...I want to take care of her. I want to give her the world."

"Okay, so do we need to sit down and go over all the plans again? Just to reassure ourselves that we're not making a mistake?"

Standing, Will refilled his coffee. "Now that I know I'm not the only one freaking out? Yeah."

It certainly didn't help him come to any long-term

conclusions where he and Tessa were concerned, but right now, he had to deal with his issues one at a time.

And this one just happened to be the most convenient to handle.

He only wished the rest of them were.

* * *

The weekend was finally here and Tessa couldn't wait to go out and get her Christmas tree. It was something she and Trevor started doing in those last precious years, and this was the first time she didn't feel overly emotional about it.

For the last two years, she always picked smaller trees since she had to carry it in and set it up by herself. But this year Liam was going tree shopping with her and promised that he'd help her pick out the biggest one she could fit in her living room and set it up for her. It was beyond exciting.

As she danced around the house while blasting Christmas music, she happily envisioned what it was going to look like and how beautiful it was going to be. As she sang along to Elton John's "Step into Christmas," she thought about all the things she might need to purchase. She knew she'd need more lights and ornaments than she currently had, but that would be tomorrow's project. She was in the middle of belting out U2's version of "Christmas, Baby Please Come Home" when Liam walked in. She was in such a good mood that she danced her way over to him and encouraged him to sing along with her.

Grinning, he shook his head. "Nuh-uh. I don't sing."

"Party pooper!" she said before finishing the song.

Once it was over, she lowered the volume and turned to face him. "So you never sing?"

He shook his head.

"Not even when you're alone in the car?"

"Nope."

"How about when it's someone's birthday? Do you sing along to the 'Happy Birthday' song?"

Grinning, he stepped in close and wrapped his arms loosely around her. "Most of the time I just silently mouth along. Singing is totally not my thing."

"That's just sad, Liam. I get that not everyone has a good singing voice, but that's no reason not to sing."

"That's exactly the reason not to sing. Why torment everyone around you when you can't carry a tune?"

"Just for the fun of it! To make you feel good!"

"Trust me, my poor singing skills would not make me or anyone else feel good." He placed a quick kiss on the tip of her nose before releasing her. "So...ready to tree shop?"

She was practically bouncing on her toes. "Yes! I could barely focus on anything else today! Fortunately, we had a lot of practice time for the winter concert so it kept me in the holiday spirit. I still hate how we don't have the funding to make the auditorium look the way I wanted it to, but I know the parents will understand."

"I'm sure they will," he reasoned. "They're going to be there to see their kids sing. I'm sure if you had absolutely zero decorations, they'd still be thrilled."

"Maybe. It just adds to the whole experience when there are twinkly lights and giant snowflakes hanging from the ceiling." She sighed. "I wanted to have a whole display of Christmas trees and one of those giant sleds—you know, like Santa uses."

Liam started to say something and stopped himself.

"Wow," she said with a grin. "I'm impressed."

"What? What did I do?"

"You totally wanted to roll your eyes and remind me

179

that Santa isn't real and yet you held it in!" She clapped enthusiastically. "Bravo!"

This time, he did roll his eyes and then grinned before pulling her back into his arms and kissing her soundly. "There. Better?"

Laughing, Tessa pulled out of his embrace and walked around gathering her coat, purse, and keys. "You couldn't keep it in, right?"

"I could have, but I figured you'd appreciate my honesty more." Together, they walked out the door and across the yard to his truck. "I've passed quite a few tree lots on my way back and forth to work every day. I'm actually kind of surprised that our little town has so many of them."

"I've gotten my tree at Mr. McCay's lot over on Barnford the last two years," she told him. "But I'm open to looking at the others if you want to."

They pulled out of the driveway and Liam shrugged. "Growing up, we always had an artificial tree, so I've never gone tree shopping. You're the one in charge of this outing."

They'd talked about how he'd never had a live tree before and she loved how he was going to experience it for the first time with her. "Then let's start at McCay's and if you don't find one you love there, we can go to one of the others."

"Find one I love?" he asked with a small laugh. "Tessa, it's a tree. As long as it's green and doesn't have any bald spots, it will be fine."

Sighing loudly, she looked over at him. "Do you have to be like this all the time? Can't you just pretend to be excited about this?"

She caught his frown before he seemed to relax. "You're right. Sorry."

Reaching over, she held his hand and within minutes,

they were pulling up to the tree lot. "Ooh...he's got a great selection this year and it looks like we got here at the perfect time!" Climbing down from the truck, she waited patiently for him to join her. "Ready?"

Liam walked around the truck and, taking her hand in his, they made their way toward the eight-foot tree section.

"Liam!" someone called out, and they both paused and looked around. A couple walked toward them and Tessa was surprised to see Liam smile.

"Jackson Coleman! Holy shit! How are you?" They walked toward each other and shook hands before giving a traditional bro hug.

"Doing great! It's been a while. How are you doing?"

"Things are good," he replied, his arm loosely draped around Tessa's waist. "The work on the resort is coming along and..."

"Wait...resort? What resort?"

"Oh, right! I guess it's been longer than I thought!" Liam said with a small laugh. "Will Jameson and I are building a fishing resort here in Laurel Bay. It was something I've been mulling over in my head for a few years and Will and I are making it happen. So, what about you? What have you been up to?"

Smiling, Jackson pulled the pretty brunette standing beside him in close. "Well...first, this is Savannah James, my fiancée," he said proudly. "Savannah, this is Liam Donovan. He's the buddy whose apartment I was living in when I first came home."

"Oh, wow!" she said, shaking Liam's hand. "It's so nice to meet you!"

"It's great to meet you too, and congratulations!"

"We actually owe a bit of thanks to you," Jackson went on. "If I hadn't come here to Laurel Bay instead of going

181

home to Magnolia Sound, Savannah and I wouldn't have met the way we did."

"Really?"

They both nodded. "We actually met at your parents' pub," Savannah said. "We both showed up there for dinner one night and Jackson walked over and introduced himself." She and Jackson smiled at each other, and it was easy to see just how in love they were.

"That's awesome!" Liam said and then seemed to realize that Tessa was standing beside him. "Oh! Sorry! This is Tessa Sullivan. Tessa, this is Jackson and Savannah. Jackson and I served together in the Marines."

Reaching out, she shook Jackson's hand. "It's nice to meet you." Then she turned to do the same to Savannah. "And congratulations on your engagement."

"Thanks!" Savannah said and then paused with Tessa's hand in hers. "Should we be congratulating you too?"

"What?" she and Liam asked at the same time, but then Tessa instantly realized what was going on.

Gently, she pulled her hand back. "No," she said sweetly. "No, Liam and I are not..."

"Not what?" Liam asked, thoroughly confused.

"It's nothing," Tessa said softly.

"I'm...I'm sorry. I guess I just thought...well...I assumed," Savannah awkwardly tried to explain, but fortunately, Jackson changed the subject.

"So who's doing the construction on the resort? Any chance it's Coleman's?"

"Um...no," Liam replied, still obviously confused. "We sort of lucked out with a smaller company since we're not building anything large. All the cabins are the size of the average tiny house. Will designed them and is helping build them. We've had to deal with a lot of engineers with clearing the land and putting in plumbing and..." Pausing, he laughed softly while shaking his head. "You'll have to come and check it out. What are you doing with yourself these days?"

"I just joined the Laurel Bay Fire Department," he said proudly.

"That's awesome! Good for you! I thought for sure you would have done something back in Magnolia."

Shrugging, Jackson explained, "I did too, but...Savannah and I sort of fell in love with the town and it's only a few miles away." He shrugged. "We bought a house over off of Soundview Drive, and Savannah works right here in town too. My cousin Parker opened up a day spa..."

"Alloro," Savannah supplied and then smiled at Tessa. "Have you been there yet?"

She shook her head. "Believe it or not, I don't think I've ever been to a day spa."

"Seriously?" Savannah's eyes went wide. "Then you need to come in! We do massages, and facials, and all kinds of pampering. Every woman needs to treat herself to a little relaxing time. If you ever want to try it, you can call and ask for me." Reaching into her purse, she pulled out a business card and handed it to Tessa. "You can book an appointment online too, if you prefer."

"Thanks!"

"Listen, we'll definitely all have to get together for dinner at the pub sometime," Jackson said. "But they were tying up the tree for us and it looks like we're good to go, so..." He shook Jackson's hand and then hers. "It was nice to meet you, Tessa, and hopefully we'll see you again soon."

She smiled and watched them walk away before turning toward the eight-foot tree section again. "Okay, let's see what we can find!"

Liam stopped her before she'd gone even two steps. "What was that all about earlier?"

"When?"

All he did was stare back at her blandly.

Sighing, she held up her left hand.

The one where she still wore the rings Trevor had given her.

"I guess she just assumed that..."

"Yeah. Got it," he said stiffly before walking over to the trees.

Hanging her head, Tessa took a moment to tell herself that it wasn't a big deal and other than it being awkward for a moment. It was a natural conclusion for someone to see them together as a couple and then see her wearing an engagement ring and wedding band and assume he was the one who gave them to her. It was silly, really. She seriously hoped he didn't take this as some sort of pressure for them to be more than what they were.

Even though she seriously wished they were more than sex buddies.

Ugh...is that the label I want on this?

No, it wasn't, but unfortunately, it didn't seem to matter how much time they spent together, Liam wasn't falling in love with her and he certainly didn't talk about his feelings.

So why aren't I?

It wasn't the first time this had occurred to her, but...she didn't want to rock the boat. What if she blurted out that she was falling in love with him and he got all weird and said that his work was done and simply walked away? How awkward would it be to have to see him all the time since he lived right next door? She didn't mind it back when they hated each other because she just thought he was a massive jerk then. Now she knew how kind he could be when he wanted to be and how loving and sweet and...

Inwardly, she groaned.

I am in big trouble here...

With a fortifying breath, she trailed after Liam and saw him simply walking by tree after tree after tree.

"Sometimes you need to pull them away from the others to get a good look at them," she told him when she caught up. "See? Look." Picking one tree, she awkwardly pulled it away from the rest, lifted it slightly, and slammed the trunk on the ground to force the branches to open a bit. She almost fell over, but Liam didn't seem in any hurry to help her. "See how much fuller it looks now?"

He shrugged and kept walking.

With another sigh, she put the tree back before going after him. Stepping directly in front of him and blocking his path, she snapped. "Are you going to be like this the entire time? Because if you are, I'd rather you just leave."

"Excuse me?"

Nodding, Tessa did her best to sound cocky. "You heard me. If you're just going to be a jerk, you should go. I'll call for an Uber or something and come back and get my own darn tree."

Crossing his arms, he stared down at her and looked ready to argue, but clearly decided against it.

"Tessa, look, I..."

"No, you look," she retorted, poking him in the chest. "This was supposed to be something fun to do, and you stomping around glaring at everything and everyone is ruining it. So either snap out of it or go home because I'm here to get a tree and you're not going to take that from me."

Liam's lips twitched slightly before he reached out,

hauled her into his arms, and kissed her soundly right there in the middle of the tree lot.

Okay, so maybe we're not just sex buddies...

"Sorry," he murmured against her lips when they reluctantly broke apart. "Come on. Show me how to pick out the perfect tree. Then we'll pick up some stew from the pub before going home and decorating."

"Ooh...I do like the thought of grabbing dinner from the pub..."

He nodded. "Then that's what we'll do. And for dessert, we'll have cookies and cocoa and admire our awesome Christmas trees."

"There's no way we're going to be able to decorate them both tonight," she told him. "Actually, we probably need to let them both acclimate to being inside overnight before we even start."

"So...wait...we're just going to bring them home and put them in their stands and...that's it?"

"Yup! But we can organize the ornaments and make sure we have enough. I know you haven't had a tree of your own, right?"

With another nod, he said, "There is a shopping spree in my future, I'm guessing."

Tessa contemplated this information for a moment. "Okay, new plan. We get the trees and bring them home. Then we'll hit the stores and buy at least some ornaments to get you started and some filler ones for me since this will be the biggest tree I've ever had."

"And then dinner?" he asked.

"Definitely. I think by that time we'll be more than ready to eat, but it will probably be late. I hope we'll still be able to get food from the pub."

"Tessa, my parents own the pub. I can go in there at any

hour and get something to eat. Trust me. It won't be an issue."

Smiling, she grabbed his hand and started walking again. "I do trust you, Liam. Always."

And...she did.

Mostly.

She just wasn't sure she could trust him not to break her heart.

Chapter Twelve

It was after ten, both trees were in their stands and in their separate homes, there were shopping bags filled with ornaments and lights scattered everywhere, and they had just finished dinner.

He was beyond exhausted.

If anyone would have asked, Liam would have told them after over ten years as a Marine that he'd be just fine tackling these little holiday tasks.

But he was wrong.

So, so very wrong.

Tessa was cleaning up their dinner dishes and Liam was out in her yard with Phoebe, who he swore was smirking at him.

"I can handle this, dog," he told her. "I just needed a few minutes to rest. In five minutes, I'll go in and decorate both trees if I have to."

All she did was sniff at him and scamper away.

As much as he hated to admit it, he needed to sit down.

Slowly, he lowered himself into one of the Adirondack chairs. It was cold out and he knew the dog wouldn't need to be out there for too long, but...getting off his feet for a few minutes was necessary. He'd worked a full day today at the warehouse with Will building one of the cabins, came home and showered and then met up with Tessa to go get their trees.

And then...

The rings.

Yeah, he had held in what was bothering him. He wanted to tell her—hell, he'd walked away from her to figure out what he was going to say—but then she confronted him and told him to leave.

That had been more than a little unexpected and it threw him a bit.

Afterwards, he didn't want to ruin their night because he'd been looking forward to it, but now...now all he could think about were the damn rings.

Why was she still wearing them and why didn't he notice it until tonight?

Probably because they were just part of who she was and she'd been wearing them since he'd met her. Tonight, however, was the first time the significance of her wearing them really hit him.

Scrubbing a hand over his face, Liam let out a weary sigh because something had to give. They were living in this little bubble right now. While he was enjoying their bubble because it meant no one could give him grief or dole out advice – even though they kind of were – maybe it was time to just say what he felt and deal with whatever came next.

Leaning back in the chair, he closed his eyes and told himself he just needed a minute. Then he'd take Phoebe back into the house and he and Tessa would sit down and talk.

Really talk.

Only...the next time he opened his eyes, Tessa was staring down at him with amusement. "What's going on?"

"You were asleep."

Sitting up straight, he looked around. "No, I wasn't. I just shut my eyes a minute ago."

With a soft laugh, she held out her hand to him. "I was inside finishing the dishes and then cleaned up the kitchen and made cocoa from scratch and before I knew it, about twenty minutes had gone by. I called out to you but you didn't respond and that's when I came out here and found you sleeping."

He accepted her hand and stood, but he still wasn't fully convinced that he had fallen asleep. Phoebe was in her arms, and together they went back into the house. "So, um..."

"Give me just one minute," she said before walking away and putting the dog in her bed. Then she came back, took his hand, led him to the bedroom, and gently pushed him onto the bed. "Stay right there."

As if he were going to leave...

When she came back into the room five minutes later, she was carrying a tray with a plate of cookies, two mugs, and a warming carafe. "Tessa..."

With a serene smile, she placed the tray on her dresser before standing in front of him. "That's for later," she told him before she kicked off her shoes, peeled off her sweater and shimmied out of her jeans.

He wasn't feeling tired anymore.

In nothing but hunter green satin, she looked sexy and festive and Liam's hands twitched with the need to touch her.

So he did.

And he kept touching her until they were both naked

and under the blankets. That's when he stopped and simply looked at her face; her beautiful, flushed face.

The words were right there on the tip of his tongue. It was the perfect moment to tell her how he felt, but she must have taken his hesitation for something else because the next thing he knew, Tessa gave him a playful shove and she was straddling him.

She was breathtaking in that moment and, rather than steal her thunder, he gently grasped her hips and let her take the lead.

And it was everything.

* * *

By two the following afternoon, Liam's tree was done.

He still didn't see what the big deal was about the whole decorating thing, but maybe that was just him.

"You don't have any other decorations?" Tessa asked as she looked around.

"No, why?"

"What about outside? Lights? A wreath? Maybe an inflatable snowman or something?"

Chuckling softly, he shook his head. "Haven't we been over this? I'm not someone who's into all that. It seems crazy to go through all that trouble for one day."

"But it's not just one day. It's the season! Don't you remember what it was like driving around town when you were younger and looking at all the decorations? I mean, every kid loves that!"

He shrugged. "I guess, but...not me. I suppose they're fine to look at, but—again—it just seems like a lot of work for such a short amount of time. Besides, we both know you're going to go overboard and anything I do is going to look ridiculous next to it, so…"

"Well, that's just sad. It's not a competition."

Putting the last of the empty ornament boxes away, he turned to face her. "This is me, Tess. I have a tree because…well, because. The holidays just don't excite me. They're not that big of a deal. I'm glad to be home and all, and I'm looking forward to spending Christmas with my family, but…it's just a day."

Her eyes went wide before her expression turned to mild annoyance. He knew she wanted to argue more, but she kept it to herself.

"So are we ready to go over and tackle your house?" he asked, hoping that would cheer her up and take some of the focus off of himself.

She instantly smiled and Liam said a silent prayer of thanks for that. "Definitely! But…be prepared. I have a lot of stuff."

"I figured that."

"No…no, I don't think you realize. Um…it normally takes me a week to get it all set up—inside and out. I don't expect you to help with all of it because I'm sure it will make you crazy, but…"

"Tessa?"

"Hmm?"

"I am more than ready to help you with all of it. I'll hang lights, get on ladders, inflate whatever needs to be inflated." Stepping in close, he wrapped her in his arms and kissed her, loving the way she melted against him. "Whatever you need me to do, then that's what I'll do."

With a happy little hum, she got up on tiptoes and kissed him back. "Are we still talking about decorating, or…"

He loved how her mind worked. "Let's just say that I'm

looking forward to being rewarded for being a good boy today and helping with all of this."

"Rewarded, hmm? Then we better get started," she said with a teasing glint in her eyes before leading him out the door.

They had taken most of her decorations down from her attic earlier before going to his house, and Liam was surprised when she told him there was more out in her shed.

"Do you want me to bring them to the front yard?"

She seemed to consider it for a moment. "Actually, I know you'll think I'm silly, but I need to write up a plan. Give me five minutes to take Phoebe out and..."

"I can take her out if you want to start the list," he offered, even though he didn't think a list was necessary.

"No, but thank you. I need a few minutes to get it all organized in my head. Why don't you see if there're anymore cookies in the freezer and then we'll get started?"

Liam watched as she picked up the dog and walked out the back door. After a quick look in the freezer, he found a bag of sugar cookies and pulled them out. It was kind of cute how she always seemed to have a batch on hand and he was happy to benefit from it.

Her phone was on the island next to where he put the cookies, and it dinged with a reminder. Curiosity had him looking over and in bold letters it said, "Chat with Trevor."

"What?" he whispered before the screen went blank. Two minutes later, the reminder appeared again and something like dread sank to his stomach like a dead weight.

The rings.

The reminder.

But really, what stuck the most was the chatting part. How was she chatting with him?

Then he looked around and wondered if there was an urn or something that he hadn't noticed before, or maybe Trevor was buried nearby and she went to the cemetery? Or...

"Okay," Tessa said a little breathlessly as she walked in the door. "I think I've got it all worked out. Are you ready?"

Honestly? He wasn't so sure anymore.

But when he saw how excited she looked, the only thing he could do was smile and say, "Let's do this!"

* * *

Icicle lights hung outside? Check.

Inflatable snow globe in center of the yard? Check.

Front porch decorated with wreath, lanterns, and Welcome Santa sign? Check.

Tomorrow she'd pick up the poinsettias she ordered from the florist, but for now, the exterior of the house was done!

Inside, she found Liam putting the last of the lights on the tree.

And there were a lot of them.

"Oh, look at how bright and twinkly it is!" she exclaimed as soon as she shut the front door. "Oh, Liam, it's amazing! Thank you!"

He smiled but kept on working.

Walking over to the TV, she turned it on and went to the channel that played holiday music so it would be more festive while they finished decorating. Sam Smith was crooning "Have Yourself a Merry Little Christmas" and Tessa couldn't help but smile because right now this was everything she loved about the holiday—the trees, the music, the decorating! This was seriously the best time of year.

"Trevor always did the lights and I never realized how big of a job it was until I had to do it myself. If you weren't here right now, stringing the lights would probably take me all day!" Her face actually hurt from smiling, but it was all just so much better than she imagined. The tree was eight feet tall and fortunately her ceiling was nine feet, so she was still going to be able to put her angel on top. Liam had opted for a star on top of his, but she liked her angel.

When he stepped away from the tree, he studied it without looking at her. "There's still one more set that we can add if you want it, but I think this looks good."

He was right, and as much as she wanted to say go ahead with the last set, maybe it would be a bit of overkill. "No, this is perfect. Thank you!"

Walking over, Tessa hugged him and loved when his arms wrapped around her. "So, can we check tree lights off the list?"

She knew he was teasing, but she loved being able to cross tasks off the list once they were done. Already they had accomplished so much and if they kept going at this pace, there wasn't a doubt in her mind they'd get it all done today.

That sort of thing hadn't happened since before Trevor got sick.

"I'll tell you what, I'll let you check it off while I start opening all the ornament cases," she told him with one last quick kiss.

"I'm going to grab something to drink," he said as he headed to the kitchen. "You want something?"

"If you could grab me a bottle of water, that would be great! Thanks!"

The ornaments were her actual favorite part of the entire process. She'd been collecting them for years and so many of them held a deep, emotional meaning to her. When she and Liam shopped yesterday, she purchased one of those mega Christmas ball packs because she knew she would just be using it for filler since the tree was so much bigger than her previous ones.

Now that she knew she could fit such a large tree in the house—and hopefully had someone who was interested in spending more than just this holiday with her—she could start adding to her collection again.

And maybe have them be ornaments that matter to *them* rather than just to her.

Glancing over at Liam, she saw him staring intensely at the tree.

"What are you thinking right now?" she asked lightly.

"That you maybe didn't buy enough ornaments yesterday."

"Oh, don't worry about that. I already have a ton. The ones from yesterday were just filler." Opening up the first case, her heart kicked hard in her chest for a moment. There were two right on top that were from the last trip she and Trevor took together.

She must have been staring at it for longer than she thought because Liam called her name as if he'd said it more than once.

"I'm sorry. What?" she asked, looking up at him.

"You just seemed a little lost in thought. Are you alright?"

Coming to her feet, she nodded. Picking up an ornament, she held it up to him. "Trevor and I bought this when we went on that hot-air balloon ride." Since the ornament was a miniature hot-air balloon, it was probably self-explanatory. "Anyway, I opened the case and saw it and just..." Then she shook her head. "Sorry."

Placing it on the tree, Tessa stepped back and smiled before reaching for the next one.

"This one I got when Trevor and I swam with the dolphins." Again, it was a dolphin with a Santa hat on it, so it was self-explanatory. Hanging it on another branch, she began going through the case, explaining where she got each ornament and why she loved it. Not all of them had to do with Trevor, but a lot of them did. When she noticed that Liam hadn't moved from his spot, she paused. "Everything okay?"

All he did was nod and picked up another case. "Should I start with this one?"

"Um..."

Raking a hand through his hair, he looked at her.

"I kind of have a system."

He let out a long breath. "Of course you do."

And this time, it didn't sound like he was teasing; he was clearly annoyed.

"Most people have a system, Liam," she said defensively. "I know that this case has my favorite ornaments and I like them to be showcased in the front of the tree. Then the next one has..."

"How about you handle the ornaments, then? Is there something else I can do? Anything else that requires a ladder or something to be hung or put back in the attic?"

Looking around, she motioned to a box in front of the fireplace. "There's lighted garland in there that gets hung on the mantle and then the stockings, if you wouldn't mind..."

"I'm on it." He moved across the room without another word.

They worked silently through multiple Christmas songs

and Tessa was so enthralled with hanging her ornaments that she could almost forget about how grouchy Liam was being.

"How's this?" he asked flatly.

Turning, she looked at the mantle and wanted to smile, but the look on his face stopped her. Putting down the ornament she was about to hang, she knew something was up. "Okay, out with it."

"Excuse me?"

Nodding, she repeated herself. "Out with it. If you don't want to be here, then go. I thought you'd be able to unclench a bit and have fun, but obviously that's not happening."

"Kind of hard to have fun when I'm the third wheel," he murmured.

"Third...? Um, what?"

Taking a step toward her, he nodded. "I feel like a third wheel here, Tessa!"

"I don't know what that even means," she replied, thoroughly confused. "It's just the two of us here."

"Is it? Because it's more like three—me, you, and Trevor." Pausing, he raked a hand through his hair again until it was in total disarray. "I feel like I shouldn't be here!" he yelled after a moment.

"That's crazy," she said, reaching for his hand, hoping to calm him down. "Of course you should be here. I want you here!"

"For what? To hang lights? Reach all the hard-to-reach places with the ladder? Because other than that, me being here is just awkward."

A twinge of panic crept up her spine.

"Liam, where is all this coming from? I don't understand what's happening right now."

Now he started to pace and she couldn't keep up with everything he was saying—it ranged from not being able to help with the ornaments to all the stories about her and Trevor and then the incident at the tree lot yesterday.

"That was all a misunderstanding yesterday," she interrupted. "Savannah made an assumption and I cleared it up. It wasn't a big deal. I thought we were over that and moved on." And honestly, she couldn't understand why he was getting so upset.

"How could we move on?" he demanded. "We never even talked about it!"

"Then we can talk about it right now like two adults," she said, still trying to be the voice of reason. "It didn't have to come to all of...you know...this."

"That's just it, Tessa, it shouldn't have had to come to this! We're sleeping together and you're still wearing those rings!"

"Okay, again, can we please just calm down and talk about this? We can sit down and forget about decorating for now. I really don't see what the big deal is..."

"I just said what the big deal is!" Liam's voice grew louder and louder with each word. "Why are you still wearing them? I mean...I don't get it! We're involved... we're...we're..."

"We're sleeping together," she tartly reminded him. "Yeah, I got that."

He arched a dark brow at her. "And...?"

"And what? It seemed to me like this was all part of some big plan of yours to help ease me back out into the dating world! You and I never talked about this being anything serious! From where I'm standing, it shouldn't matter if I'm wearing Trevor's rings, since you're clearly not interested in dating me seriously!"

"Where the hell did you get that idea?" he snapped and then seemed to realize what he was saying. "Okay, fine. That's how it all started, but I thought you realized it stopped being like that a long time ago!"

"How would I know, huh? The one time you took me out, it was to your parents' pub and it was weird as hell!"

"It wasn't that weird and we've done other things, Tessa," he tried to reason.

"Seriously? Other than the Christmas tree lot, ornament shopping, getting takeout, and eating dinner at each other's houses, what exactly have we done? Where have we gone?" And before he could he try to answer, she barreled on. "Nowhere. We don't talk about relationships and we don't talk about feelings unless it's you telling me that something I'm feeling is wrong or ridiculous, so..."

His expression was thunderous, but fortunately, he didn't argue.

And she wasn't sure if that was a good thing or not.

Then neither of them were talking, and that definitely didn't seem like a good thing.

"I can take off the rings, Liam, but I'm not taking them off for a guy who's just sleeping with me because he's trying to be a good friend." She shrugged.

"That sounds like some kind of ultimatum," he murmured.

It was crazy how much that one statement hurt.

Swallowing hard, Tessa shook her head. "Just stating a fact. I'm not a mind-reader and I had no idea this bothered you so much or that it bothered you at all. These rings have been on my finger every time we've been together and you never said a word. Now suddenly they're a big issue."

"It's not just the rings," he said, raking a hand through his hair. "I can't...I just can't keep competing with a ghost."

She felt like she'd been kicked in the gut.

"What?" she whispered.

"I'm never going to measure up," he said, and for the first time since they started this discussion, his tone was a little sad. "Everywhere I look in this house, he's there. The pictures, the things the two of you bought, the Christmas ornaments, the holiday decorations, the stories..." With a mirthless laugh, he added, "Even your phone."

"My phone?"

"Earlier, when you took Phoebe out and I was in the kitchen? Your phone dinged with a reminder," he told her. "It said, 'Chat with Trevor' and I don't think that was a one-time thing."

There was no point in lying, so she simply shook her head but refused to explain herself to him. This was her life, and Trevor was an important part of it. What did he expect her to do, just forget the man who was a huge part of her world just so he didn't have to feel uncomfortable?

"I genuinely wanted to help you move on in the beginning," Liam went on. "It was a little selfless then. But then... then it became more and I should have said something or told you how I felt, but...everywhere I turned people were telling me I wasn't good enough for you and I let them convince me to keep my feelings to myself."

"Why would anyone tell you that? Liam, that's ridiculous!" Taking a step toward him, Tessa wanted to reach for him, but he held up a hand to stop her.

"They said I was too serious and too much of a control freak, that I'd steal your joy away." He let out another mirthless laugh. "I didn't want to believe them, but...they're right."

"No! No, they're not! You're not stealing anything from me!"

He took one step back and then another. "For whatever reason, you are holding on to Trevor; it gives you comfort to schedule chats with him and to surround yourself with mementos and stories and memories. I'm not asking you to forget him, but I also can't be a part of it. I need to know there's a future, but I don't see how that's possible when you refuse to let go of the past."

Tears stung her eyes, but she didn't know what to say.

Her fingers toyed with the rings and she knew she could take them off and put them away in her jewelry box, but...it was more than that. It was deeper and everyone had warned her it was happening and she'd refused to listen.

"Liam, I..."

"I can't do this anymore," he said, his voice low and gruff. "And I don't think I should. There's nothing wrong with you, Tessa, and there never was. We see life differently and I know I was a complete jackass about it all, but...you shouldn't have anyone holding you back from the way you feel. And I know I'm going to because..." He motioned to the room around them and she knew exactly what he meant.

Looking up at him, she didn't stop the tears from falling. And when he walked over to her, she thought that maybe— just maybe—he had changed his mind. Cupping her face, he looked down at her and she swore he was going to kiss her and tell her that everything was going to be alright.

But he didn't.

"Be happy, Tessa. Keep sharing your joy and laughter and optimism everywhere you can. The world needs more people like you."

She whispered his name, but...

"I should have been honest with you from the get-go. I

changed the rules and now I'm the one who can't seem to live by them, so..."

This time he did kiss her, but on the forehead.

"Take care of yourself."

Numb and more than a little dumbfounded, she watched him grab his coat and as he walked out the door, she wondered just how the day had gone so far off the rails.

Chapter Thirteen

Liam tossed his coat on the sofa and kept walking until he was in the kitchen.

And he felt completely gutted.

He could have saved himself a lot of grief and heartache if he'd just ignored all the things his siblings said to him and went with how he actually felt.

"Great time to realize that, jackass," he murmured as he opened the fridge and looked for something stronger than water to drink. Unfortunately, other than a ridiculous amount of takeout containers, there wasn't anything there.

Now that he thought about it, it had been a while since he went grocery shopping.

Only...right now, he was more than likely going to order even more takeout or go to the pub rather than shop for food.

Glancing over at the kitchen clock, he saw it was almost seven. The pub would probably be crowded and maybe that would work in his favor because he knew he'd be terrible company if he had to sit and have a one-on-one conversation with anyone.

A sound by the front door took him by surprise and he was shocked to see Tessa coming through the door. "Tessa, what are you...?"

"Oh, no. You don't get to talk," she snapped as she stomped over to him. "You had a whole lot to say a few minutes ago. Now it's my turn."

Shit.

"I will not apologize for having a life before I met you, Liam Donovan," she said, and he hated the tremble in her voice. "I have lived and I have laughed and I have loved. It's not a crime. And maybe I do cling to the past for a little comfort—to look back on memories that are precious to me and make me smile. I'm not going to hide any of that just so that you or whoever else comes along doesn't have to feel awkward. I would never ask you to forget a part of your life just because I don't understand it."

"I understand that you loved Trevor," he countered. "I really do. But...it's just everywhere and you don't see it. I don't see how you might ever move forward when you keep choosing to surround yourself with the past!"

"I'm not surrounding myself..."

"You are," he said sadly, not wanting to fight with her about this. "Nothing I can say is going to change your mind about it, and that's fine. It was wrong of me to try because... well...it just was. I found that I just enjoyed being with you and thought that...that everyone was right and you'd end up hating me again."

"That's just it, Liam. I don't hate. It's just not who I am. Did you annoy me? Yes! You were mean and arrogant and condescending, and you intimidated the heck out of me! But I didn't hate you."

He started to relax, but...

"But I'm beyond disappointed in you and I feel like I

can't trust you," she said sadly. "You tell me your feelings changed, but you never said a word. There were things that were bothering you that you never shared. I can't be with someone like that. It's too much work and I'll always feel like I'm waiting for you to snap or freak out over something I don't see coming."

"Tessa..."

"You're so afraid of being vulnerable. You always want everyone to look at you like you're the guy who's always in control and, by doing that, you're going to miss out on some amazing things in this world. And for that, I pity you."

Liam could see the tears in her eyes and wanted to go to her and comfort her, but she must have sensed it and immediately held up a hand to stop him even as she took a step back.

"I cling to a happier time while you cling to no one but yourself. I don't see where that makes your way any better than mine."

And with that, she left.

He didn't go after her; he didn't say a word. Once the front door closed behind her, Liam hung his head and allowed himself a solid minute to simply get his emotions under control. And then he did what he always did—stood a little straighter, let out a long breath, and moved on because...well...he had to.

Growing up, he didn't have time to sit and wallow when things didn't go his way because he had chores and responsibilities, like helping with his siblings. In the military, you had to keep moving forward even when you watched some of your good friends die senselessly.

So here he was, in his kitchen, vowing to move on after losing the woman he saw himself spending forever with.

How ironic was that?

From the moment he met her, he couldn't wait to get away from her. But once he got to know her, all he wanted was to be with her.

And in the end, he'd lost her.

"Clearly everyone was right. I wasn't good for her," he muttered before stalking across the room, grabbing his coat and keys, and walking out the door.

As much as his family was largely the reason he was in this current predicament, he knew they didn't mean it, and it was pointless to be angry with them. After all, he could have proved them wrong, but he didn't.

The drive across town was short and, as predicted, the parking lot of the pub was full. Pulling around to the back, he parked next to his father's truck and climbed out. Walking in through the kitchen wasn't something he normally did, but it just seemed easier right now.

"Liam!" his father called out when he spotted him. "What are you doing sneaking in like that? Who are you trying to avoid?"

It would be wrong to say everyone—especially as he was the one showing up where there was guaranteed to be at least a handful of Donovans. Shaking his head, he walked over and gave his father a quick hug. "The parking lot was mobbed, so I figured it would be easier to do it this way."

"Smart boy," Shane said as he flipped a couple of burgers. "I'm guessing you're hungry if you're showing up at this hour. What can I get you?"

"Actually, I think I need a drink first," he admitted with a mirthless laugh. "A strong one."

Rather than ask questions, his father nodded toward the door to the dining room. "Go. Your uncle will hook you up. Then come on back and I'll have a nice bacon cheeseburger waiting."

Funny, that was exactly what he was going to ask for. "Thanks, Dad."

As predicted, it was crowded out in the dining room and Liam did his best to smile and nod at anyone who said hello. By the time he made it to the bar, he realized that maybe this was a mistake. He didn't want to talk or smile. He wanted to be alone.

"Liam!" Uncle Ronan called out. "Good to see you! What can I get you? A beer?"

"Let me get a little Irish Whiskey," he said. "A double?"

Ronan arched a graying brow at him but said nothing.

"Hey! Any chance you can give us a hand tonight?" Jamie asked as he walked over and picked up an order of drinks. "We're slammed and Danny called in sick."

"Not tonight, bro," Liam told him. "Sorry."

"Order up!" someone called out, and fortunately his brother didn't stick around to try to convince him to stay and work.

Ronan put his drink down in front of him with just a hint of disapproval. "Make sure you eat something with that," he said before walking away to help a customer.

With his head down, he headed back to the kitchen and was thankful that no one tried to stop and talk to him. But when he slid through the door, he found Patrick back there with his father.

"You're not the only one looking for a meal and unwilling to try to find a parking space," Shane said with a laugh. "Sit! This will be fun having a bit of a boys' night here in the kitchen. I'm sure Jamie will whine about not being included, but I'm training him to take over this place so I can take your mother on a nice vacation."

"Seriously?" Patrick asked. "You'd trust him to run the pub? He's a doofus."

Shane laughed softly. "You want to run it?"

"Hell, no! But I'm not sure Jamie can handle it."

Liam pulled a stool over to one of the long stainless steel prep tables and sat down.

"What about you?" his father asked him. "You think Jamie's up to it?"

He shrugged. "Other than you and Uncle Ronan, he's here the most. I'd hope he's learned something after all that time."

Shane looked over at Patrick and shook his spatula at him. "See? You should be a little more supportive, like Liam. I'm sure it would help with Jamie's confidence if he knew both his brothers believed in him."

"Oh, good grief. Jamie doesn't need any help with his confidence, Dad," Patrick argued before turning and glaring at Liam.

"What? What did I do?"

"You are such a damn suck up," his brother said before muttering a curse.

"How the hell am I being a suck up?" he snapped with more heat than he intended, but that was probably because he was itching to fight with someone.

"You and your politically correct answers! You and I both know Jamie's a screw up who is easily distracted! Would you trust him to run your business?"

"That's not a fair question! He's never worked in what I do! Of course I wouldn't trust him to run it!"

"Boys..." their father warned, but it was all he said.

"And what is your deal lately?" Liam demanded. "You seem to have a problem with everyone and have something snarky to say about all of us. What the hell is that about?"

"You want to know what my problem is?" Patrick snarled right before he shoved Liam in the shoulder.

Hard.

Coming to his feet, Liam shoved him right back. "Yeah. I want to know."

Before either could say a word, Shane had them both by the scruff of the neck and dragged them to the back door before pushing them out. "Fight it out outside and don't come back in until you do!"

Stumbling, Liam took a moment to get his bearings, but Patrick was on him in the blink of an eye. "I am sick and tired of *perfect* Liam who always says and does the right damn thing! You're exhausting to be around!"

He was fairly certain his eyes were bugging out of his head. "Do you even hear yourself? When the hell have I done anything like that?"

"All the fucking time! God, you don't even realize it, do you?" Patrick said with a maniacal laugh. "Do you have any idea how much it sucks to constantly be compared to you? You were the good student, the great athlete, the perfect son, the perfect soldier." He sneered at him. "Then you come home and all everyone talks about is how great you are and all the big things you're doing for the town! Well, newsflash, buddy! I was doing big things for this shitty freaking town while you were gone and no one was ready to throw me a parade over it!"

"I have no idea what you're even talking about! No one's throwing me a parade, Patrick!"

"Trust me, if they could, they would. You come home like some freaking hero returning from war and every little thing you do is big news! I had to grow up in your damn shadow and while you were gone, I finally had a life! Now you're back and..."

The string of curses that flew out of his mouth were beyond colorful as he paced back and forth. When he stopped and was practically toe to toe with Liam, the look on his face was fierce.

"I have been working my ass off trying to build a small local real estate empire so I can make a name for myself rather than simply being Liam Donovan's younger brother. And you had to come home and steal that from me."

Holy. Shit.

"Pat, come on. You know that wasn't my intention," Liam said as some of the fight went out of him. "For years I hadn't given much thought to what I was going to do when I came home. The plans for the resort were sort of an idea I'd been thinking of but wasn't sure if I could make it happen. Will's architectural engineering skills were like the final piece of the puzzle. This had nothing to do with you. You have to believe me."

Pacing again, his brother mumbled a bunch of stuff under his breath before stopping in front of him again. "Do you want to know why I didn't do anything when Arianna moved into your apartment?"

He shook his head.

"Because I thought it was funny. I knew it would make you bat-shit crazy and I thought it would be hysterical if you came home and found her there."

"Um..."

"That was my first thought, then I decided I didn't want to get involved because no matter what I found for her, Mom wasn't going to approve or if God forbid something happened, I'd somehow get blamed."

"Yeah...I get that."

"And then there's Tessa," Patrick went on and Liam inwardly groaned. "Do you have any idea how the guys in the town have been practically standing on their heads to get her attention? Ever since she moved to town, men have been trying to ask her out. She never said yes to anyone until you."

"Um..."

"I seriously wanted to punch you in your stupid face just on principle! Does everything come easy for you? Can't you just be a mere mortal like the rest of us?" With a disgusted sigh, he walked away.

With a weary sigh of his own, he followed.

At the far end of the back lot, Liam caught up to him. "Do you have any idea the kind of pressure I've had to live with?" he asked without really waiting for an answer. "Being the oldest of five kids wasn't anything I asked for. I would have loved to do anything else but work at the pub or babysit the bunch of you. I can't help that I was a good student or that I was good at sports and you know what? It's shitty of you to even call me out on that because you were even smarter than I was and beat my touchdown record!"

Grinning, Patrick went, "Oh, yeah..."

"I went into the Marines to get away from all of this," he went on. "I didn't want to be Shane and Kate Donovan's son everywhere I went. I wanted my own damn identity! I fought hard for it!"

"Then why come back, huh? You could have gone anywhere in the world after you were done with the service. Why here?"

"Because believe it or not, I missed everyone! I thought it would be nice to come home to my family, but ever since I did, nothing's gone right and all any of you have done is give me shit!"

Now it was his turn to pace.

"I find out my baby sister thinks I'm an ogre, my best friend lied to me for a year also because he thought I was an ogre, Ryleigh thinks I'm an uptight pain in the ass, Jamie does nothing but mock me, and you hate me. On top of that, Tessa and I broke up. So...yeah. I guess I should have gone somewhere else!"

Muttering his own string of colorful curses, Liam decided he wasn't hungry and was just going to go home.

He was halfway to his car when Patrick called out, "What did you do to screw it up?"

That was it.

That was the last straw.

Turning, he pretty much lunged at his brother and hit him square in the jaw and before he knew it, he was on the receiving end of Patrick's fist. They yelled, they shoved as they hurled insults, and as good as Liam thought he was at fighting, his little brother got in some solid punches.

"Not so perfect now, are you?" Patrick snarled as he landed a hard hit on Liam's ribs.

"What's the matter? Jealous?" Liam shot back, mimicking the move.

"As a matter of fact, yes! Happy?" And with one final shove, Patrick took a breathless step back. "You have everything, Liam, and it's effortless for you." He breathed heavily as he wiped sweat from his brow. "I work my ass off and it's still not enough to compete."

"Dude, I don't want to compete with you, I swear! I just wanted to come home and be with my family again." Dropping his arms to his sides, he gave up. "Hate me. Punch me. Hurl every insult you can think of at me if it makes you feel better." Shaking his head, he sighed. "I'm just...I'm done. I'll sell the property to Will and sell the house and just...go. Would that make this better? Would that make you happy?"

Patrick studied him hard for a solid minute before he seemed to relax. "And let you be the bigger person?" he said with a small laugh. "Shit, I'd never be able to live with that."

And in that moment, Liam knew they were going to be alright.

Eventually.

His brother reached out a hand first and when Liam shook it, he hoped it was a step in the right direction.

And just because he could, he pulled Patrick in and hugged him.

Laughing harder, his brother pulled back and said, "You always have to do me one better. Is it any wonder I want to punch you in the throat most days?"

"You're right, you're right." Together, they started to walk back to the pub door.

"So, did you totally blow it with Tessa, or is there a chance she'll take your sorry ass back?"

"I really think you have a thing for her. Because it seems to me you're a little fixated on her and it's pissing me off."

With a small chuckle, Patrick shook his head. "I think she's a great person and incredibly sweet, but I have never been tempted to ask her out and I'm not attracted to her, so don't worry."

"Then why have you been on my case about her?"

"I told you. It just pissed me off that you managed to do something that no other guy in town has for the last two years. You're annoying. Deal with it."

When they stepped into the kitchen, all banged up and a little bloody, Shane took one look at them and pointed to the bathroom. "Clean up and don't let your mother see you looking like that. Go."

It didn't matter that they were two grown men; neither was willing to take on Shane Donovan.

Because even at fifty-five, he could still take on both of his sons without breaking a sweat.

* * *

Her desk at school was decorated to look like a gingerbread house.

She had bought a few meager extra decorations for the holiday concert stage, and her chorus group sounded wonderful.

And she'd never been more miserable.

All week long, Tessa had done her best to be upbeat and not let anyone see how her heart was broken and that she was miserable. But every day she made sure she was home long before Liam drove by so there would be no chance she'd have to see him.

Eventually it was going to happen; they lived next door to each other and there was only so long you could go without catching at least a glimpse of each other. But for now, she'd go to whatever extreme measures were necessary to avoid him.

Like calling in sick on Friday so she could drive down to Charleston and surprise her mother and maybe get some baking in with her and her sisters.

She'd packed up her car and left home just after seven that morning—right after she watched Liam's truck pull away. Part of her wished he would have at least tried to talk to her this week just to see if she was okay.

But he hadn't.

It was one thing to lose someone you loved and couldn't talk to them because they were well and truly gone. It was quite another to lose them but they were still there within reach and wouldn't talk to you.

"All of this sucks," she murmured.

All week long, she'd moped around the house. It didn't matter how cheery her tree looked or how many of her favorite holiday specials were on TV or how much Christmas music she played; she was miserable.

And that made her even angrier with Liam because he ruined her favorite holiday.

The drive felt like it took ten times longer than usual and by the time she drove into the city limits, she was ready to scream. Turning onto the main road that would lead her to her parents' home, she drove by the florist and decided to stop. With Phoebe in her arms, she walked in and made a couple of purchases before letting the dog do her business and getting back in the car.

"One more stop, baby girl, and then I promise you'll be able to run all around the yard, okay?"

All Phoebe did was yawn and curl back up in her carrier.

Her detour extended the drive by fifteen minutes, but it was something she needed to do.

The sky was gray and it seemed fitting as she drove through the cemetery gates. The last time she was here was the day of Trevor's funeral. After that was when she decided she could talk to him anywhere because the thought of standing at his gravesite meant facing a reality she never wanted to face.

But today she knew just how much that decision cost her.

Parking at the end of the lane, she let out a sigh before picking up the wreath she just purchased. "Here we go," she whispered as she climbed from the car.

Trevor's plot was the sixth one in and there was a poinsettia there. Placing the wreath beside it, she took a step back and fought hard not to cry.

"It seems silly to not know what to say considering I talk to you every day, but I feel like now that I'm standing here with you, my words should maybe be different. More reverent or something like that." She sighed. "Oh, Trev, I've made a mess of things. I know I've been crying about it all week, but I don't want to keep crying about it. I don't know what to do, and all I know is that I am clueless when it comes to men. Why can't they all be as sweet and understanding like you were?"

Of course there was no answer.

"I'm sorry I never came here," she said quietly. "It was all...too real. Too final. I think everyone's been right all along and I've been living in some kind of bubble or suspended sense of reality. I'm just afraid if I don't hold on to you with both hands that you really will be gone. And then where will I be?"

Tessa dropped to her knees and knew she was losing the battle with crying and didn't even try to fight it. It had been a while since she'd let herself cry over Trevor, so it was only fitting that she did it here today.

After several long minutes, she straightened and attempted to pull herself together. A few cars had passed by but one parked in front of hers, so she didn't want to be sitting here blubbering with an audience. It wasn't until she noticed a familiar face that she got to her feet.

Wiping her face, Tessa got to her feet and forced herself to smile. "Hey, Mrs. Scott," she said softly. "How are you?"

"Oh, Tessa! Let me look at you!" Trevor's mom held her in a fierce embrace before pulling back and smiling at her.

Then she wiped away a few stray tears.

"How are you?"

"I'm okay," Tessa forced herself to say, even though she felt anything but.

"Hmm..." Stepping away, she put another potted poinsettia down by Trevor's headstone. When she turned, she studied Tessa for a moment. "Let's try that again. How are you?"

Mrs. Scott had been a second mother to her, so it was no wonder she could see right through her.

"Right now? Kind of a mess. And not just because I'm here visiting."

Nodding, they each stepped a little farther away from the plot. "What's going on?"

Ugh...where did she even begin?

And then, as if it had a mind of its own, her mouth just ran away and blurted out the entire story of her and Liam—from the moment they met at her cousin's wedding right until she stormed out of his house seven days ago.

"I remember the day Trevor told us he was going to ask you to marry him," his mother began. "We all tried to talk him out of it." At Tessa's shocked expression, she laughed softly. "Not because we didn't love you, Tessa, but because we did. His father and I told him it wasn't right because it would put a lot of extra pressure on you. It's hard enough losing a friend; it's even harder to lose a spouse."

That...actually made sense.

"We were so thankful for you because you made a really rotten and unfair situation bearable," she went on. "I don't think we could have been so positive and upbeat for Trevor the way that you were. I cried all the time and my husband used to get frustrated with me because he never wanted Trevor to see that. You kept him laughing and smiling right up to the end, and I never thanked you for that."

And just like that, she was crying again.

"I wish I would have cried more," she admitted. "Maybe if I had, I would have grieved properly and been able to accept that he's gone. Everyone has been harping on me for years about how I haven't dealt with his death, and I always said they were wrong. But maybe...they were right."

Mrs. Scott pulled her in for another hug. "We each have to grieve in our own way." When she released her, she said, "I talk to him every day."

"Me too," Tessa said with just a hint of awe. "He used to tell me how much he loved to hear about my day, so...I still share it."

Reaching out, his mother took one of Tessa's hands in hers. "It's okay if you *don't* talk to him every day. If he knew how much this was affecting your life, what would he tell you?"

She knew, but didn't want to say it out loud.

"He'd tell you he wanted you to be happy. If being with Liam makes you happy, then you need to make it work."

"But...I can't just never talk about Trevor again or...or just throw everything away that reminds me of him! How is that fair?"

"It doesn't sound like that's what he was asking," she said gently. "It sounds like he's looking for a way to fit into your life and you've filled it so much with Trevor that there isn't room for someone else." Pausing, she gave Tessa's hand a small squeeze. "There were three things Trevor used to always say about you."

"Oh?"

Nodding, she explained, "First, he treasured your friendship."

"I felt the same about his."

"Second, he would do anything to make you smile. It gave him great joy whenever he could do something for you."

She felt herself blush even as her heart kicked hard in her chest.

"And third, he hoped you'd find the man who would love you the way you deserved to be loved." She let that sink in for a minute. "I think he always hated the fact that the two of you never had...you know...those kinds of feelings for each other, but he used to talk about how he hoped the perfect man would come along. I don't know if that person is Liam, but you're never going to know if you don't fully put your heart out there. Trevor wanted you to be happy and he'd hate it if he were the reason you weren't."

"You make it sound so simple..."

"Believe me, I know it's not. I've gone to a lot of support groups and spoken to several counselors because grief is...it's hard. I'm not trying to make light of your struggles, Tessa, but I know that if my son were standing right here with us, he'd tell you it's okay to let him go. He'd tell you that he's in a better place and knows that you love him, but it's okay to love somebody else too."

"I...I don't know if that's what's going to happen," she said quietly. "Liam is..."

"Tessa," Mrs. Scott gently interrupted. "You don't have to have it all figured out today. Just know that whatever you decide, Trevor would support it." Then she hugged her again. "The thing to remember is, you have your whole life ahead of you and that life doesn't have to be in Laurel Bay."

"But..."

"And it doesn't have to be here in Charleston either. Whatever it is you decide, just know you have people who love and support you." Squeezing her hand, she said, "Now, how about you and I go and grab a cup of coffee and warm up? It's chilly out here."

"I've got Phoebe in the car and..."

"Then come back to the house with me for a little while

and I'll make us some coffee or cocoa or whatever you'd like."

Smiling, she accepted. "Thank you. I think that sounds like a wonderful idea."

Later, she went to her parents' house and spent the weekend laughing and baking and talking all about her upcoming school concert. Her sisters had joined them and it was the best weekend she could remember sharing with them in a long time.

If anyone noticed a change in her, they didn't say anything. But when she said goodbye to them all on Sunday morning, it felt like they were all a little bit lighter —cheerier.

And Tessa felt like maybe she was going to be okay.

She'd driven home without giving much thought to the time, but when she turned onto the block, she noticed Liam pulling into his driveway too.

Neither said a word; they barely exchanged a glance. But when Tessa had her luggage and Phoebe in the house, she breathed a large sigh of relief. She'd seen him and kind of looked at him, and the pain wasn't nearly as bad as she expected.

As she got ready for bed that night, she walked over to her jewelry box and stared down hard at it.

Then, before she could second-guess herself, she removed the engagement ring and wedding band and gently placed them inside. Closing the lid, she let out a shaky breath before whispering, "Thank you for giving them to me, and thank you for understanding that it's time to take them off."

Tomorrow started a new week and the final preparations for the holiday concert and for the first time in over a week, Tessa knew she could give it all of her attention. Decorations or no decorations, she was going to make it the best concert Laurel Bay Elementary had ever seen.

Chapter Fourteen

Liam was miserable and was apparently spreading that mood around everywhere he went.

When he got to the job site in the mornings, everyone groaned.

If he stopped at the pub on the way home, people scattered to avoid him.

But the worst was when he got home on Thursday and Phoebe had somehow gotten away from Tessa and was running around in the yard. He'd gone to pick her up before she ran into the street and got hurt, and she snarled at him and immediately ran back to Tessa's porch.

"Great, even the friendliest dog in the world hates me. Awesome."

He'd been working overtime just to have something to do and with the weekend looming, he was already trying to think of somewhere he could go just so he wasn't sitting at home thinking about Tessa and wondering if she was okay.

Since she walked out of his house, he'd only really seen her once. It was across the yard and neither of them said a word, but...he missed her.

Like heartbreakingly missed her.

With a sound that was part moan and part whine, he collapsed on his sofa. With his head thrown back and his eyes closed, he seriously tried to think of how he could keep living in this house with her right next door hating him.

Only...Tessa didn't do hate.

"That's just it, Liam. I don't hate. It's just not who I am. Did you annoy me? Yes! You were mean and arrogant and condescending, and you intimidated the heck out of me! But I didn't hate you...but I'm beyond disappointed in you and I feel like I can't trust you."

He really liked this house, but...he didn't love it. He certainly didn't love it enough to stay and make Tessa miserable, so he reached for his phone, typed a quick text to his brother, and asked him to start looking for a new house. Yeah, it would suck packing up and moving again, but...it was the right thing to do.

When he didn't get a response right away, he assumed his brother was busy.

"And I should probably get something to eat," he murmured as he stood up. He didn't want to go to the pub; hell, he didn't want to go out at all.

The whole town could breathe a collective sigh of relief knowing he and his foul mood would not be bothering them tonight.

In the kitchen, Liam rummaged through the refrigerator and ended up throwing away about a hundred dollars' worth of takeout leftovers. When he was done, what remained was dismal at best. Slamming the door shut, he went through the pantry to see what he had there and it was equally slim.

"Cereal it is," he grumbled, but when he opened the

refrigerator and took out the milk, he realized it had gone bad.

That was when he snapped.

The cereal box was thrown, the milk carton crashed into the sink and splashed everywhere, all while he cursed his life, his luck, and how unfair it all was.

"I'm a good person, dammit! I took care of my family and friends! I served my country for years! What more am I supposed to do?" he cried out, although for the life of him, he had no idea where he thought the answer was going to come from.

With a curse, he walked out the back door to his yard to try to just breathe. It was a cold December night, but the sky was clear and full of stars. Maybe if he sat outside for a little while, something would come to him—either about his shitty life or dinner. At this point, he wasn't going to be picky.

He never did any work on the yard, so all he had outside were a couple of Adirondack chairs that he'd purchased after seeing how great they worked in Tessa's. Sitting down, he shivered a bit and pondered going back inside for a coat, but figured he deserved to be cold and uncomfortable.

Arms crossed, head thrown back, he did his best to simply let his mind go blank. And it was working until he heard voices coming from Tessa's yard.

"This is gorgeous back here," someone was saying. "It's like a tranquil retreat."

"That's what I was going for," Tessa replied. "Although it's not nearly as nice to hang out outside in the winter, I still decorate it so it's festive when Phoebe and I come out here."

"Well, this will be a huge selling point," the other person was saying. "When you're ready, we'll get some pictures of the yard at night all lit up and some during the day so potential buyers will see how beautiful it all is." She paused. "And you're thinking of putting it on the market in January?"

Wait...Tessa's selling her house? What the hell?

"I figured it was best to wait until after the holidays. Once I put all the holiday decorations away, you can come in and take pictures."

Liam's heart kicked hard in his chest because he knew he was the reason Tessa was going to sell the house she loved and moved from a neighborhood that loved her.

And that's why he had to track Patrick down and get his house on the market as soon as possible. If he could beat her to the punch, she'd see that she didn't need to leave. He'd go and make life easier for her.

Quietly, he waited until he heard Tessa go back into her house before he got up and went into his. He forgot all about not wanting to go out and walked through the house grabbing his phone, keys, and coat so he could go to the pub and hopefully track his brother down and get things started.

Pulling the front door open, he jumped back and almost screamed when he found Ryleigh standing there, poised to knock. "Jesus, Ry! You scared the shit out of me!"

Grinning, she gave him a small shove back into the house and out of her way. "That wasn't my plan, but a serious perk," she said, shutting the door behind her.

"Um...what are you doing here?"

"Oh, I drew the short straw and was told to come over and make sure you were home and then sit on you if you wanted to leave."

"Yeah, that wouldn't stop me, but I don't understand anything else that you said."

Sighing dramatically, she took off her coat and tossed it on the couch. "Patrick got your text while he was at the pub. Now everyone's on their way over, so..." She shrugged and then planted herself in front of the door. "I don't actually *want* to sit on you, but I've taken a lot of martial arts classes and could do some serious damage to you if you try to leave."

That made him chuckle. "It's adorable that you think that, but you can relax. I'm not looking to leave."

She looked him up and down with a smirk. "So you often wear your coat around the house and carry your keys?"

Groaning, he made a face at her. "Okay, fine. I was *about* to leave, but now I'm not. Is anyone bringing food?"

"That's why I was sent ahead. Mom's making up trays right now and calling in coverage."

Muttering another curse, Liam walked over and collapsed on the couch. "Everyone's coming? Seriously?"

"When you drop a bombshell like putting your house up for sale, what did you think would happen?"

"I don't know. Maybe Patrick would do his job and have some sort of client confidentiality? Maybe?"

Now it was her turn to laugh. "Now look who's being adorable now," she said before walking over and sitting next to him on the couch. "Is this because you and Tessa broke up?"

Ugh...he hated talking about his personal life, but obviously nothing was sacred in this family.

"Yeah," he murmured. "I've already messed with her life, and I don't want to keep doing it. It's awkward as hell and..." His head lolled back against the cushion. "I hate this."

"Which part—the breakup or the fact that we're all

going to gather around and talk about it?" she teased, and her smile was just a touch devious.

"You know, if you're not careful, I could total deflect some of this onto you and remind Mom how you're still single," he countered and watched as her eyes narrowed.

"You wouldn't."

"Keep teasing, and I will."

Frowning, Ryleigh studied him hard. "Can I ask you something before everyone gets here?"

"Depends. Will you broadcast whatever I say later?"

She shook her head. "Trust me, I feel your pain."

"Okay, then. What's up?"

She twisted a bit in her spot. "Do you love her? Is that why you want to move away?"

It was pointless to deny it, so he nodded. "I didn't think it would feel like this, but...yeah."

"Then why aren't you trying to win her back? What could have possibly happened that you can't work it out?"

Liam told her the whole story because...well...he just needed to tell someone. He'd shared some of the details with Patrick after their parking lot brawl, but not every-thing. When he was done, he waited for the critique, for Ryleigh to tell him what he did wrong and how much he screwed up.

And waited.

And waited.

Turning his head, he looked at her. "Aren't you going to say anything?"

"I'm not sure what to say. That is a truly complicated situation."

That was not what he was expecting her to say. "So, what would you do?"

Ryleigh seemed to consider what she was going to say.

"I don't think it's a deal breaker, Liam. I think if you love her, then you find a way to make it work." Pausing, she frowned at him again. "You are the worst at communicating, and it sounds like you never actually talked to her about how you felt until you had one foot out the door."

Now it was his turn to frown. "What's happening here?"

"What do you mean?"

"How is it my kid sister—the one who used to either keep her nose stuck in a book or would throw said book at my face—turned out to be so damn smart?"

She practically preened. "Because my nose was always stuck in a book. I got the best of both worlds—I'm smart and I know how to kick some serious ass if I need to."

"You have three brothers; we can kick anyone's ass you need us to," he reminded her.

"I know, but it's fun watching people underestimate me."

Before she could say anything else, the Donovan family was coming through the door.

Without knocking.

It was loud and chaotic and it felt...right.

This was why he had come home to Laurel Baby. His family—as annoying and interfering as they could be—were also the most loving and supportive people on the planet.

Standing, he walked to the kitchen where his mother was setting up food. Liam leaned in and kissed her cheek. "Thanks, Mom. This is...*ow!*"

She smacked him upside the head, just like she used to do when he was a kid.

"You think you can just go and join the Marines and stay gone for almost twelve years and then come home for a few months and move away again?" Kate said, advancing on him even as he was backing away. The rest of the family cleared a path for them.

"I'm not leaving Laurel Bay, I'm just...this house just isn't the right fit for me," he said with a bit of hesitation.

"You broke the heart of the nicest girl in this town and now you're running away like a coward!" she said with disgust. "I raised you better than that." Turning her back on him, she went back to setting up food. "Everyone, eat before it gets cold!"

He got a few minutes' reprieve while everyone made themselves a plate and then did their best to find a spot to eat at his small kitchen table.

"Not even a decent place to eat," his father said as he shook his head. "Maybe we should have done this at the pub."

"If I'd known everyone was coming over, I would have had more options," he murmured as he walked to the garage and grabbed a folding table. Patrick and Will were right behind him grabbing some chairs. It still wasn't enough for everyone to have a seat, but it would be fine.

"I can't believe you're going to sell this house already," Arianna said. "It's so cute and has so much potential and..." With a soft gasp, she looked at Will. "We should buy it!"

"What?!" everyone said.

"Oh, stop being dramatic. You all know Will and I are looking for a place and we haven't found anything we like. But we both thought this house was...you know...kind of great, right?"

Nodding, Will looked around. "It definitely needs work..."

"And furniture," Shane chimed in.

"Okay," Jamie called out. "For the sake of moving things along because the pub is actually kind of busy tonight and some of us are supposed to be working, can we forget about Liam's lack of furniture and focus on why we're here?"

"Ryleigh?" their mother said.

"He's still in love with Tessa and is moving because it hurts to be this close," his sister said.

"Hey!" he snapped at her. "What the hell?"

"Dude, you've been gone for too long. This is how we work. Deal with it," Ryleigh said with a sweet smile before taking a bite of her dinner.

"Great! So everyone knows my pain. Awesome," he said as he placed his dinner plate on the counter. "Why are you all here then?"

"Because you clearly need help," Arianna said. "You've spent most of your life doing things to help all of us. Now it's our turn to help you."

Shit.

That was...kind of sweet.

"Plus, we're tired of you moping all over the place," Jamie chimed in. "I swear, every time you walk into the pub, everyone gets depressed. It's enough."

"I'm more than happy to help you find another house," Patrick offered, "but I think you're jumping the gun here. If you can work things out with Tessa, maybe the next move will be a place for the two of you."

His eyes went wide and a sense of panic nearly choked him. "Already? Seriously? I mean...it's too soon! We haven't been together that long! We...we..."

"Your mother and I got married six weeks after our first date," his father said before reaching over and kissing his wife's hand.

"And Will and I fell in love on our first date," Arianna reminded him. "And if it hadn't been for you, we could have been together sooner."

231

"Are you ever going to let that go?" Liam asked.

She pretended to think about it. "Depends on whether you screw up our plan."

Liam looked around the room. "Wait...so there's a plan? You all already have something worked up?"

"Follow all of our instructions, and we can guarantee that Tessa will take you back," Ryleigh told him confidently.

"But...how?"

"First, eat your dinner," his mother reprimanded. "Then we'll talk."

"But..."

"Oh my God! Are you *already* not following instructions?" Jamie laughed. "I told you guys he was going to screw this up!"

There was no way he was going to prove his little brother right, so after making a dramatic zipping motion across his lips, Liam picked up his plate and ate every last bite.

* * *

The holiday concert was two days away and Tessa was feeling good about the whole thing. As she walked down the hall toward the school auditorium, she went through the checklist in her head to make sure she wasn't forgetting anything.

There was a flurry of activity going on at the end of the hall, and she picked up her pace to see what was going on. Making her way through the crowd of teachers, she walked into the auditorium and froze.

"What the...?"

"Oh, Tessa!" Principal Channing called out. "We just

received this donation for the holiday concert! Come and show us where you want it all placed!"

Slowly, she made her way down the aisle toward the stage.

There were a half-dozen fully decorated Christmas trees, dozens of giant snowflakes, easily a dozen red and white poinsettias, and a giant Santa sleigh filled with wrapped gifts. Climbing up onto the stage, she looked around in wonder. "I don't...I don't understand. Who did this?"

"Kate and Shane Donovan," he told her with a smile. "Donovan's Pub. Isn't it fantastic?"

She wanted to be upset that Liam shared this information with his parents, but...her auditorium was going to look fantastic! Making a mental note to stop by the pub on the way home, Tessa immediately went to work instructing volunteers on the placement of everything.

It took two hours because of the giant snowflakes, but when she stepped out into the auditorium would sit and looked around, tears stung her eyes. "It's perfect," she whispered. "Absolutely perfect."

"This all looks amazing, Tessa," Kelly Riley, the school art teacher, said. "That was very generous of the Donovans to do this. And the fact that the trees are artificial means we can use them again next year!"

"Definitely!"

"So, how did the Donovans know about the concert? Are they friends of yours?"

Nodding, she fought back a wave of sadness. "They are and they are seriously some of the best people."

"And their food is delicious," Kelly added with a laugh. "Which reminds me, I need to get home. Eric's cooking for me tonight and I don't want to be late. Have a good night!"

"You too, Kelly! And thanks for the help!"

Tessa walked back up to the stage and simply marveled at how everything looked exactly as she had imagined it and knew she needed to go to the pub right now and thank Shane and Kate. Hopefully she wouldn't run into Liam, but if she did, she'd thank him too for making all of this possible.

Out in the parking lot, she was about to get in her car when Principal Channing jogged over. "Oh, good, Tessa. I was afraid I'd missed you."

"Is everything okay?"

Nodding, he gave her a nervous smile. "I sort of have a rather...unorthodox favor to ask."

That sounded...awkward.

"O-kay..."

"I'd like to do something a little...spontaneous that will surprise my wife for our anniversary."

"Oh?"

"It's actually on Thursday and she was upset that it's the night of the holiday concert and that I have to be here, so..."

"Oh, Principal Channing, if you need someone else to go up and make the announcements, I'm sure no one would mind!" she assured him.

"It's tradition," he said lightly, "and it's important for me to be here to show support for the students."

"That's incredibly sweet of you."

"Anyway, her favorite Christmas song is 'Christmas, Baby Please Come Home.' They played it at our wedding and...well...I'd really love it if I could sing it to her at the beginning of the concert."

It was also the song she had tried to get Liam to sing with her.

Tessa hoped her smile didn't look too forced. "You want...to sing? At the concert?"

He nodded.

"If you don't have the sheet music or if you don't think you can play it, I have the instrumental version that we can play and I can just sing along to that. What do you think?"

I think this could be incredibly awkward...

"I didn't realize you enjoyed singing," she said instead.

"Well, I'm not very good at it. But what I lack in talent, I more than make up for in heart. So what do you say? Would you mind lending me the stage for a few brief minutes?"

Like she could say no to her boss.

"I think it will be a wonderful surprise," she said with a smile. "And I think we should maybe use your instrumental version and I'll play along on the piano. I bet the kids will get a real kick out of the whole thing."

He chuckled softly. "Oh, I'm not sure about that, but I'm willing to try." Smiling, he opened her car door for her. "Thanks, Tessa. And have a good night!"

"You too!"

Within minutes, she was driving across town toward Donovan's Pub and sang along to the radio so she wouldn't be able to obsess about whether or not she'd run into Liam.

The parking lot wasn't too crowded when she pulled in and there was no sign of his truck, so...she breathed a sigh of relief. Inside the pub, she spotted Mrs. Donovan first and smiled when the older woman came bustling over to hug her.

"Oh, Tessa, sweetie, how are you? Did you get the decorations?"

Tessa squeezed her extra hard. "You are like a guardian angel!" Pulling back, she couldn't help but smile. "I took a bunch of pictures so I could show you how beautiful it all looks! The kids are going to be thrilled!"

"It was our pleasure. When Liam told us how the school had cut your budget, well...Shane and I could not let that happen! All of my kids were in the chorus in elementary school. Arianna's the only one who stuck with it all the way through high school though." She made a tsk-tsking sound. "So, we have a lot of fond memories of the holiday concerts."

"Wait...even Liam? He sang in the chorus?"

"Oh, yes! As his mother, I'm allowed to say that he wasn't very good, but he did it because it was what we expected of him." With a bit of a giggle, she whispered, "Although I think he just didn't want to do it because when he was older, I'd occasionally hear him singing when he thought no one was listening, but...I'm always listening." Winking, she added, "Either way, once he described what you wanted to do and how you had limited resources, Shane and I knew we had to do something."

"I am just so thankful. Truly. You've made this the absolute best concert the school has ever seen—certainly the most festive and magical!"

Smiling, Kate gave her a gentle pat on the cheek. "I love seeing you so happy, Tessa. It makes my heart feel good." Looking around, she motioned for her to follow. "Come and sit. Ryleigh and I were going to have something to eat. You'll join us!"

"Oh, um...okay." She kept glancing around, but there was no sign of Liam.

And now she wasn't sure if she was happy or disappointed.

They sat in a corner booth—or rather, Tessa sat, and Ryleigh immediately joined her.

"Shane made his famous shepherd's pie," Kate told her. "Would you like that or would you prefer something else?"

"That actually sounds fantastic! Thank you!"

"I'll have that too, Mom."

"Hmm...no. I think you should have the spinach salad with the grilled salmon. I'll tell your father to go easy on the butter."

"Mom!" Ryleigh hissed. "Stop it! I'm a grown woman and I can certainly eat what I want for dinner."

"Fine, have the shepherd's pie, but don't come crying to me when the last of your friends gets married and you can't find a plus one to take to their weddings." And with a huff, she turned and went to the kitchen.

"Ugh, she makes me crazy!" Ryleigh groaned. "Are all mothers like this or do I just have rotten luck?"

"I'm probably not the right person to ask right now. In my eyes, your mother's a hero. She kind of saved my little holiday concert at school."

"Oh, right. The decorations! They got there today?"

Nodding, Tessa pulled out her phone and showed Ryleigh the pictures. "They're perfect! Like if I could have gone shopping and picked it all out myself, I would have gotten the exact same ones! I practically cried when I walked into the auditorium and saw them."

"I'm glad. Liam mentioned how bummed you were that the school cut your budget, so I'm glad my parents could help."

She nodded again and had to fight the urge to ask how Liam was doing.

But clearly, she was transparent.

"He's a mess, you know," Ryleigh softly told her. "I mean, he's always a little surly, but since the two of you... you know...he's even worse. I don't know what happened between you guys and I'm not asking you to tell me, just... just know that Liam's one of the good guys. He sticks his foot in his mouth a lot, but ultimately, he's someone you can rely on."

Sighing, Tessa studied her hands rather than look directly at Ryleigh. "You have to say that. You're his sister."

"Um...actually, I don't. Look over at the bar. See Jamie?"

Tessa nodded.

"He's a complete doofus and I would encourage no one to get involved with him. He's cocky, arrogant, completely self-centered, and too good-looking for his own good. Basically, he's exhausting." Then she scanned the room again. "And then there's Patrick. See him in the corner talking to the older guy in a suit?"

Again, she nodded.

"Patrick's a workaholic. He's determined to rebuild this entire town and make a name for himself. It's very admirable, but he's clueless. I wouldn't set him up with anyone I know either because he'd end up ignoring them because he's too busy practically making love to his phone." She groaned and then shuddered. "But Liam? All of my friends had crushes on him. He's got that serious and broody thing going for him, but deep down, you know he's not a douche."

Unable to help herself, Tessa laughed out loud as she looked at Ryleigh. "Oh my goodness! That was...wow!"

"All I'm saying is, if you're even remotely thinking of giving him another chance, you should."

She considered her next words very carefully.

"It took me a long time to open myself up to getting involved with anyone," she began. "And Liam brought out a lot of strong feelings in me. Most of them weren't good."

Nodding, Ryleigh said, "Sounds about right."

"But he also proved that first impressions aren't everything."

Kate put a couple of glasses of wine on the table before excusing herself again.

"I'm someone who loves to talk, Ryleigh. I believe communicating is one of the most important things in any relationship. Anyone can hop into bed together and have a good time, but if that's all there is, what's the point?"

"That depends. Are there a lot of orgasms?" she teased, causing Tessa to laugh again. "Sorry, that was childish of me. Go on."

"Liam doesn't talk about anything personal. I knew all about his military career and everything about this fishing resort project, but I had no idea how he felt. I don't want a superficial relationship with anyone. When I'm in a rela-tionship—whether it's platonic or romantic—I'm completely in. Liam holds himself back and...and I can't live like that."

"I get it, but..."

"And he's so uptight! He refuses to just have fun! He wouldn't even sing Christmas songs with me! I mean... everyone sings Christmas songs!" She laughed. "I get that most military guys are a bit more...reserved, but I just wish he would have loosened up even a little and showed that he had even a teeny tiny whimsical side."

"Now you're looking for a unicorn," Ryleigh said flatly. "That doesn't exist. I've never met a guy who would will-ingly sing or show his...whimsical side." She sighed dramati-cally. "And if I did, I'd totally date him."

"Sleigh bells ring, are you listening?" A deep male voice sang out, and Ryleigh groaned.

"Ew, Ryker! Knock it off!" she snapped before hiding her face in her hands.

Tessa looked up and saw a guy who looked a bit scary grinning at them. He had dark hair and both arms were covered in tattoos. "Um…"

"Just ignore him and hopefully he'll go away," she mumbled. "Jeez, what is wrong with him?" Looking up, she glared at the guy. "And stop listening to my conversations, creep!"

He held up his beer in a toast to her before facing the bar again.

"Anyway," Ryleigh said after a minute. "Just…think about it. About Liam. Okay?"

It was pointless to argue right now, especially when she spotted Mrs. Donovan walking toward them with a tray loaded with food.

"I've got this holiday concert to get through, but I promise once that's done, I'll…I'll think about it."

Grinning, Ryleigh hugged her. "That's all I ask."

Chapter Fifteen

"Did I tell you we have interest from one of those big fishing blogs?" Will said a couple of days later. "They reached out and would like to do a piece on the resort. They'd like to come and scope out the property and get some before pictures and then asked if they could be part of the soft opening so they could promote us. What do you think?"

Liam was staring at the email he'd been trying to read for the last ten minutes and finally gave up. "How did they hear about us?"

"Your sister's marketing campaign. I'm telling you; Ryleigh's a genius. If we can get some free publicity from the bloggers and influencers, we can really hit the ground running."

"Are there fishing influencers? That doesn't seem like it's a thing."

"Yeah, I'm not really sure, but it seems like there are influencers for everything. If one or two of them want to do a blog post or some kind of TikTok video about the resort, who am I to argue?"

"I agree," he said and went back to reading the email.

"So, any big plans for tonight?" Will asked with a knowing grin on his face.

"Shut up."

"Oh, come on!" he said with a laugh. "Are we seriously not going to talk about this?"

With a huff of annoyance, Liam closed his laptop and glared at Will. "I'm going to watch Tessa's concert tonight. I'm going to present her with a massive bouquet of flowers and pretty much beg and grovel for her to take me back. There. Happy? We talked about it."

"Dude, come on. I know we all ambushed you the other night, but…are you sure you're up to this?"

"Believe it or not, I'm perfectly capable of talking to Tessa. By showing up at the concert and giving her the flowers in front of everyone, she'll see that I'm comfortable going public with our relationship."

"And public groveling, so…that's got to work in your favor."

Frowning, he shot Will a glare. "I've got this under control. Trust me."

But his friend didn't look the least bit convinced. "I know you say that and I heard everything you said at your place, but…are flowers going to really be enough? I mean… are you suddenly okay with how she's still kind of hanging on to this Trevor guy?"

Standing, Liam paced a bit, his hands raking through his hair in frustration. "Who am I to say how someone's supposed to grieve, huh? I never lost a best friend or anyone that I loved. We lost buddies while we were deployed and it was awful, but it wasn't ever anyone who was so deeply entrenched in my life," he explained and saw Will nod. "You lost your mom not even two years ago. Are you saying you don't think about her or have reminders of her anywhere?"

"I think about her all the time—especially since I met Arianna. I think my mom would've loved her and it sucks that she's not here to meet her." Shaking his head, he let out a long breath. "I didn't have time to fully grieve because of my commitment to the military. I don't know if things would have been different if I'd been home while she was sick and right there with her when she died."

"Exactly. Who the hell am I to give her shit about this?" he said with more than a hint of self-disgust. "God...I think about the things I've said and I can't believe she didn't kick my ass to the curb sooner."

"Well, yeah. We're all wondering that," Will said with a small laugh. "But...I guess I just want to make sure you're going back with both eyes open. Nothing's changed in the last week or so. She's not going to miraculously be over her grief and her house isn't going to be stripped of memories that you aren't a part of."

"I know," he said solemnly. "And I don't expect any of that. I guess I just wanted to feel like there was room for me in her life, but...that's on me for not talking to her about it."

"Believe me, I know that talking about feelings and shit is not our strong suit, but other people need it."

"Like my sister?" he teased.

"Actually, your sister is more like you than you think. She's kind of comfortable with not talking about her emotions because she thinks she's got everything under control. And to be honest, it pissed me off in the beginning. I mean, I get that I should have talked to her when I realized she was your sister and all that, but once I landed here in Laurel Bay and we were dating..."

"Sneaking around," Liam corrected with a grin.

"Whatever," Will snapped. "Once I was here, it was like there was one miscommunication after another and I hated it. Now we know we have to talk, and sometimes it totally sucks. But...we also haven't had any major issues since we started doing that. So...learn from me."

It annoyed him how much he was having to learn from everyone around him because it made him feel like he wasn't nearly as smart or together as he'd thought.

And that shit was humbling.

"I appreciate your concern," he said after a moment. "I really do. But...I've got to do this and if I fail, then...then I'll deal with it. I just know that I can't keep sitting around doing nothing. You all crammed that point down my throat the other night." Sitting back in his chair, he gave Will a weak smile. "I'm prepared to deal with whatever goes down. In a perfect world, Tessa will forgive me and we can go back to a better version of who we were."

"And in an imperfect world?"

"Then you're going to have to deal with me being in a miserable mood for however long it takes for me to get my shit together." Then his smile grew. "That almost seems like it could be fun."

"Don't be a dick," Will murmured as he stood. "Now if you'll excuse me, the trailer carrying cabin number four should be here any minute and I want to go oversee the install." He grabbed his phone and keys. "You want to come and check it all out?"

"Um...I'll be out soon. I've got a couple of emails to go through."

"Sounds good."

As soon as Will was out the door, Liam opened his laptop and re-read the email he was trying to focus on earlier. His initial reaction was to simply type, "No way," but...that wasn't how this worked.

He was an adult, a business owner, a veteran, and someone who was smart enough to know that there were going to be times when he was going to have to suck it up and do something he didn't want to do.

Even if it was part of the plan.

Still, as he leaned back in his chair, he wondered if there was maybe a way around this request.

Off in the distance, he could hear the truck pulling in with the constructed cabin on it. There were more than enough guys on the crew outside to help with whatever needed to be done, but there was a part of him that really enjoyed seeing the cabins go up and get put in place. Will's suggestion to build them off-site had seemed a bit convoluted, but he had to admit that things went much smoother than he had ever expected.

"I can simply pretend I didn't see the email..."

But...he wasn't a liar.

A coward at times, and a poor communicator, yes. But a liar? No.

"Shit."

And before he could second-guess himself or talk himself out of it, Liam quickly typed up the response and hit send.

Closing his laptop, he prayed he didn't just make the biggest mistake of his life.

* * *

The noise was almost unbearable.

Students were chasing each other around backstage, parents were lingering where they weren't supposed to be, and Carrie Nolan, her assistant, was hovering over Tessa's shoulder like they were conjoined twins.

"Is there something you need, Carrie?" she finally asked, forcing a smile.

"I...I just wanted to make sure I was close by if you needed anything. I know you've put a lot into this concert and want it to go off without a hitch," she said sweetly.

She was a very nice woman—a perfectly wonderful assistant—and yet right now she wished she would handle some of the chaos without being told.

But apparently not.

"Can you please round up the students and line them up by grade so we can be ready when it's time to take the stage in ten minutes? Remind them now is the time to grab a last drink of water or use the bathroom. Enlist the help of some of the parents who shouldn't be back here if you need to."

"I'm on it!" Carrie said cheerily as she walked away, and it was the first time Tessa took a relaxing breath in almost an hour.

With no one hindering her, she walked around the stage and made sure everything was in its place. The risers for the students to stand on were all secured, her piano was in its place, all the trees were lit up, her snowflakes were twinkling, and the giant sled was looking incredibly festive.

It was magical and so darn perfect that she almost cried. Again.

Although, she was fairly certain some of her emotions were still because of Liam and their breakup.

After sharing a lovely dinner with Kate and Ryleigh Donovan, Tessa had gone home and had herself a good, long think. Although, to be fair, all she'd been doing lately was thinking.

Or...overthinking.

Still, the end result was the same. Liam might not have handled things properly, but he was still right. Between spending the afternoon with Trevor's mom, the weekend with her family, and then dinner with Kate and Ryleigh, Tessa came to realize just how delusional she'd been in her grief. Trevor wasn't a martyr; he was just a man. He was a man whose life had been unfairly cut short, but...he'd also been far from perfect.

And her house had become a bit of a shrine to him.

So, in the last few days, she made some changes and put things away. Photos had gone into scrapbooks where she kept some of her most cherished memories. Memorabilia had gone into the hope chest in her guest room, and some of the assorted knick-knacks had simply been put away. It was okay to keep them and maybe pull them out once in a while, but there was no need to surround herself with them every day.

It was time for new memories.

New memorabilia.

New knick-knacks and ornaments.

And once this concert was over, she was going to go home, let Phoebe out, and then march over to Liam's house and demand that he talk to her and give her a second chance.

"Tessa!" Principal Channing called out as he walked onto the stage looking extremely...um...festive.

Ugly sweater festive.

Oh, Lord...

"Hey!" she said sweetly. "Look at you! You certainly got into the holiday spirit!"

"My wife bought this sweater for me and insisted the students would get a kick out of it," he said proudly. "Oh, and this!" He put a Santa hat on and for a man in his 60s, he certainly seemed to be extremely confident in looking... well...silly.

Meanwhile, she had opted for a long black wool skirt, black boots, and a red sweater.

And a Santa hat.

The two of them standing beside each other must look utterly ridiculous.

"I love that you got into the spirit of things," she told him. "Are you ready for your big solo?"

"I am!" Glancing around, he asked, "So...I'll be standing over here, right?"

"Yes, it's the same spot you'll be doing your opening remarks." Then she realized there was one tiny detail they hadn't discussed. "Will you be singing before or after them?"

"Before," he said as he straightened his hat. "I figured that's how we'd open the show. I'll sing to my sweet Rachel and then kick off the concert before joining her in the front row. Will that be okay?"

"I actually believe it's perfect. Your wife is a lucky woman. Most men wouldn't go to such extremes to do something so romantic."

"Well...I have to admit, I had a little help coming up with it, so I can't take all the credit."

Reaching out, she gave his arm a gentle squeeze. "It's still such a wonderful gesture."

"Tessa!" Carrie called out. "We need you!"

"If you'll excuse me, Principal Channing," she said apologetically. "And remember, the curtain will open in five minutes."

"*Tessa!*"

"Um...hopefully," she murmured. "Just...watch for my cue."

He gave her a thumbs-up before she turned and walked away.

Rushing across the stage, she breathlessly looked around. "What's up?"

"Okay, um...Jessica Roland threw up and sort of ruined her dress. Her mother is taking her home, but they won't be back in time to sing."

"Oh, no! I hope she's okay!"

"It was her nerves, her mom said. So...there's that."

Something about the way she said "there's that" told Tessa there was more. "And...?"

"Eric Bailey will only wear his tie on his head," she went on. "His parents are talking to him right now."

"O-kay...anything else?" she asked, laughing nervously.

"Just..." She paused. "Don't freak out, okay?"

Tessa's eyes went wide as she waited for what else could possibly go wrong.

"Mrs. Perkins—you know, the old music teacher you replaced—caught wind of Principal Channing's opening number and she's insisting on being the one to play the piano for him."

"What?! Why? Why would she want to do that?"

"She claims that they used to do the faculty talent show together and she'd like to surprise him and...and...I don't know what to tell her! She's kind of scary."

Tessa instantly spotted the woman in question and plastered a smile on her face as she walked over. "Hey, Mrs. Perkins! It's so nice of you to join us tonight. Carrie says you'd like to play the piano during Principal Channing's song."

"I'm going to have to insist," the older woman said

firmly. "Damon and I go way back and as much as I'm sure you're a fine pianist, I know he'd want me to be the one playing for him."

Was this woman for real?

"Um..."

"Now, if you'll excuse me, I'm going to take my seat. Why don't you get your student calmed down and lead them out onto the risers? It's showtime!" Then she walked away, leaving Tessa and Carrie staring after her, dumbfounded.

"Did that woman just steal my thunder?" she whispered.

"I think she did," Carrie agreed.

"Should I do something? Maybe go over and ask her to step aside, since this is my show?"

"Tessa, I think you'd have to physically remove her from the piano bench and we both know that's not going to happen."

"So I'm supposed to just let her steal the show?"

"It's one song and maybe it's for the best. This way you can stand back here with me and cringe a little. I can't imagine Principal Channing being a great singer. And that sweater is very distracting."

"Hmm...maybe. Still, it's not right."

"No, but it *is* seven-thirty and we need to get started, so..."

"You're right. You're right." And with a huff of annoyance, Tessa got everything in motion. She had the students in their places and then gave the stage crew the cue to raise the curtain. On the opposite side of the stage, she motioned for Principal Channing to take his spot.

Turning her back on the stage, she walked back to where Carrie was standing as the first notes began to play—

both on the piano and the recording they were using for backup.

"It's Christmas...baby, please come home..."

"That doesn't sound like Principal Channing," she said, and noticed that Carrie was grinning like a loon. "What...?" Then she turned and gasped.

There, in the center of the stage, stood Liam Donovan wearing a red sweater with a snowman on it, a Santa hat, and...he was singing.

"The snow's comin' down...I'm watchin' it fall...Lots of people around...Baby, please come home..."

"What in the world? What is happening right now?" she whispered.

"Just...enjoy," Carrie said before giving her a quick hug.

"They're singin' 'Deck The Halls'...But it's not like Christmas at all...I remember when you were here...And all the fun we had last year!"

Tears stung her eyes and she wanted to run out on the stage and hug him, but right now all she could do was stand there and watch this incredible man leave his comfort zone so completely—so publicly—so he could show her how he felt.

At least, she hoped that's what this was all about and that he hadn't lost a bet or anything.

Focus, Tessa!

Liam smiled as he sang as if it were just the two of them. He only had eyes for her, and it was the greatest moment of her life.

"Pretty lights on the tree...I'm watchin' 'em shine...You should be here with me...Baby, please come home..."

Wait...who was singing the chorus with her? She wondered. Was it the recording or...

"Look at my Arianna and Ryleigh singing up there to

251

support their big brother!" Kate Donovan said as she walked up beside her. "It's just like when they were little kids!"

Now Tessa had to wonder if she was even awake or if this was some kind of dream. "Mrs. Donovan! What...?"

"Shh...it's his big finish!" she murmured softly.

After another chorus of "Baby, please come home," there was a rousing round of applause. She knew he was going to come over to her and she couldn't wait to hug him and tell him how wonderful and exciting it was, but...he didn't move. Instead, he faced the audience.

"I'd like to thank all of you for humoring me and letting me take a few moments to sing a song to the most amazing woman in the world. You all know her. She's the happiest and most uplifting person I've ever met. She comes to this school every day with pure joy in her heart because she gets to teach music to your children." Pausing, he smiled at her. "You might not believe this, but she loves singing all the time—not just here at school. Personally, I never met anyone who just found so much delight in simply singing a song. The last time I truly sang, it was on this very stage when I was a student here. Oh, sure...maybe I've sang a bit of a song here or there according to my mother, but this stage was the last time I sang a complete song. Until tonight."

There was another round of applause.

"And I did it because Tessa Sullivan asked me to sing with her not so long ago—we were decorating her Christmas tree and I refused to do it. And I've regretted it ever since. So, tonight was a chance for me to sing for her," he went on. "With an audience, otherwise no one would believe her."

Everyone laughed.

"So, thank you again for humoring me. Now, I'll pass the mic to Principal Channing so I can go and grovel to my girl. Have a great night and enjoy the concert!" Liam said as he walked off the stage and right into Tessa's arms.

"Oh my goodness!" she whispered against his neck and he lifted her into his arms. "That was amazing! I can't believe you did all that for me!"

"We helped," Arianna said as she walked over to join them, followed by Ryleigh and Will, but Liam didn't seem ready to put her down yet.

"Okay, you three, let's go take our seats and we'll all celebrate at the pub after the concert. I made some nice pies," Kate said as she herded her family away.

And still Liam didn't put her down.

His arms felt incredible around her and Tessa wanted to kiss him and gush over his song, but...

"Liam," she finally said. "I need you to put me down. The concert..."

Slowly, he lowered her to her feet and gave her the sexiest smile she'd ever seen right before he kissed her. It was deep and wet and so full of naughty promises that her knees threatened to give out.

When he lifted his head and caressed her cheek, he said, "Go and do what you have to do, but know that I'll be waiting right here to bring you home."

Her cheeks heated and she hoped she could remember how to play the piano or how to do anything that she needed to for the concert.

Although...Mrs. Perkins was already at the piano...

No! Bad Tessa!

Reluctantly, she took her place at the piano and caught the knowing look in Mrs. Perkins' eyes.

"You're a lucky girl, Ms. Sullivan. Not many men would go to such lengths to prove their love." Squeezing Tessa's hand, she walked away.

"May I present to you," Principal Channing was saying, "Laurel Bay Elementary's favorite music teacher, Ms. Tessa Sullivan!"

Smiling brightly, she walked out to the center of the stage and faced the audience to a loud round of applause.

"Thank you, parents, students, and faculty, for joining us tonight for our annual holiday concert. I had prepared a big speech, but I think we're all ready to hear all the hard work your babies have done for tonight. So may I present to you the Laurel Bay Chorus and our holiday celebration!"

After that, Tessa played through all eight songs the full chorus sang and the three solos they prepared. The kindergarten class put on a short play before everyone was back on stage for the big finale. When they were done, the applause was deafening and one of the sweetest sounds she'd ever heard.

Liam singing to her would forever be at the top of the list, though.

Before she knew what was happening, he strode out onto the stage and gave her the biggest bouquet of roses she'd ever seen in her life. Kissing her hand, he stepped back and led a second round of applause.

Once the curtain closed, it seemed like a monumental task to make sure all her students were safely with their parents and for her to do a final sweep of the backstage area. And through it all, Liam stood and patiently waited for her.

"Oh my goodness," she said when it was finally just the two of them. "What a night!"

"The show was great, Tessa," he told her. "You did an incredible job and should be very proud."

"The kids did all the work and I'm so proud of them. They deserve all the praise." He helped her put on her coat, but there was something she couldn't figure out. Turning, she asked, "How did you pull this off? And how did you get Principal Channing in on it?"

Grinning, Liam took her by the hand and led her toward the exit. "He and my dad are good friends so..."

"I can't believe he agreed," she commented, and as they walked out the door, they thanked Carl, the school resource officer, and wished him a goodnight.

"I know my mother mentioned the pub," he said as he walked her to her car, "but if you'd rather go home..."

That was exactly what she wanted, but she felt a bit guilty. "I kind of think I need to at least stop by and thank everyone again. They donated all the decorations and really made my vision come to life. So...would you be disappointed if we stopped there for a little while?"

Pulling her into his arms, he smiled down at her. "Do you promise that we'll only stay for an hour or less?" he teased.

"I promise," she replied. "Believe me, I'd really like to be home right now with you and hear all about how you came up with this plan tonight." Pausing, she just took in the sight of him. "Liam...I'm...I'm dazzled. No one's ever done anything like that for me and..."

He placed a finger over her lips. "We'll talk about it all when we get home." At her car, he paused. "How about we actually swing by the houses on our way? This way you can let Phoebe out and then we can take just one car to the pub. What do you think?"

"That's brilliant!" Going up on her toes, she kissed him quickly before pulling back. "I'll see you there!"

Feeling beyond giddy, Tessa started her car and was out of the now-empty parking lot in the blink of an eye. The drive was short and as she turned onto their block, it was almost blindingly bright.

"What in the world...?" She knew her own decorations were bright and several neighbors had gone equally overboard with their lights, but she'd never seen it quite like this before.

She hit the brakes hard in front of Liam's house.

It was like he had matched everything she had in her yard and on her house and doubled it.

Laughing hysterically, she pulled into her own driveway and then made her way through the maze of inflatable reindeer until she got to where he had just pulled his truck in.

"So?" he asked proudly. "What do you think? Impressive, right?"

"Oh my goodness, Liam! What did you do?"

Walking over, he put his arm around her and turned her to face the yard. "Well, obviously I had to put lights on the house."

"Um...how many sets did you use?"

"I'm not sure...maybe, twenty?"

"*Liam!* My house only took five!"

He shrugged. "Then I got the inflatable Santa and all the reindeer..."

"They really are cute," she said.

"But then I saw Santa's Workshop and had to get it because, well...it made sense. Then I got the giant mug of cocoa with the gingerbread man because it made me think of you."

"And the snowmen?"

He grinned. "They match yours, so I thought it would be cute if we twinned a little. Your snowmen are guarding your walkway and now so are mine!" He hugged her. "Adorable, right?"

"Beyond adorable," she told him before kissing his cheek. "But I really need to get Phoebe out if we're going to get to the pub and home at a reasonable hour. Tomorrow's a school day so I need to be up early."

"Actually...you don't."

"What do you mean I don't? Tomorrow's Friday. I have classes."

"Principal Channing gave you the day off and Will told me not to come in either, so...we've got all night to do whatever we want." Waggling his eyebrows playfully, he took her by the hand and led her across the yard toward her house.

The laugh was out before she could stop it. "So basically I've been in the dark on just about everything. Do I have that right?"

Liam considered her for a moment while she opened the front door. "Maybe a little, but it was done with the best of intentions. I'm sure if you want to go to school in the morning, you can..."

She never let him finish.

Dragging him into the house, she shut the door and kissed him the way she'd been wanting to ever since he finished singing.

Maybe they'd get to the pub, maybe they wouldn't.

All she knew was that right now, this was exactly where they were supposed to be.

Chapter Sixteen

"How did I not know this was going to happen?" Will asked an hour later when Liam and Tessa finally showed up at the pub.

"Because you have a big mouth, baby," Arianna said. "And you were either going to dog poor Liam about it or try to talk him out of it."

"I wouldn't have done either of those things," he argued, but he was smirking so everyone knew he was lying.

"Did anyone happen to take a video?" Jamie asked. "I can't believe no one told me this was going down!"

"You definitely would have dogged him about it," Ryleigh said with a laugh. "And poor Liam was nervous enough."

They were crammed in the corner booth with barely any room to breathe, and yet it was the happiest he had ever remembered being. Tessa was pressed up against him with his arm around her, and they were laughing and joking with his family while eating a variety of appetizers.

"I wasn't nervous," he countered. "I just didn't know if I was going to be able to do it without um...you know..."

"Throwing up because you were nervous?" Jamie asked as he reached for a fried pickle chip.

"Oh, stop," Arianna said. "Like you'd ever be able to get up and do something like that."

"Me? I've gotten up and sang karaoke plenty of times!"

"That's different," Ryleigh told him. "Liam went out there in front of the entire school and sang to win Tessa over. You just get up and sing karaoke hoping to get laid." Then she shuddered and reached for her own pickle chip.

Turning his head, his lips gently brushed against Tessa's ear. "So...did I?"

She smiled and hummed softly. "Did you what?"

"Win you over?"

Pulling back a little, she nodded. "Definitely. That whole thing was my love language."

"Bad singing is your love language?" he teased, kissing the tip of her nose. "Good to know."

"It wasn't that bad. Everyone loved it."

"Yeah, but people also seem to enjoy watching train wrecks, so..." Jamie supplied before sliding out of the booth. "I'm going to grab another plate of these. Any other requests?"

"How about some cheese fries?" Liam asked. "Or sliders? Or both?"

Everyone laughed and as Jamie walked away, Patrick walked in and joined them. "Sorry I'm late," he said as he slid into the booth. "I'm guessing by the goofy grin on your face and the fact that Tessa's here that you didn't scare her off with your singing."

"That's right," Liam said, feeling a bit cocky. "She loved it."

All his brother did was roll his eyes before holding up his phone. "I guess we could take your word for it since she's sitting right here and not denying it, but for those of you who would like to rewatch the action, I've got it all right here."

"Wait, *what?*" Liam asked as he sat up straighter.

"And it's up on YouTube. But don't tell Jamie. I'm gonna try to make some money off of him first before letting him know it's out there for all the world to see."

"Oh no..."

"Stop," Tessa said, kissing his cheek. "It was amazing and now we can always look back on it! Thank you, Patrick!"

The teasing went on for several minutes and then they all sat back and laughed when—in true Jamie fashion—he practically begged Patrick to let him see the video. They haggled and eventually he handed over fifty bucks for the right to see it.

And as soon as it was done, Patrick informed him of its location on the internet.

"Dude, you suck! Dammit!" He stormed off with a round of colorful cursing while the rest of them continued to crack up.

"You know, that never gets old," Liam said. "He is way too gullible."

"I know, right? And Mom and Dad think he's going to be able to handle running the pub? Even short-term?" Patrick asked.

"Yeah, but...someone's got to do it," Ryleigh chimed in. "And when we're not here setting him up to look like a doofus, he does kind of take it seriously, so..." She shrugged.

They ate and talked for at least an hour when Liam decided it was time to go. Fortunately, no one stopped them and he only had to get ribbed a little more about how maybe he should sing the rest of his apology to Tessa or maybe start a caroling group.

Jerks.

It wasn't until they were walking up to Tessa's door a few minutes later that he felt a little nervous. When they were here earlier, she had pretty much destroyed him with a quick and fierce seduction. It had taken him completely by surprise but was totally worth it.

Now he knew they were going to have to talk and he was afraid his mouth was going to get him in trouble again.

"I know we just finished eating, but would you like something to drink?"

"Thanks, but I'm good." Sitting on the sofa, he motioned to the spot next to him. "Do you need to let Phoebe out?"

"I think she's okay for right now. We weren't gone that long."

Nodding, Liam took a moment to gather his thoughts. When he looked up at her, he said, "I'm sorry. I never should have dumped all my hang-ups on you the way I did. It wasn't fair to you and it was just..." Pausing, he sighed. "I've never done this before. I've never been in love with anyone and I feel like I never know what to say or what to do."

"Liam..."

"Things always came easily to me. As the oldest, all my siblings were compared to me. In school, I did really well and everyone was compared to me."

"Liam..."

"But here? Suddenly, I felt like I was being compared to someone, and it freaked me out. I know I should have handled it better, but it was all new to me!" With a growl of frustration, he leaned back against the cushions. "I know singing a song doesn't change anything, but I wanted you to see that I can do the things that you like and that I'm willing to try." Turning his head, he looked at her and his heart ached just looking at her beautiful face. "You're everything, Tessa. From the moment you fell out of that tree, you changed me. Tempted me. Please tell me I didn't screw things up for us."

With a serene smile, she placed her hand on his thigh. "Can I ask you something?"

"Anything."

"Do you like me?"

His eyes went wide. Was she crazy? "Why would you even ask me that? Of course I like you! I love you! Don't you get it?"

"When we met..."

"I was a complete jackass," he interrupted. "Seriously, I was the worst and I know it. I'm sorry for the way I acted at that wedding, but...I was wrong. I should have looked at you and appreciated your upbeat personality and the joy you felt in celebrating." He squeezed her hand. "I've never met anyone who embraces every aspect of life and...I don't think I'll ever get to that level, but I see how much happiness you bring to everyone you meet."

"Not you..."

"At first," he reminded her. "But I need it. I need that kind of thing in my life. I don't want to be the guy that people don't want to talk to or the neighbor nobody likes. I've been in charge of so many things in my life, Tessa, that sometimes I forget that not everyone needs me to be that way."

"You are a bit bossy..."

"And let me tell you something else. I have never—ever

—done anything like I did tonight for anyone else. And do you know why?"

"Because no one dared you to?"

Okay, so she wasn't going to make this easy. Fine.

"Because I never wanted or needed to. Tonight was about me proving to you that I am capable of change. If that's not enough, then tell me what I need to do because I'm committed to this, Tessa. I'm committed to *you*."

Her smile deepened a bit. "Well...you were already well on your way to making things up to me by singing at the holiday concert."

He nodded.

"Then you really got my attention with all the decorations in your yard."

He nodded again.

"But...do you know what sealed the deal?"

Shaking his head, he held her hand tightly in his. "Tell me. Tell me, beautiful girl."

"You said you loved me," she said dreamily, resting her forehead against his. "Those three things combined were more than I ever expected."

It was crazy how fast his heart was beating and how relieved he felt. He'd gone into combat in war-torn countries and yet this moment with this woman felt like the greatest challenge of his life.

And he'd won the greatest prize ever.

Her heart.

At least...he thought he had.

Lifting his head, he looked at her. "Okay, my turn. Can I ask you something?"

She nodded and gave him a shy smile. "Anything."

"How do you feel about me?"

"Um..."

Wouldn't it be a bitch if he'd just spilled his heart out to her only to find out she wasn't in the same place?

Holding his breath, Liam waited for her to explain.

The look of pure panic on Liam's face made her realize her mistake.

"Oh my goodness, Liam," she said, reaching up to cup his jaw. "I love you. So much! I was so afraid to…"

But she never got to finish because he hauled her into his lap and kissed her until she was gasping for breath. When they broke apart, she hummed with appreciation.

"I thought you were just trying to be a good guy when this whole thing started with us," she admitted. "I never did date a lot and I thought that maybe this was something friends did for one another." She laughed softly even as she shook her head. "But every meal we shared, every time we just sat around talking…I fell a little harder for you. And that day at the cabin? I couldn't believe someone like you would even want someone like me. Even if it was just as a friends with benefits thing."

"I tried telling myself that's all it was going to be," Liam told her solemnly. "But I was lying to myself and I knew it. Then I realized how unfair I was being to you because you genuinely trusted me."

"So you never wanted me to date anyone else?"

"Never. Why do you think I took you with me to the pub that time?"

"I knew it!" she said with a laugh. "You were acting so strangely that night and you made me think I was going crazy!" She punched him in the arm lightly. "Your whole family thought we were dating all the way back then?"

"All the way?" he repeated with amusement. "It wasn't that long ago and, Tessa, we were dating. It didn't matter if neither of us were brave enough to put a label on it. The fact was that we were dating. From the moment you kissed me, you were mine."

"Mmm...that's good because that was the moment I decided you were mine, too."

"Really?"

"Actually, no. Sorry," she said quietly. "It took me a little longer, but that's only because I obsess over things and didn't realize there was even a chance of this going anywhere for us."

Caressing her cheek, the look on his face was one of pure tenderness. "I have another admission."

"Oh?"

"I, um...I heard you talking to the real estate agent last week."

Drat. She had forgotten about that whole thing. "Liam, I..."

"But the funny thing about that is that right before I overheard you talking, I had just texted Patrick that I wanted to put my house up for sale."

"What? Why would you do that? You just bought it!"

"Because you love this house, Tessa. You made it a home and put your stamp all over it." He looked around the room and then frowned.

"What's the matter?"

"Something's different. What did you change?"

Carefully, she climbed off his lap and sat back and watched as Liam stood and began walking around. "I didn't notice anything earlier, but there's something just...different. Did you move the furniture around?"

"Nope."

He studied her Christmas tree and the mantle before heading for the dining room.

And stopped.

Turning around, he walked back over to the fireplace and looked at the built-ins. "Tessa," he said sadly. "What did you do?"

Rising, she went to him, wrapping her arms around his waist. "It's confession time for me too." With a small sigh, she explained. "You were right about everything. I wasn't living. I had created a safe little bubble for myself that actually turned into a shrine without me even realizing it. My family had been trying to tell me for years, but I wouldn't listen. Then you said it and it just made me angry. That's when I realized that maybe...maybe I had. After all, if everyone I knew was seeing it, it had to be there."

"Sweetheart, I never should have said anything. It's your house and like you said, you had a life before me and..."

"Liam, no. I'm glad you said the things you did because I needed someone to come out and just put it bluntly."

"No," he whined softly. "I shouldn't have..."

"Listen to me," she said as firmly as she could. "I am always going to be someone who looks on the bright side of everything. I am always going to cheer for the people around me to succeed and I'm going to want to celebrate everybody's achievements. But it's time for me to also start living a life for me and not the one that Trevor didn't get to live."

His expression saddened.

"I'm always going to miss him, but...you were right when you said he wouldn't want me to live like this. So... thank you."

Pulling her in close, he kissed the top of her head. "I'm so sorry. You never should have had to make that choice."

"The only one to blame is me." Stepping out of his arms, Tessa walked him around the house and pointed out the small changes she made. And when they ended up in the bedroom, she showed him the final one.

Holding up her left hand, she wiggled her fingers.

"Those were the first to go and I can't believe I was insensitive enough to keep them on while you and I were..."

"Don't," he said. "I think we're both done apologizing." Cupping her face in his hands, he smiled lovingly at her. "Are we good?"

She nodded. "We're good."

"Do you love me?"

"So much, Liam."

"That's good because I love you too." Glancing toward the bed, he winked playfully at her. "I know we kind of sort of made up earlier, but how about we do things properly right now and I promise to make things up to you all night and then again all day tomorrow?"

"Wow, look at you being all braggy about your stamina!"

"Let's just say I'm hopeful," he said bashfully before sitting on the bed and pulling her into the vee between his legs. "Don't sell this house, Tessa. It's great and you've put so much work into it."

"But I don't want you to sell yours either! You've been doing all kinds of work on it and..."

"And it's not a home," he told her. "No matter what I do to it, it's never going to be a home. Will and Arianna would like to buy it when I'm ready. They're already planning to restore it back to the way it was when it was built and maybe even putting a treehouse in the yard when they have kids."

Her heart melted.

"Where do you think you'll go?" She knew exactly where she wanted him to be but felt like maybe it was too soon to say anything.

And that's exactly how all their problems started, she realized.

"Would you consider maybe...living here with me for a little while?"

Frowning, he seemed a bit stumped. "You mean until I find another place?"

Silly man.

"No, I mean until *we* find another place."

"Tessa...you love this house."

"I do, but...I think the memories I made here before I met you weren't so great. I think it's time for a genuine fresh start. One that we make together. What do you think?"

The frown turned into a look of pure gratitude. "Are you sure? You're not just saying that because..."

"Because I love you and we were practically living together already?" she finished. "Liam, everything about our relationship has been a bit untraditional. All I know is that when I'm with you, I'm happy. When we're apart, I miss you. This is fast and it's scary, but..."

"But my parents got married six weeks after their first date," he said, sounding oddly confident in that statement. "Will and Arianna fell in love on their first date. Donovans don't do anything slow. So if you're sure about this..."

Nodding happily, she climbed into his lap until they fell back against the mattress. "I am 100% sure!"

"Then we need to celebrate," he told her, his voice taking on the sexy gravelly tone that she loved so much.

"I agree. Repeatedly."

"That's my girl."

And this time when they kissed, it was sweet and slow and beyond satisfying.

If they could end every day like this, Tessa knew she'd be a happy woman.

As Liam rolled her onto her back and covered her body with his, Tessa knew this was right. He was the man for her, and she couldn't wait to start this new phase of their relationship.

* * *

It was amazing how much better the holidays were when you were spending it with someone you loved.

She and Liam went Christmas shopping together and then wrapped gifts that night at home. He had very little patience for actually doing the wrapping, but he was a good assistant.

They went to several holiday parties that the neighbors were hosting and everyone praised how festive the two houses looked—even if they were bright enough to be seen from space.

They went to dinner on Sunday at his parents' home and it was loud and boisterous and beyond wonderful. The subject of where she was going to actually spend Christmas came up, and Tessa had to admit that she was torn. She'd always spent the holidays with her family, but this year, it was important for Liam to be with his. So when she got home that night, she'd called her mother and broke the news to her.

Tessa had a feeling her mother would have put up more of a fight if she hadn't shared how she'd fallen in love and how she was staying in Laurel Bay to be with Liam. At some point they'd have to figure out a holiday schedule, but it wasn't necessary just yet.

By the time she'd gone to school Monday morning, she and Liam were big news. She lost count of how many teachers came in to congratulate her or to gush over how romantic it all was. It should have gotten tiring to keep repeating the story, but it didn't. Every time she thought of him singing to her in his red sweater and Santa hat, she couldn't help but smile. And her students had come into class singing "Christmas, Baby Please Come Home" and laughing hysterically.

Someday they'd understand how it wasn't silly, but for now, she enjoyed their laughter.

The winter break started in two days and normally she wasn't overly anxious and counting down, but this year, she was. The thought of having two whole weeks with Liam was exciting. Construction was stopping on the resort for the holidays as well. The weather was bordering on frigid and they figured a two-week break would do everyone a lot of good.

Their plan was to go out as much as possible and do some of the things Liam had missed the most while he had been in the service. They were going to visit her family for a couple of days between Christmas and New Year's so he could meet everyone. She was excited to introduce him to her parents and she knew they were probably breathing huge sighs of relief that she was finally moving forward with her life.

And honestly, so was she.

Tessa was packing up at the end of the day and grabbing her satchel when her cell phone dinged with an incoming text.

Liam: Hey! Have you left school yet?

Tessa: Just getting ready to. Why? What's up?

Liam: I was hoping you could stop by the site.

He had mentioned a new style of cabin that had just been delivered. It had a sleeping loft and she had mentioned how she'd only seen those on HGTV. They were originally not going to go with that style, but opted to try just one.

Tessa: Does this have anything to do with the cabin with the loft?

Liam: I guess you'll have to come and find out for yourself.

Tessa: Hmm…

Liam: Everyone's gone for the day. We started our holiday break early, so…

Then a picture arrived. It was a selfie and Liam was shirtless and she could see a ladder leading up to the loft.

Tessa: Very tempting, Mr. Donovan.

Liam: You think so? I think it's even better in person.

Tessa: Do I need to stop and pick anything up?

Another picture appeared. This time, it was a couple of mugs and a plate of cookies.

"Damn! It's like he knows all my weaknesses!" she said with a laugh.

Liam: And if that's not enough...

One final picture appeared.
Another selfie.
Now he was in just his briefs and a Santa hat.

Tessa: I'm on my way!

There was a playfulness to Liam that was emerging, and she was loving it. So if driving across town to the construction site so she can run her hands all over his incredibly sexy body was what she had to do to keep encouraging this side of him, then...she'd have to do it.

"The sacrifices I make," she said with a giggle as she practically ran to her car.

Life was good.

And in a few minutes, it was going to get even better.

Epilogue

New Year's Eve:

The pub was jam-packed.

The music was loud, and everyone was laughing and having a good time. It was hard to believe he hadn't spent one of these here with his family in over eight years. But now, as he looked around, Liam knew without a doubt that he was happy to be home.

Beside him, Tessa was wearing a pair of snug jeans and a sequined top.

And a tiara.

He had no idea where that idea had come from, but she and Ari and Ryleigh each had one. Then he caught sight of his mother and noticed she was wearing one too. Either way, they were all smiling, so all was good.

Will walked over and shook his hand. "Happy New Year, bro!"

"Happy New Year! How was San Francisco?"

"It was great, but I think next time we go to see my aunt, we'll go after the holidays are completely over. Arianna was so eager to come home because she didn't want to miss this party that I feel like she never really relaxed."

"You were only gone for three days. How much relaxing could she do?"

Shrugging, he snagged a glass of champagne off of the tray Jamie was carrying. "Have you guys talked any more about the house?"

"When's your lease up?"

"April."

"Then let's aim for that so you can move without breaking your leases. You know Tessa and I aren't in a hurry. But if there's anything you guys want to do on the house, just let me know."

"Thanks. I'll talk to Ari about it."

"Talk to Ari about what?" his sister asked as she joined them, straightening her tiara as she snuggled up to her fiancé.

"Any work we want to do on the house before we move in."

"Ooh...that could be exciting!"

"What's exciting?" Tessa said as she mimicked Arianna's pose and snuggled close to Liam.

He repeated the conversation to her and motioned for Jamie to bring them another two glasses of champagne. It was almost midnight and he didn't want them to be the only ones without drinks.

"You know, you're allowed to go behind the bar and get your own damn drinks," his brother reminded him.

Just then, Patrick joined them and after saying hello to everyone, he turned to Jamie. "Hey, can you get me a glass of champagne?"

"You guys suck!"

"Maybe we should get our own drinks," Tessa suggested.

"Hell no!" Ryleigh said as she made her way into their

little circle. "He fired one of the waitresses this afternoon and now he has to work."

"Why'd he fire her?"

"Something about him dating one of her best friends and never calling her again. Apparently, she was just here to spy on him because her friend is a bit of a psycho."

"Wow, that's a lot of drama for our little pub," Patrick commented, but he was totally amused.

"Hey, Ryleigh," someone said, and they all turned and watched as some guy, who looked a little like he was part of a biker gang, stood there smiling. "Can I buy you a drink?"

"I'm sorry, I know it's cold out, but has hell frozen over?" his sister asked sweetly.

Liam was about to step in, but Tessa held him back.

All the guy did was tip his head at her. "Can't blame a guy for trying. Some day you're going to say yes."

"Not in this lifetime," he heard Ryleigh murmur.

"Um...do you need us to talk to this guy?" Patrick asked as he glared at the guy's retreating back.

"Nah, he's harmless. Annoying, but harmless. Could you imagine the look on Mom's face if I ever went out with a guy like that?" Then she laughed and laughed and laughed until it got awkward.

"Anyone else think Ryleigh's had enough to drink tonight?" Arianna teased.

Jamie came back and handed them all drinks, including one for himself, and a few minutes later, their parents joined them. Uncle Ronan was behind the bar and called out, "Okay, everyone, ten seconds to the New Year!"

Liam pulled Tessa even closer as they counted down with everyone.

"Ten...nine..."

She smiled up at him, and for a woman who was always smiling, it was different now—softer.

Peaceful.

And he loved that for her.

"Three...two...one! Happy New Year!" Turning her in his arms, Liam lowered his head and kissed her soundly.

"We get it! You're happy! Get a room for crying out loud!"

Yeah, Ryleigh definitely had enough to drink.

Lifting his head, Liam smiled down at Tessa. "Happy New Year, beautiful girl."

"Happy New Year to you too. It's going to be the best one ever."

"Absolutely. I promise to do everything in my power to make that happen."

"Liam?"

"Hmm?"

"Do you love me?"

"More than anything."

"Then that's all I need. Mission accomplished."

He knew she meant it, but he had a few more tricks up his sleeve for the coming year. And he couldn't wait to surprise her with them all.

Who will be the next Donovan to
fall in love?

Find out in

Save Me

Chapter 1

I wonder if fish get thirsty...

"So that's how I found out I have a shellfish allergy," Jarod Milner, the world's most boring date explained.

Ryleigh Donovan wished someone would come and save her from the worst date of her life, but apparently no one in her family could sense her extreme unease.

No matter how many times she tried to catch their attention.

Having dinner at her family pub was never her first choice when she went out with a guy, but tonight's date was really more of an ambush.

Her mother had called and said they were having a problem with their computer and because Ryleigh was sort of a tech-geek—or as she preferred to be called, a tech *goddess*—she had agreed to come to the pub to check it out. As soon as she arrived, her mother immediately ushered her over to a booth and introduced her to Jarod the periodontist.

"I wasn't too upset about it, because I never liked fish," he went on and Ryleigh swore she was going to go back into the office, upload a virus onto her parents' computer, and then leave on a two-week road trip without her phone.

That would teach them.

Actually, it wouldn't. It didn't seem like anything would. She'd begged, pleaded, and carried on about how she did not want to be set up with anyone—and especially didn't want any surprise dates—and yet, here she was.

"It's also why I never go out on a boat. I get seasick."

I wonder if fish get seasick?

Seriously, she'd had her share of bad dates, but this one was going at the top of the list. The reigning champion had been the time she'd gone out with Leo, the accountant. He'd talked numbers all night and lectured her about her financial status and how far behind she was on her retirement fund. She was 24 at the time and told him she wasn't worried about retirement just yet. Then he'd gotten annoyed by her so-called snarkiness and walked out—sticking her with the bill.

Oh, how she'd practically kill to have Jarod walk out right now because of her snarkiness...

Although, it was hard to be snarky when you couldn't get a word in because he had done nothing but talk about himself all damn night.

Yeah, she was definitely putting a nasty virus on the office computer as soon as she was done here.

With a sigh, Ryleigh glanced around the pub hoping to catch someone's eye who would read her desperate need for help.

Uncle Ronan was busy chatting with Joe Denton. No doubt talking about the upcoming Super Bowl. Her brother Jamie was making drinks behind the bar while talking to some blonde who'd been coming in here more and more lately. He didn't look too happy, so there was zero chance of him even paying any attention to her. None of her other siblings had shown up to get something to eat, and her mother was suspiciously absent.

You better be guarding all your electronics, mom, because I'm gunning for them...

The door to the pub opened and in walked Ryker.

No last name—or maybe no first name—just...Ryker.

He hadn't spotted her and this was possibly the one and only time that she wished he would. Normally, it was like the man had a tracking device on her because he seemed to easily find her in a crowd. It just figured that when she would finally willingly accept his flirting and offer of a drink and he didn't even look at her.

I cannot catch a break!

"So what about you, Ryleigh? When was the last time you went to the dentist?"

Ugh...kill me now...

"About six months ago," she lied. "No cavities." With a big smile, she showed off her teeth. "I'm an excellent brusher."

He frowned and made some sort of disapproving sound. "Your gums look a little red and inflamed." Moving in closer, he reached out to touch her face and she instantly pulled back.

"Yeah, um...we're not going to do that," she told him firmly. "Not here in the middle of the pub, and not anywhere." Glancing around again, she waved Jodi, their server, over. "It was nice meeting you, Jarod, but...I need to go. Have a nice night." Sliding out of the booth, she grabbed her purse and smiled stiffly at Jodi. "Have you seen...?"

"She's in the kitchen," Jodi whispered. "Hiding." With a

wink, she put the bill down on the table and blocked Jarod from going after her. "I'll just take that when you're ready."

Ryleigh didn't waste any time storming into the kitchen. "Mom! What in the world?"

Her mother, ever the innocent, stood by the sink pretending to be washing dishes.

"The water's not on and there isn't even anything in the sink!" she snapped, slamming her purse down on the stainless-steel workstation, causing the contents to fly out everywhere. Muttering a curse, she frantically scooped it all up before facing her mother. "How could you do that to me?"

"Do what?" Kate Donovan asked sweetly. "Fix you up with a very nice, respectable man?"

"He just tried to put his hand in my mouth!"

Kate looked at her oddly. "Why would he do that?" Then she paused. "Oh...because he's a dentist. It's what they do."

"He's not a dentist, he's a periodontist, and yes, there is a difference because he described it for over 45 minutes! And I don't care what he does for a living, you don't put your fingers in someone's mouth in the middle of a restaurant!"

"We're really just a pub; we're not very formal..."

"Mom!" she cried and stomped her foot. "That's it! Enough! You need to stop with this! I don't want you fixing me up with anyone! Ever!" Her voice grew louder with each word and yet her mother's expression was completely serene. "I'm serious. If you ever do this to me again, I'll... I'll...I'll mess up your computers!"

"Don't be so dramatic, Ryleigh," Kate said wearily. "Besides, we know a dozen people who could fix the computer."

This was getting her nowhere.

Again.

If she was going to put a stop to this, she was going to have to do something drastic.

She just had no idea what that was just yet.

Picking up her purse, she glared at her mother. "This isn't over. From now on, I'm not coming here when you call with some sort of emergency. You're like the boy who cried wolf. I don't trust you, and I'm never going to believe you again."

A loud sigh was her mother's only reaction.

"Why can't you just leave me alone on this?"

"Because you have terrible taste in men, and I'd like to see you settle down. You're not getting any younger and I want grandchildren."

"Need I remind you that Arianna and Will are planning their wedding and I'm sure Liam and Tessa won't be too far behind? I don't see why I'm the only one you're fixated on."

Kate stepped in close and gave her a soft pat on the cheek. "Such a pretty girl. Why can't you find a man to go out with more than once?"

There were so many answers to that question, but the only one to come out was, "Because you keep fixing me up with jerks and weirdos! If you'd just leave me alone and let me date who I want, I guarantee you I'd go out on more than one date!"

It was amazing lightning didn't come down from the sky and zap her right there on the spot. She'd gone out with several men of her own choosing and none of them had resulted in second dates either.

Was she a little picky? Maybe. But she wanted a man

who was intelligent, funny, good looking...someone who understood her geeky side and didn't mock her for it.

And definitely someone who didn't stick their fingers in her mouth over dinner.

"Ryleigh," her mother began patiently. "You see this as me picking on you, but I'm your mother and I see how you push people away. You're too young to be this set in your ways. No one is perfect and maybe if you stopped trying so hard to show the world how much you know, you could let someone in."

On the surface, it sounded like the perfect thing a mother should say to her daughter.

But Kate Donovan was no ordinary mother.

"Maybe you could put the same effort into doing your hair and buying some decent clothes as you do into proving how smart you are and..."

And there it was.

Inwardly, she sighed.

Liar.

No, inwardly, she raged.

Seriously, she really loved her mother; hell, she loved her whole family. But all Ryleigh truly wanted was for them to love her where she was at instead of focusing on where they thought she was lacking.

And maybe not so much *they*, as one specific person.

"I'm leaving," she said firmly. And I think it would be best if we didn't talk for a few days." Purse in hand, she walked across the kitchen and slammed her palm against the swinging door on her way out. Luckily no one was on the other side of it—because that would have ruined her glorious exit.

With a small huff, she didn't make eye contact with

anyone on her way across the crowded room. The only thing she did notice was that Jarod was gone.

Good riddance.

"Ry!" Jamie called out.

So close...

Her brother came jogging over and, for once, he wasn't quite his jovial self. "You okay?"

"Yeah, why?" she murmured.

"You were looking pretty fierce when you came through the doorway and I just wanted to make sure you're alright."

That was kind of sweet.

"Just...just mom stuff," she told him. "Did you see how she ambushed me tonight?"

He nodded. "I did, but...I sort of had my own thing going on."

"Then I guess I should be asking if you're okay."

With a shrug, he replied, "I guess. This is the first time I've ever had a breakup that just won't end."

She fought the urge to roll her eyes. "Yeah, it's tough to be you," she mumbled and fortunately, he grinned.

"So, what was wrong with the guy tonight?"

"The list is endless, but the highlight was when he tried to put his fingers in my mouth to inspect my gums."

"No!" And then the rat-bastard laughed.

Hard.

"And you want to know what the worst part is?"

"You mean that wasn't it?" Jamie asked with another laugh.

"That mom still doesn't think she did anything wrong! Why isn't she bugging you about this breakup? Why isn't she harping on Patrick to settle down? I mean...why is all her energy on me?"

He instantly took a step back. "I'm not touching this with a ten-foot pole. Look, I'm sorry she's bugging you, but as long as she's doing that, my life is easier, so..."

Leaning in, Ryleigh shoved him.

Hard.

"You suck." And with that, she stormed away.

For once it would be nice if someone took her side. She was a good person who always stepped up to help her friend and her siblings, and this was the thanks she got. No one was willing to do the same for her.

It wasn't fair and it wasn't right and she was just so damn done with it all.

Shoving her way through the crowd, she practically sagged with relief when she got to the door.

And slammed her hand against that one too for one last glorious exit.

Not that anyone would notice.

* * *

Ryker noticed.

Hell, from the moment he first laid eyes on Ryleigh Donovan, he'd noticed everything about her. From her long auburn hair and green eyes to her defiant attitude and sensual curves.

She was trouble with a capital T and apparently, that just added to her appeal.

For months he'd been doing his best to get her to go out with him and she'd shot him down every time. Most guys would take the hint and move on, but Ryker had a feeling that her bravado was all an act.

Actually, he was pretty damn sure of it.

When he'd walked through the door tonight and saw her sitting in the booth with that dufus who looked like every uptight loser he'd ever despised, he'd almost turned and walked right back out.

And yet...Ryleigh was out with him.

Because Ryker spent so much time at Donovans Pub, he knew her mother was constantly trying to fix her daughter up with nice, upstanding guys.

Which totally left him out of the picture.

On the surface, Ryker was basically every mother's nightmare; tattoos, long hair, beard, and extremely rough around the edges. If that guy was Kate Donovan's idea of the perfect guy, then there wasn't a snowball's chance in hell of her ever considering him.

And that was a damn shame because he knew he'd treat Ryleigh better than any man alive. Hell, he'd treat her like a damn princess if given the chance.

He thought about the way she'd stormed out of the pub and wondered why he was still sitting here nursing a drink when he could potentially go after her and make sure she was alright.

Tossing a twenty down on the bar, he nodded to Ronan before making his way out the door. There was a chance she was long gone, but he was hopeful.

Just like he was hopeful every time he tried to start a conversation with her.

He loved her snark and dry wit; and admired the way she didn't seem to tolerate anyone's bullshit.

Even his.

Out on the sidewalk, he glanced in both directions, raking a hand through his out-of-control hair. He was about to mutter a curse when someone beat him to it.

"Dammit! Dammit, dammit, *dammit!*"

A slow smile crept across his face as he made his way toward the parking lot. There, he found Ryleigh standing next to her sensible little Toyota, stomping her foot in frustration. Doing his best to appear casual, he slowly made his way over to her.

"Hey, beautiful," he drawled. "Is everything okay?"

Her green eyes shot daggers at him. "No, everything is most definitely *not* okay," she snapped. "I dropped my keys back in the kitchen and I am not going back in there!"

That...wasn't what he was expecting.

"Why not?"

With a groan, she fished around in her purse again before replying. "Because I had a fight with my mother and made a big stink about how I didn't even want to see or talk to her for a few days. If I go back in there, it completely nullifies my glorious exit. Dammit!"

"Glorious exit?" Leaning against her car, he studied her. "I don't think I've ever heard anyone describe leaving that way."

"Trust me, in that moment, it was awesome. If I have to go back in to grab my keys, it will look like I did it on purpose and..." She groaned again before digging in her purse one more time.

Gently, Ryker took the bag from her hands. "It's not that big, Ryleigh. They're not in there. Do you have a spare set somewhere?"

Her shoulders sagged as she nodded. "At home, but... ugh...I hate that I did this! Now I'll have to call for an Uber to go home and back and..."

"You don't need to call for an Uber."

"Uh, yeah, I do, because I certainly don't want to walk

there and back. It's already dark out and it's a mile each way..."

"I'll drive you."

Her eyes went a little wide as her mouth moved with no words coming out.

He liked that he caught her off guard.

"It's not a big deal. And, like you said, it's only a mile away. What's it gonna take? Ten minutes tops?"

"Ryker..."

"Do you want to go back inside and have everyone think you're caving?" Honestly, he had no idea if that even applied to the situation, but he gave it a shot.

"Absolutely not!" she told him. "But...um...I don't mind calling for a car." Holding up her phone, she made a bit of a show of pulling up the app. "You don't need to drive me anywhere, but...uh...thanks."

With a careless shrug, he straightened. "No problem. I knew you'd be too embarrassed to accept my help, so...have a good night." Turning, he started to walk away.

"Embarrassed? Why on earth would I be embarrassed?"

Ryker hid his smile as he turned to face her again. "You know...after being on a date with someone else earlier and then essentially sprinting from the table, I just figured you'd want to avoid anyone who witnessed that."

Throwing her head back and exposing that neck that he'd love to lean in and press his mouth to, he fought the urge to stay where he was. Her little growl of frustration was kind of adorable, and when she straightened, she looked mildly pissed.

"He tried to put his fingers in my mouth! Trust me, it was in his best interest for me to get away from the table as fast as humanly possible."

"Why would he put his fingers in your mouth? Was it like a third date or something?"

"*Ew!* No! And is there really a date rule on when it's appropriate to put your fingers in someone's mouth in the middle of a restaurant?"

If they were talking about the two of them, yes. But when it was her and some other random guy, absolutely not.

"I wouldn't say rule..."

"Never mind," she quickly interrupted before turning her back and looking at her phone.

Ryker wasn't stupid; he knew she was going to be too stubborn to accept a free ride from him based on...whatever preconceived notion she had about him

But he refused to accept that.

"Ryleigh, this is crazy. I'm right here, my car is literally five feet away. You can be home in fifteen minutes. Just let me do this for you."

It was insane how nervous he was and found himself holding his breath. He'd asked her out at least a dozen times and she'd always turned him down. But this wasn't a date.

This was a chance for her to get to know him.

The way she looked at him told him she was considering it.

"I just...I don't want you to read anything into this," she began carefully. "I know you've asked me out before..."

"Pfft, please. I'm not dense. This isn't a date. This is just me helping you out. I know that."

Her eyes narrowed slightly. "I don't even know your name."

"What are you talking about? You know my name."

"No, I know *part* of your name. There's got to be more to it than just Ryker."

Shaking his head, he said, "Nope."

"Seriously?" she deadpanned. "So that's it. Just Ryker. No last name?"

"Maybe that is my last name," he countered.

"And your first name?"

He grinned. "Just one name."

"So...you're *Ryker* Ryker?" she asked with one brow perfectly raised.

When she said it like that, it sounded ridiculous, but he was enjoying the banter. "No, just the one name. You know, like Adele, Cher or Madonna."

Her lips twitched. "Are you saying you're like...an aging pop diva?"

I walked right into that one, didn't I?

"Or like Bono, Sting, or Prince," he corrected.

"Do you sing?" she asked.

"Um...what?"

Nodding, she once again asked, "Do you sing? I mean... the single name and the comparison to all these musicians, I'm assuming there's a connection."

Unable to help himself, Ryker laughed. "Ryleigh, I'm just offering to take you to pick up your keys so you can take your car and go home and save face with your family. Do you want my help or not?"

She eyed him warily. "Fine. I do. But I'm texting my sister and my best friend Ivy. If anything happens to me, they're going to make sure bad things happen to you."

"Consider me warned," he told her before walking over to his truck.

"Um...maybe this isn't a good idea."

With a weary sigh, Ryker turned to face her. "Why now?"

"There's no way I can get into that truck! It's like...I'd need a ladder to climb in!"

Fine, the truck was a little on the high side. The Ford had been modified quite a bit, but...it was temporary. He was only driving it until he found something else.

"No ladder, Princess. There's a step and I can help you up." Walking up behind her, Ryker opened the door and held a hand out to her. The look she gave him told him she was not happy about it, but when she finally put her hand in his, he felt like they'd finally taken that first step into friendlier territory.

Only took six months, but...who's counting?

It took every ounce of willpower he possessed to not put his hands on her ass to help her that last little bit, but it was close. She smiled nervously at him once she was seated, and Ryker jogged around to the driver's side and climbed in.

"Okay, where to?"

Ryleigh didn't come out and give him the address, she simply started giving him direction. "Make a left out of the parking lot and go down to Elm and make a right."

He did as she instructed.

"So...this fight with your mom. It was bad, huh?"

"To me it was."

"You don't think it was to her?"

Shaking her head, she said, "Go down to Peachtree and make a left."

He nodded.

"My mother like to...instigate," Ryleigh went on. "And when she pushes me to where I'm a ranting lunatic, she just smiles and looks at me like I'm crazy. It doesn't matter how many times I ask her nicely not to interfere in my life or set me up with strange guys, or ambush me like she did tonight, she doesn't listen. It's exhausting and...*ugh*. I'm just done."

"Is she like this with all your siblings?"

She shook her head. "Nope. Just me."

He found that a little hard to believe, but as he turned onto Peachtree, he waited her out.

"Go down about a mile and my apartment complex is on the right."

"I didn't realize there were apartments back here."

"It's a small building; only four units. None of them are particularly big. I have a two bedroom, but the second bedroom is tiny so I use it as an office."

"Okay, I have to ask...why is your mom like this with only you?"

She sighed loudly. "I wish I knew," she said sadly. "I really wish I knew. She was over-protective of Arianna, but still fixed her up with a couple of Jamie's friends. Liam joined the Marines a year after high school, so she didn't have a chance to do anything to him. And when he came home, he got involved with Tessa so..."

He nodded.

"Patrick is like...I don't even know. It's like she's a little intimidated by him and so in awe of his business accomplishments that she doesn't want to bother him. She whines every once in a while how she wishes he'd meet someone, but she never truly bugs him about it."

"And Jamie?"

"Jamie's just...Jamie," she said. "He's got a new girl-friend every week and she thinks he'll eventually find the right girl and settle down."

"I mean...I guess that makes sense," he reasoned, "but..."

"Tonight I told her that if she'd just leave me alone and let me date who I want to date, everything would be fine."

"So...date someone."

Turning her head, she glared at him. "Oh, gee, Ryker. That's brilliant. Why don't I just date someone?" Rolling her eyes, she straightened in her seat as they pulled up to her building.

And then instantly groaned.

"What? What's the matter?"

"If I don't have my car keys, I don't have my house keys!" she cried. "Dammit!"

He was beginning to see how that was her go-to reaction to things.

"Does your landlord live in the building?"

"No."

"Do you have a complicated lock on your door?"

She blinked at him like he was crazy.

Without waiting, Ryker climbed out of the truck and jumped up into the bed. His toolbox was back there, and he quickly rummaged around for what he needed before climbing over to help Ryleigh out.

"What are you doing?" she asked.

"We're going to get into your apartment, get your keys, and take you back to get your car."

"By breaking in? I don't think so," she said with a snort.

"Would you rather go back to the pub and see the smug look on your mother's face?

"No." There was a definite huff of annoyance after that, but she held out her hand so he could help her down. "I can't believe I'm going to let you pick my lock..."

There was a very dirty comeback on the tip of his tongue, but he held it in.

They walked up to the second floor, and Ryleigh simply stepped aside and held her phone up like a flashlight for him. In less than a minute, he had the door open. As he straightened, he stared down at her. "Tomorrow, get a better lock."

For a moment, he thought she was going to argue, but all

she did was walk into the apartment and back out in less than a minute. "Thank you," she murmured.

The drive back to the pub was primarily spent in silence because he couldn't believe that she didn't have more safety precautions in place in her home. Anyone could break in even if they didn't have the know-how that he did.

As if reading his mind, Ryleigh blurted out, "I have a deadbolt that I use every night, so...it's not like anyone can just get in."

"You need something better in general," he replied. "If you want, I can pick something up and install it tomorrow." His voice was gruff and a little harsh, but he hated thinking of anything happening to her.

"No, but...thank you. I'll pick something up myself."

He pulled back into the pub parking lot and parked, but didn't move to get out. Twisting in his seat, he figured this was his chance to say what he needed to say and hoped she wouldn't laugh in his face.

"Here's the thing, Ryleigh," he began. "I like you. I think you're pretty and have a wicked sense of humor and I'd like to take you out sometime. We've been doing this dance for several months and I don't think you ever take me seriously, but I'm telling you right now that I am serious. I'd like the chance to take you out on a real date—not here at the pub—and I think you should give me a chance."

There.

He'd said it.

She studied him for several long moments and for the life of him, he had no idea what was going through her mind. But if he had to venture a guess, he'd say that she was trying to come up with yet another way to turn him down, even though he'd saved her ass tonight.

The silence dragged on until he thought he'd go mad.

"Look, um…"

She held up a hand to stop him. "Okay," she said confidently. "Let's do it. I'll go out with you."

And Ryker was fairly certain his jaw hit the ground.

Get your copy of SAVE ME here:
https://www.chasing-romance.com/save-me

And check out the entire DONOVANS series here:
https://www.chasing-romance.com/the-donovans-series

Also by Samantha Chase

The Donovans Series:

Call Me

Dare Me

Tempt Me

Save Me

The Magnolia Sound Series:

Sunkissed Days

Remind Me

A Girl Like You

In Case You Didn't Know

All the Befores

And Then One Day

Can't Help Falling in Love

Last Beautiful Girl

The Way the Story Goes

Since You've Been Gone

Nobody Does It Better

Wedding Wonderland

Always on my Mind

Kiss the Girl

Meet Me at the Altar

The Engagement Embargo

With this Cake

You May Kiss the Groomsman

The Proposal Playbook

Groomed to Perfection

The I Do Over

The Enchanted Bridal Series:

The Wedding Season

Friday Night Brides

The Bridal Squad

Glam Squad & Groomsmen

Bride & Seek

The RoadTripping Series:

Drive Me Crazy

Wrong Turn

Test Drive

Head Over Wheels

The Montgomery Brothers Series:

Wait for Me

Trust in Me

Stay with Me

More of Me

Return to You

Meant for You

I'll Be There

Until There Was Us

Suddenly Mine

A Dash of Christmas

The Shaughnessy Brothers Series:

Made for Us

Love Walks In

Always My Girl

This is Our Song

Sky Full of Stars

Holiday Spice

Tangled Up in You

Band on the Run Series:

One More Kiss

One More Promise

One More Moment

The Christmas Cottage Series:

The Christmas Cottage

Ever After

Silver Bell Falls Series:

Christmas in Silver Bell Falls

Christmas On Pointe

A Very Married Christmas

A Christmas Rescue

Christmas Inn Love

The Christmas Plan

Life, Love & Babies Series:

The Baby Arrangement

Baby, Be Mine

Baby, I'm Yours

Preston's Mill Series:

Roommating

Speed Dating

Complicating

The Protectors Series:

Protecting His Best Friend's Sister

Protecting the Enemy

Protecting the Girl Next Door

Protecting the Movie Star

7 Brides for 7 Soldiers:

Ford

7 Brides for 7 Blackthornes:

Logan

Standalone Novels:

Jordan's Return

Catering to the CEO

In the Eye of the Storm

A Touch of Heaven

Moonlight in Winter Park

Waiting for Midnight

Mistletoe Between Friends

Snowflake Inn

His for the Holidays

Wildest Dreams (currently unavailable)

Going My Way (currently unavailable)

Going to Be Yours (currently unavailable)

About Samantha Chase

Samantha Chase is a New York Times and USA Today bestseller of contemporary romance that's hotter than sweet, sweeter than hot. She released her debut novel in 2011 and currently has more than eighty titles under her belt – including THE CHRISTMAS COTTAGE which was a Hallmark Christmas movie in 2017! She's a Disney enthusiast who still happily listens to 80's rock. When she's not working on a new story, she spends her time reading romances, playing way too many games of Solitaire on Facebook, wearing a tiara while playing with her sassy pug Maylene...oh, and spending time with her husband of 32 years and their two sons in Wake Forest, North Carolina.

Sign up for my mailing list and get exclusive content and chances to win members-only prizes!
https://www.chasing-romance.com/newsletter

Start a fun new small town romance series:
https://www.chasing-romance.com/the-donovans-series

Where to Find Me:

Website:
www.chasing-romance.com
Facebook:
www.facebook.com/SamanthaChaseFanClub
Instagram:
https://www.instagram.com/samanthachaseromance/
Twitter:
https://twitter.com/SamanthaChase3
Reader Group:
https://www.facebook.com/groups/1034673493228089/

Made in the USA
Monee, IL
10 December 2022

20877872R00180